Praise for *Of Starlight and Bone*

———

"Packed with non-stop action, this SF adventure is sure to keep readers turning the pages!"

—Maria V. Snyder, *New York Times* bestselling author of *Navigating the Stars*

"This fast-paced space adventure kept me turning pages right up to the exciting conclusion. I wanted to run away on a spaceship and spend more time with the characters, especially the engaging and relatable cyborg lead."

—Jordan Rivet, Author of *Wake Me After the Apocalypse*

OF STARLIGHT AND BONE

EMILY LAYNE

OWL HOLLOW PRESS

Owl Hollow Press, LLC, Springville, UT 84663

Of Starlight and Bone
Copyright © 2023 by Emily Layne

Library of Congress Cataloging-in-Publication Data
Of Starlight and Bone / E. Layne. — First edition.

Summary:
Aurelia must deal with the stigma of being part machine, which is why she's dead-set on proving her worth. But as she uncovers an unfathomable darkness hidden in the depths of the galaxy that threatens everything she holds dear, something in the system catches her scent, and she knows it will stop at nothing to catch its prey.

Cover: Les Solot

ISBN 978-1-958109-12-0 (paperback)
ISBN 978-1-958109-13-7 (e-book)

For my husband, Jeff. Of every love story in every galaxy, ours is my favorite. I'm yours.

————

CHAPTER ONE

---

09 Aug 3319, 14:19:08
Ancora Galaxy, Planet 04: Babbage,
Expansion District

Aurelia Peri had failed to stop her target from fleeing out of the alley, and now, against specific orders, she was creating a scene. Humid wind plastered tangles of red hair to her skin, renegade strands from her rope braid. She spat some out of her mouth with a grimace.

"Come on, come on," she hissed to her borrowed ride. The cycle hummed as she opened up the throttle, bearing down on the running man meters ahead. He shoved people aside, throwing a glance behind him. Fresh blood ran from his nose and upper lip, the vivid crimson clear even through the blur of foot traffic separating them on the open-air skybridge.

"Stop by order of the DISC taskforce!" she shouted as pedestrians leapt out of her cycle's path into the protective glass guard rails. Birdie, a lithe white poodle and Auri's assigned partner, loped just ahead, snarling and barking at anyone who didn't scramble away fast enough.

Auri could've sent Birdie to tackle the man and pin him in place, but this was her first assignment. She wanted—no, needed—to prove she was capable. Not just to her captain and fellow DISC agents, but to herself.

The man reached the end of the skybridge. Instead of taking the escalator back to ground level almost thirty stories below where the chase began, he staggered through the doors of the connected building. Birdie bounded after him.

"*Kuso*," Auri swore. She reached the building's entrance heartbeats later, leaping off the cycle. It powered down as the doors whooshed open, and she sprinted through. The suddenly cool air brought out goose bumps along her organic skin. Birdie, tongue lolling, waited in the center of a walkway surrounded by cubicles of tinted smart glass. Curious heads poked out from the tiny offices, showing varying degrees of interest and concern.

Auri flashed a smile that she hoped looked confident. At the end of the hall, her target slid open a door and disappeared behind it, leaving a dripping red handprint on the glass.

She ran, Birdie at her heels, the tails of her dark green coat dancing at her back. A manager shouted, "No dogs!" as she passed his office, furnished with a sleek designer sofa in front of a curved steel desk. He leapt out of his hover-chair and jogged into the hall.

Auri bared her forearm to him, the barcode on her skin warming as the c-tact lenses in the man's eyes processed her DISC agent badge. His reprimands shriveled into silence, though his mouth still hung open like a faulty shuttle door.

The other side of the bloodied glass revealed a flight of steps, slick with decades of dust. Smeared footprints and droplets of blood led upwards. Auri's mechanical leg propelled her up each flight even after her organic leg began to burn with fatigue. The bang of another door opening and closing echoed through the space. She pushed herself harder, faster.

A black glass door loomed at the top of the final flight of steps. She yanked it open. Glaring sunlight burned her organic eye, oppressive humidity replacing the cool air. She blinked away tears and focused on the silhouette of her target, hunched in the center of the building's tiled roof, heaving labored breaths.

Her c-tacts whirred with facial recognition tech available for DISC agents on active missions. Information coalesced at the left corner of her vision, adding to the identification information available to any citizen of the Ancora Federation.

Tanaka, Hiroki, DOB 14 Sep 3276
R. Loc.: Kaido, Ushi District
Cattle Ranch Hand
Wanted: Alive

Auri heaved in a lungful of air that was part relief and part exhaustion. At least she'd been chasing the right man. After all, this was an emergency transfer of a COF, a Class One Fugitive. If she hadn't been the only agent nearby when Agent Hillsdale slipped getting into his shuttle and broke his leg, Auri might still be back on Rokuton. The Military Police Brigade, MPB, had been after Hiroki for days. He'd finally popped up on Babbage and they wanted to seize the opportunity. Hillsdale said he'd inform the captain of the transfer according to protocol and to "get the hell onto your shuttle."

She couldn't screw this up. For both her *and* Agent Hillsdale's sakes.

"Tanaka Hiroki," she began. "I am Agent Peri Aurelia of the DISC taskforce." She paused midway to catch her breath. "You are under arrest for the murders of Tanaka Marie and Tanaka Hana. You have the right to—"

Hiroki gripped the sides of his face, torn and dirtied fingernails digging into his skin. "It wasn't me. I would never... I *never*." The lawn furniture and potted plants placed about the roof acted as mute witnesses to the man's pleas. Auri forced herself to remain detached, calm.

"Mr. Tanaka," she soothed, taking a hesitant step forward, Birdie following. "I promise you will have the opportunity to plead your innocence in court."

But even Auri knew the judge would find this man guilty. Her brief perusal of his case file on her flight over hadn't uncovered any other suspects.

But now that she got a good look, his current state didn't match the violent criminal she had imagined when Hillsdale transferred the file. Hiroki wore threadbare rags streaked with blood, both dried and recent. His right forearm bore a gouge along his barcode. Crimson oozing from the wound splattered the tiled rooftop. The effort to obliterate his identifying marker, an illegal action in itself, had been a waste because he hadn't sliced deep enough. His nose and lip, cut from a fall on the escalator earlier in her chase, had stopped bleeding but left his face a gory mess.

How this man escaped Kaido and navigated Krugel's Curve was beyond her.

"No, no, no," Hiroki moaned, shaking his head. Sweat and oil-dampened hair clung to his forehead. Fear burned hot in his eyes as his body tensed to run.

"Don't move!" Auri shouted. "Birdie, detain!" Her partner darted forward, cutting off Hiroki's only escape: an entrance to the nearby skybridge, this one mercifully devoid of pedestrians.

Auri hefted her disc free from its holster across her back. At her touch, the weapon grew from plate-sized to tire-sized. A hazy ring of blue electricity buzzed across its rim, the disc set to stun. She tightened her grip on the rubber handle in the center. "Mr. Tanaka, come with me peacefully. Enough running. You're only making things worse for yourself." She took another step forward, nerves jangling in her stomach.

"They'll kill me. They'll put me in the dark." He backed toward the edge of the roof, one hand squeezing the gaping wound over his barcode. Blood ran in rivulets over dirtied skin. "Attica chokes you, breaks you, and eats you whole."

Auri resisted the urge to roll her eyes at the familiar phrase attached to the Federation's notorious prison. She was too concerned about the ever-shrinking gap between Hiroki and the roof's edge.

"No one is going to kill you," she said.

Lie. The judgment for the atrocities Hiroki committed was death. But facing this man and his malnourished body, wrinkles around his mouth, and eyes lined with blood and grime, what else could she say?

"They should've killed me. Monsters hiding inside human flesh. Chomp, chomp, chomp." Hiroki broke into a strangled, manic laugh. The heels of his worn *geta*, traditional Japanese sandals, scraped the tile. "Bit right through them, bones snapping. Gobbled them up."

"Gobbled them up?" she repeated, shivering despite the heat. A copper tang tainted her mouth, and the world darkened at the edges. Faraway echoes of hungry snarls and terrified screams made her muscles tense. Pain burned deep in the socket of her right armpit where her robotic limb connected to muscle.

Birdie's growl freed Auri from the clutches of the phantom cries. She tightened her grip on the disc, thankful her prosthetic hand couldn't sweat. Hiroki stared at her, chapped lips slightly parted.

"They will come for us all," he wheezed.

Auri shook her head, fighting the urge to retch. Her focus splintered between Hiroki and the strange hallucination she'd just had.

"Listen," she began. "I don't—" Hiroki straightened as if he'd reached a decision. "Wait!" She darted forward, her boots sliding on the smooth tile. "Stop!"

Hiroki took a step back into empty air. He appeared to hover as Auri ran, fighting against the viscosity of time to reach him.

She shouted his name, abandoning her disc as she leaned over the ledge, stretching out a hand. He was already too far. His eyes seemed to meet hers as he fell: limbs splayed, fingers curled. His lips moved, but Auri couldn't hear him over the roaring in her ears and Birdie's barking.

Hiroki hit the water roadway thirty floors below with a bone-breaking smack.

CHAPTER TWO

News drones zoomed overhead, controlled by cameramen back in cushy studios. No doubt the networks' viewers would get a lovely picture of the hologram *MPB line do not cross* tape and the massive crowd gathered behind it. Policemen loitered about the sidewalk lined with blooming trees and iron benches, and a hover-boat dredged the canal in front of Auri…

Hunting for a broken body.

As Auri rushed down thirty floors after Hiroki's suicide, passing boats had shoved the man's body deeper into the canal system. She could've commissioned a gondola driver and retrieved the corpse herself, but that would've taken too long. Within hours, Hiroki's body would drift out of the district's canals into the darker waters between Babbage's floating cities, anchored like enormous ships. Impossible to recover. For the sake of time, she had called in the local police. An embarrassing admission of incompetency in the hope of fixing things as best she could.

When Auri boarded her shuttle yesterday, she never imagined her first mission would end in such a spectacular failure. The eager excitement of seizing Hiroki and returning to her captain's praise and Agent Hillsdale's appreciation had bled away. Now she was trapped in a living, humid, media-filled nightmare.

But at least the officers around her seemed to be enjoying themselves. They chatted to the drones as the operators relayed questions through the machines' tiny speakers. Those on the boat snacked on melting watermelon popsicles while a specially designed crane combed through the trash-lined bottom of Expansion District's waterways.

Auri's skin was covered in a slick sheen of sweat and murky water droplets, courtesy of the boat's kickback spray. The DISC-mandated short-sleeved blouse and bow around her neck clung to her, revealing more than she thought appropriate with her vest unbuttoned. But she was too hot and too upset to put her coat back on or button the vest. Her body felt painfully small for her soul, the aching, squirming thing longing to curl in on itself and hide. What would Agent Hillsdale say when he found out? And the investigation to follow…

If it wasn't for Birdie at her side, she might have submitted to her desire to run. Instead, she knotted her fingers into the soft white curls atop the dog's head, hair cropped short per regulation.

"We've got something!" An officer clenching a popsicle stick between his molars leaned over the boat's bow. The crane emerged, its three-pronged claws wrapped around an object, liquid streaming into the water below.

Yes, Auri thought, swallowing around the lump in her throat as a limp form was dropped onto the sidewalk a few meters away. *Object is the correct term.*

Hiroki's corpse met the bare requirements of being called "human." Chunks of flesh and extremities had been sliced away by passing propellers. His dark eyes remained whole, still open and staring.

Staring at her.

Hiroki's words, his pleas for understanding, replayed in her mind: "*It wasn't me. I would never… I* never." Why would a man choose this fate over Attica? Over a painless, instant death?

Auri caught herself before she could ponder his proclaimed innocence further. The evidence in the case file was clear, and her emotional response would be pointless.

The drones surged forward, snatching close-ups of the massacred corpse. Auri released Birdie, scrunching her hands into fists. She could almost hear the newscasters' commentary as the live footage played: "We warn you that this video contains graphic content that may be disturbing for some viewers." And all the viewers at home, instead of changing the stream, would lean forward, intrigued.

Small faces peered at her from the crowd, children sneaking peeks around their parents' legs. One little girl with dark skin, hair a beautiful halo around her head, waved at Auri excitedly, as if the whole situation was such fun. The parents seemed too preoccupied trying to see what the crane dredged from the canal's depths to think that the sight might not be appropriate for their children.

"Thank you!" Auri shouted to the officers who clustered around the body. She was barely loud enough to be heard over the crowd and drone of the motor. "I'll take it from here." She yanked her uniform coat off the bench where she'd draped it and shouldered her way through the gawkers. She gently spread it over Hiroki's corpse. The jacket's tails were long enough and the man's body small enough that his entire form was covered, except for the bloated, discolored tips of his toes.

Drones buzzed in her face, whipping up stray hairs, and relayed their questions.

"Was this a suicide?"

"Can you comment on the DISC taskforce's failure to capture 27.5 percent of criminals in the last six months?"

"As a cyborg, what are your thoughts on the Cyborg Bomber on Aurora?"

Auri turned away from the drones. Her inadequacy had already cost a man his life; she didn't want to feed any negative press about DISC agents. Newscasters were experts at twisting footage to meet the Federation's—and their—agendas.

"Senior Officer Krane," she called over her shoulder to the supervising officer.

He approached, gray hair buzzed close to his skin, blue uniform tight across his chest. "Yes, Agent Peri?" His voice was rough as sandpaper, eyes suspicious as they roamed over her. It was an expression Auri was used to. No one trusted her overabundance of mechanical parts.

Back on Earth, over a millennia ago, all humanoid robots had been decommissioned due to a programming bug that caused them to turn against their masters. The cyborg prejudice worsened after the Cyborg Bomber incident six years ago. Especially for Auri. Many of his victims had been the parents of students in her class. Considering the Bomber had been quickly executed for his crimes, she and other cyborgs remained the perfect target for that hate.

"I am identifying this body as my assignment, Tanaka Hiroki." The words were soot in her mouth, despite the relief she felt saying them. Regulation required her to stay to identify Hiroki for the local police, her personal report, and the subsequent investigation. "I'm leaving the body in your care. I'll be filing your name in my report." *In other words, don't lose this body or screw up because my captain will have your name.*

Officer Krane gave a gruff nod. Auri turned away only to stop when he called out, "Your jacket?"

She glanced at the dark green material, its golden buttons and scarlet threading matching her pants and black knee-high boots. The idea of picking up the jacket to reveal Hiroki's body made her organic skin icy. She never wanted to touch that jacket again. She had enough spares back home.

"Keep it." She grimaced, then whistled for Birdie.

The poodle trotted over as a whispered comment from one of the officers caught Auri's attention: "You think she'd be a little less stoic, the clank. No messy court trial. The investigation won't even give her a bad mark, being the GIC's adopted daughter."

"You can't trust clanks," another replied. "Their mechanical parts poison their brains. Maybe she killed the poor bastard."

She gritted her teeth at clank, the derogatory term for cyborgs. "Come on, Bird." The pair stepped through the hologram police tape and into the crowd. Many onlookers stepped aside after their eyes met hers. One of Auri's eyes was human, a deep blue and beautifully normal. The other…

It was a close replica, but not perfect. The blue was a little too light, the pupil not quite matching, the sensors in the iris almost transparent—all together, clearly cyborg.

Something tugged at her hand, and she tensed and spun. The little girl who waved earlier smiled up at her, an enormous backpack looping over her shoulders. Auri relaxed and tried to smile back.

"I like your red hair, *Agent-san*." She bowed, the backpack sliding up to bump the back of her head.

Auri grinned despite her fatigue and the heat, tucking a stray lock behind her ear. She always got along better with children, their innocent hearts too young to nurture the world's prejudices—or its fears. "Thank you. I like yours too."

"Your doggie is pretty. But she's working so I can't pet her, right?"

Auri glanced at Birdie where she sat at her feet, still as a statue, brown eyes on the little girl. "That's right. Did you learn that in school?"

"Nadoka!" a voice called from the crowd. "Nadoka, where are you?"

The little girl turned, her pink cotton dress swaying around her knees. "That's my mama. Bye, *Agent-san*. Bye, *Wan-chan*!"

She hurried away, squeezing through gaps in the crowd. Auri watched her go until she reunited with a petite woman laden with shopping bags. The mother patted the top of Nadoka's head, pulling a plastic-wrapped rice ball, or *onigiri*, from a bag and handing it to her. Then the mother and daughter abandoned the onlookers and hurried down a small side street.

Loneliness coiled around Auri's neck and constricted her throat. Other than their dog, a DISC agent always operated alone, which Auri liked most of the time. But even off the job, there was no one to comfort her. She turned back to the empty sidewalk and strode away to retrieve her borrowed cycle from the skybridge.

Just hours before, she had straddled the machine filled with hope and excitement. Now she felt hollow.

A warm body brushed against her thigh, and Auri smiled down at Birdie as they rode the elevator back up to the skybridge level. "Thank you for your help today. I have a nice treat waiting for you back on the shuttle."

Birdie's ears quirked at the word *treat*, and she turned to look at Auri with pleading eyes, showing just enough of the whites to be heart-rendingly cute.

"I thought that would get your attention." Auri found the cycle where she'd left it, slung a leg over, and revved the engine.

As she rode the vehicle-only escalator down, she gazed across the canal at the sunset where it peeked between skyscrapers and their connecting skybridges. In place of drying laundry, early Obon decorations were strung between windows of opposing buildings. Each circular lantern symbolized a loved one lost, a name scrawled in kanji on the outside. In a few days the lanterns would be lit in remembrance. Some would even be launched into the sky at special festivals after hours of games, dancing, and food.

Would anyone remember Tanaka Hiroki?

She took a slow breath, mentally preparing the report she would send to her captain once she boarded her shuttle. He wouldn't be pleased that she swapped with Agent Hillsdale, especially after her failure. Her organic fingers trembled on the cycle's handlebar as Hiroki's last moments replayed in her head. She might've saved him if that hallucination hadn't distracted her, or if she'd let Birdie detain him instead of wanting to do it herself. How would she explain that?

She shook her head. If she let herself think too much, she would cry herself into a puddle. Aurelia Peri was a DISC agent. She needed to act like one.

Though she longed to escape inside her shuttle, she had one last errand. Auri rolled her shoulders and tightened her grip on the handlebars. Soon she would need to find an MPB officer to get the cycle back to its rightful owner. But for now…

"Birdie, I'll race you to the *takoyaki* vendor."

At *race*, Birdie took off down the empty sidewalk. Auri laughed. The dog had no idea where they were going.

She lifted her foot from the ground, revved the cycle's engine again, and hurtled into the sunset, murky water sloshing beside her like a ghostly reminder.

CHAPTER THREE

---

10 Aug 3319, 03:22:34
Ancora Galaxy, Planet 02: Isoroku-Patton,
LL Hangar Bldg

A yawn forced Auri's lips apart as she stumbled out of her shuttle, knapsack slung over a shoulder. Her gaze locked with an engineer waiting outside dressed in rainforest camouflage fatigues.

"Excuse me." She blinked sleepy tears out of her eyes. "Late mission."

He nodded once and shuffled off to inspect the front paneling of the shuttle. "Good morning to you too," she muttered and clomped down the metal ramp.

The hangar was unpopulated this early in the morning. Ships and shuttles of all sizes and classes stood at attention, waiting for their pilots. Auri gave her own shuttle, a Raptor Class, an affectionate pat before she walked away. It had taken good care of her, running on autopilot all the way, even through the Fed's slingshots that got her home in half the time. Not that she would've turned her nose up at manual piloting.

Much to Auri's disappointment, DISC agents received limited flight lessons, mostly emergency maneuvers or repairs.

Their assignments relied heavily on speed, and autopilot was renowned for shortening travel time. She and a few other trainees had tried—and failed—to wheedle their way into extra lessons during basic training.

But on a late mission like her current one? She'd tucked away her wounded pride and relished the ability to send her report to Captain Ishida and then sleep some in the ten hours it took to get from Babbage to Isoroku-Patton.

Her boots click-clacked on the freshly shined floor as she moved toward the nearest exit. All that lay between her and her bed was a thirty-minute transport ride from Rokuton, a nickname for the planet Isoroku-Patton, to its moon Agar.

Twenty minutes into her journey, with only a snoring janitor for company, Auri received a ping from her captain. The red flashing icon in the corner of her eye made her stomach perform an unpleasant flip. Why was he awake at this hour?

She swallowed hard and opened the message. Birdie sighed beside her, curled up on one of the plastic seats. A dog on a transport chair was technically bad form, but no one was here to complain.

Report rec'ed. Debriefing 0800, my office.

Short and to the point—nothing about the swapped case, the botched mission, the news drones. Typical Captain Ishida. Auri leaned back in her seat and spent the rest of the ride trying to ease jittering nerves over tomorrow's—*today's*—meeting.

———

The DISC bunk hall was a row of shut doors, everyone either on a mission or asleep before early morning PT. Except outside Auri's own door. She might've been concerned the lump was a pile of the other agents' dirty pajamas—one of their kinder pranks—

if Birdie's tail hadn't started wagging. Then she saw the shock of blond hair.

Auri undid the working vest around the dog's chest and back and whispered, "Go ahead."

Birdie bounded forward, tackling the pajamas and eliciting a cry of surprise. The pile unrolled, revealing a lanky man who used both hands and knees to protect himself from the over-eager dog.

"Auri," he said between laughs. "Get your dog off—ew! Her tongue went in my mouth."

"Birdie, leave it," Auri said with a smile, standing over her friend, arms crossed. "Ty, what are you doing outside my room?" Despite her faux gruff tone, her insides buzzed with happiness.

"I wanted to see how your first mission went." He pushed himself up with a grunt, grimacing as his back popped. "Every-one was gossiping about it. No one can believe Hawkeye Hillsdale gave it to you." His implication about what the others thought hung in the air between them: *Gave it to a cyborg. Someone no one trusts.* He continued, "I'm not surprised though. They should've sent you out ages ago. Heard he broke his leg in three places?"

"Uh, yeah. I was running Birdie through some training ex-ercises and happened to be the closest agent." She braced herself. "What are the gossips saying?"

He shrugged. "Well, some placed bets."

That meant a large enough pool had thought she would fail. Her happiness fizzled. She cleared her throat. "How long have you been waiting?"

"Long enough to feel like a sushi roll." He stretched his arms overhead. His tight gray t-shirt with DISC written in bold letters rode up to show a flash of toned stomach. Heat warmed Auri's organic cheek at the sight. She glanced up and was horri-fied to find Ty watching her.

His thin lips spread in a slow smile. "Are you going to tell me about your first mission? Or are you going to change the subject again? Either way, I'm sure it can't top mine."

Ty was a year older and a year ahead of her as a DISC agent. Technically, he was her brother since his father, the General-in-Chief, had adopted her. But Tyson Peri had never felt like a brother.

"It was a mess." She ran a hand through her tattered rope braid, realizing with growing embarrassment what she must look like. A subtle sniff of her shoulder revealed another horrible truth: she smelled like stale sweat. But Ty's eyes were half-lidded. He probably cared more about going to bed than Auri's body odor.

"My target jumped off a building to escape capture and—" The words to admit her strange hallucination got caught on her teeth. She closed her mouth and swallowed. "Uh, have you ever had a case like that?"

His eyes widened, coming to full alertness. "A suicide? No, but they don't exactly send us after people who fail to renew their cycle's registration. The investigation won't be bad." He patted Auri's mechanical cheek. The synthetic skin only provided the sensation of pressure, but no warmth or intimacy like organic skin, and she bit back a sigh. "But I can't promise Hillsdale won't be furious. Or the captain. Anyway, did you bring me the *takoyaki*?" He held out a hand as if he already knew the answer.

Auri snorted as she slung her small knapsack off her shoulder. Switching the conversation from furious superiors to food was fine by her. She pulled out a paper container and held it out. Even through the tightly sealed lid, the scent of spices permeated the hall. Her mouth watered, and she hated *takoyaki*. Birdie sniffed the air appreciatively, but her training kept her from snatching at the container.

"You're awesome, Aur. Thanks." He peeled back the lid and took a long whiff. "That gnarly old vendor in the Expansion District on Babbage makes the best *takoyaki*."

"If you're a fan of food poisoning, *aho*." *Dummy*. Auri keyed in her bedroom door code and slid it open. "I'll walk you to your room. Birdie, inside." The poodle trotted into the room and hopped onto Auri's bed as if she belonged there instead of her—very comfortable—dog bed.

Ty shook his head, resealing the lid as she shut the door on Birdie. "You should stick her in the kennels with the other DISC dogs. You don't see me sleeping with Busu."

"I still can't believe you decided to call your pit bull that." When they'd been assigned their animal counterparts halfway through basic, Ty had been less than impressed with his pit bull.

"It fits." He led the way along the corridor to his room a meter down. "You're getting too attached to Birdie, and it'll screw with your missions. You won't be able to put her in danger. She's not a friend. She's a tool. It's stupid to get close to a DISC dog. Have you seen their survival rate?"

The familiar argument made her sigh. Ty always warned her not to be so close to Birdie. What he didn't understand was Birdie was the only living creature Auri felt loved her unconditionally. "The General-in-Chief said it was okay to keep Birdie in my room." The words were out before she could stop them.

"Asking favors from my dad, huh?" His expression darkened, brows drawing close together. "He always liked you better."

She shook her head, trying to backtrack. "I just told him Birdie helps with my nightmares. I didn't mean—"

He cut her off with a wave of his hand. "Whatever."

They stopped outside his room, the awkward silence between them stretching. He keyed in the code on his door and slid it open. It was tidy, as protocol required, but the wall across from his bed was littered with hologram pictures of him and his friends. Auri already knew there were none of the two of them.

He started to walk inside but stopped and half turned, not meeting her eye. "Don't forget about lunch tomorrow."

She winced, regretting ever bringing up the GIC. Their father had set up weekly lunches when Auri started basic training a year ago, and they were usually spent with the GIC talking about Auri's accomplishments and Ty's failures.

Ty turned to enter his room, but she grabbed his elbow. "Um, Ty?" She glanced at him, yearning for reassurance despite the pain and anger brewing in his eyes. "Do you think the captain will really be mad? I've got a debriefing with him at 0800 tomorrow."

He looked at her hand on his arm and she let go. "Probably not. It's not like you let the guy get away. You just let him die."

You just let him die. The words echoed in her head.

"Night, Aur." He retreated into the room, sliding the door shut behind him. Auri stood outside for a beat longer, fighting to get her emotions under control.

Eventually she returned to her room, wearily tugging the door open. Birdie snored on Auri's narrow bed. The room, when compared to Ty's, was lonely and drab, hologram notes scattered on the walls to remind her of upcoming tasks.

At least her room smelled lovely thanks to the fresh flowers she'd cut a few days before. On her way to her dresser, she inhaled the scent of the powder-blue hydrangeas bursting from a glass container. Their multiple blooms formed a perfect sphere.

When she first moved into this room, she'd transformed the balcony into a garden before even unpacking her clothes. Flowers made her feel at home. Safe. Loved. Her fingers brushed the single earring she wore, threaded through two holes in her left earlobe. A delicate metal blossom hung from the front of the chain and in the back, the gold thread screwed into a green metal leaf. The GIC claimed Auri had it with her when the MPB Rangers rescued her all those years ago. Technically, wearing it was against regulation, but it was yet another allowance the GIC had made for her.

She grimaced again over her blunder with Ty. The GIC was an open wound for him, and she'd gone and dumped a shaker of salt into it. Hopefully a good night's sleep would ease the tension between the two of them. And the *takoyaki*.

She changed out of her dirty uniform and collapsed into bed, unceremoniously shoving Birdie to the floor. The poodle groaned before curling up on her bed.

"Good night, Bird," Auri mumbled. She rolled onto her side and closed her eyes.

As always, the nightmares came next.

CHAPTER FOUR

10 Aug 3319, 07:55:53
Ancora Galaxy, Planet 02: Isoroku-Patton, Moon:
Yosai, MPB Bldg

"The captain will be with you in a moment."

"*Arigato.*" Auri thanked the new secretary, fresh out of basic judging by his cropped hair and perfectly ironed fatigues. He didn't notice the parts of her that weren't human, he was so intent on impressing everyone.

After his extreme politeness to the grumpy delivery lady who'd come to take orders for lunch, Auri couldn't help asking, "First day?"

He nodded. "Obvious?"

She winked. "You'll be fine."

His gaze found her mechanic eye and fixed there. Color burned bright in his cheeks as he fumbled with the holo screen perched atop his desk—an excuse to turn away from her.

Auri knew how drill sergeants teased the new recruits in basic: "There's a cyborg or two up in the ranks, but there's one in particular you've got to worry about. She's a spy for the GIC. Her robotic ear records everything you say. And that eye of hers? Can see right through your clothes to your—"

For some, the last part had been more of a turn on than a turn off.

She looked at her hands, giving the secretary the space he craved. Rather than sit in one of the cushioned chairs lining the walls, she fidgeted. Her fingers smoothed the gold buttons running down her uniform coat and adjusted the school-girl styled bow at her neck, making sure it lay just so. She brushed the single chevron on her upper right sleeve, distinguishing her as a DISC Agent Second Class.

What would the captain say about her botched mission? Would he send her back to basic for one mistake? She could avoid Agent Hillsdale while he still convalesced at the hospital here on Yosai. But how long until he was discharged? "Hawkeye" Hillsdale was so nicknamed because his track record was perfect. As an Agent First Class, he'd been gunning for a promotion to lieutenant. Auri's screw up would reflect badly on him, even if he hadn't actually participated. His poor judgement in giving her the case might prevent him from making the jump to officer.

Instinctively, she reached for the reassuring comfort of Birdie's warm curls, only to grasp air. The poodle had been left behind, forbidden from entering officer headquarters.

The secretary's head jerked up, a newbie reaction to a ping from a high-ranking officer. His gaze darted to Auri. "Captain says you may go in."

"Thanks." She gave her jacket a final tug to straighten it and strode up to the captain's door. She slid the dark glass open, saying a polite *"Sumimasen,"* accompanied by a shallow bow to excuse her entrance.

The captain leaned forward in his chair, scarred hands folded on his desk. His wedding band glistened in the sunlight creeping through the floor-to-ceiling window at his back. Soon the windows would automatically tint to block the sun's onslaught, but this early they were clear and almost invisible, as if no barrier existed between her and the beauty of Yosai, the Forested Moon.

"Agent Peri," Captain Ishida said with a nod. "Report."

She took a breath, willing her organic knee to stop trembling. "Yes, sir." She clasped her hands behind her back and spread her feet apart, head erect. With quick efficiency, as she'd been trained, she offered the details of her mission, omitting the hallucination. All in the interest of the greater good and, yes, her career. If she recorded her hallucination and the captain used it as evidence that the DISC taskforce wasn't a good fit? That couldn't happen. No other division allowed her to keep criminals from hurting innocents *and* be spared a cyborg-hating partner.

When she finished, Captain Ishida gestured to the solitary chair in front of his desk. Auri frowned. Did his face look paler than usual? "Have a seat."

She obeyed.

After an uncomfortable silence, likely purposeful on his part, he asked, "Agent Peri, is there a reason why both you and Agent Hillsdale failed to inform me of the case swap?"

Auri curled her toes in her freshly shined boots. "I… Sir, Agent Hillsdale said he would inform you."

A muscle at his temple ticked. Wrong answer. "And what makes you, a rookie fresh out of basic, think *you* shouldn't also inform me as a courtesy?" His voice was soft, but his tone hinted at a simmering anger. "And in this case, out of common sense. The pain medication administered to Agent Hillsdale after you left rendered him unable to send so much as a ping to cancel his subscription to *The Rising Sun* newscast."

Her heart dropped into her stomach. This whole time she'd thought Hillsdale had informed Captain Ishida. She scrambled to think of an appropriate apology, even while feeling the sting of the captain's uncharacteristic anger. He was known to be a patient leader who listened to his agents. Auri could understand why he might be annoyed, but angry?

"It was a mistake, sir. I never should've taken his case."

He shook his head, letting out a slow breath. "I assign agents specific cases for a reason, Agent Peri. There were reasons why I wouldn't assign you Agent Hillsdale's, reasons straight from the GIC himself. Reasons I obviously should have passed on to my Agents First Class."

Auri opened her mouth, but the captain anticipated her question. "Reasons I'm not at liberty to disclose to you."

She yearned to press the issue, but she was already in enough trouble. "I understand. It won't happen again." She waited a beat, gauging Captain Ishida's mood, before she said, "Sir, this might sound strange." His gaze shifted to his holo screen, likely skimming the report she'd submitted to see if he had further inquiries for her. She forged ahead. "Has a suspect ever been found innocent?"

"Is there a more specific question you want to ask?" His deep-set eyes flicked to her.

She swallowed. "Could Tanaka Hiroki have been innocent? He mentioned monsters attacking his family. And his suicide—"

"*No.*" The word came out sharp with no room for debate.

Surprise left her mouth propped open, soundless. Had Captain Ishida just snapped at her? This was not the captain she had heard about, had been excited to serve under. His behavior, combined with his curled fists on the desk, made the hairs on Auri's organic arm rise.

He watched her for a beat then shook his head with a sigh. His hands relaxed on the desk. "All convicts try to blame someone. Over time you will learn this—assuming the investigation clears you. I'll be visiting Agent Hillsdale this afternoon to discuss the case and my opinions regarding the swapped assignments."

"That's not necessary!" The objection burst from her mouth, louder than she'd intended. But the last thing she needed was to get a superior agent in trouble. "Excuse me, sir. I begged

Hillsdale for the case. I took advantage of him. His leg was broken in three places, sir."

"I'm aware." The captain leaned back in his chair, lean arms crossed over his chest. "I'm bringing him in regardless. Considering the feelings among my agents after your first case and your pending investigation, I want you to take leave next week for Obon."

"Obon? Sir, I don't have any gravesites to visit. Or a home to return to. Couldn't you give this... this gift... to an agent who has family?"

The captain's features hardened, and his eyes shifted back to his holo screen. "I'm sure the GIC will appreciate it, considering your public appearance at the festival on Aurora every year. Besides, other agents can travel past Krugel's Curve. Other agents don't have a pending investigation on their file. And other agents didn't spark an illicit gambling ring with her foolish decision to take a mission not assigned to her."

Auri winced at each reason. The first one hurt the most. The GIC refused to allow Auri to take any cases that lay past Krugel's Curve, the infamous asteroid belt that split the solar system in half. It was packed with pirates and colliding space debris. He claimed he couldn't stand the thought of anything happening to her on Ancora Federation's rougher planets.

Not only had the regulation made her stand out amongst her other agents, but Auri worried he thought her incapable.

"In any case, there aren't any available cases on Rokuton, Aurora, or Babbage." The captain's voice drew Auri out of her inner turmoil. "So enjoy the leave. Dismissed."

"*Arigato*, sir. For the leave and for understanding about the assignment swap." She bowed again and marched out of the office, anger propelling her past the secretary, out the door, and onto a transport to the moon Agar.

Once back in her room, Auri let out a pillow-muffled scream. Put on leave like a disposable agent and her concerns about Hiroki's case brushed aside. She felt like a child.

She collapsed onto her bed beside Birdie. The poodle groaned and flopped onto her side, jaws parting in a yawn. Fish breath made Auri crinkle her nose.

"I feel so useless," she murmured into Birdie's ear. It twitched against her lips. The dog's head darted up, her rough tongue catching Auri's organic cheek. She laughed, propping herself upright on her arms. Outside the glass of her garden balcony, the sun shone bright over the tropical landscape.

Auri could spend the day moping in her room, avoiding Agent Hillsdale after his discharge, and eating as much junk food as the chow hall provided. Or she could prove herself capable by digging up proof to validate her concerns and present them to the GIC at lunch. More intel might even speed up her investigation.

Feeling purpose-driven once again, she hopped off the bed and changed out of her uniform, yanking a dress over her head. The wispy fabric fell to her knees and covered her shoulders, but…

Auri adjusted the neckline. The webbing of scars that snaked across her ribcage, breast, and shoulder poked out at the very edge of the fabric. The surgeons had managed to remove the scars on her face using synthetic skin, but her body remained marked. Whenever she was out of uniform, finding clothes that covered but didn't make her look like a nun posed a challenge.

The outside temperature recorded in the corner of her smart wall indicated it was sweltering, but she grabbed a quarter-sleeved jacket and slipped it over her shoulders. Better.

"Birdie," she said, scooping up the poodle's leash. "How about a walk?"

CHAPTER FIVE

---

10 Aug 3319, 10:25:05
Ancora Galaxy, Planet 02: Isoroku-Patton, Moon:
Agar, Patriot Park

The twin Tech Towers and their twenty-story, solar-panel exterior reflected a myriad of colors across the park. Paper lanterns hung across the walkway that led to the buildings, ready to be lit once night descended. People lounged in the sun, parents played with children, and DISC agents walked their dogs. The scent of food, cooked by festival vendors at the end of the strip, wafted on a warm breeze that tickled the palm fronds overhead.

Auri led Birdie on another circuit of the park, stopping underneath the Towers for the fifth time. She fiddled with her earring. The captain claimed there was nothing to Hiroki's "monster" accusations. But she couldn't shake the shadow of unease that trailed chilled fingers across the back of her neck. Checking the case intel in the Tech Towers wasn't against regulation. In fact, research was encouraged. Of course, usually the case was still active...

Birdie paused to sniff a patch of grass. The fountain in front of the Towers gave Auri an encouraging burble as if to say, *You can do it!*

Worry over the captain finding out wasn't the only thing holding her back. She hated going through the Towers' security. After the Cyborg Bomber's attack, every cyborg was required to undergo a physical search. Neither the weapon detectors nor the guards were ever happy to see her. Well, some guards were, but she avoided them.

She pressed her fingertip against the hard grooves of the flower on the earring. A man had died spouting his innocence, begging her to believe in the existence of his monsters. Hiroki was a criminal, but even criminals, outcasts... *cyborgs*... deserved compassion.

"C'mon, Bird." The pair strode toward the Tech Towers' entrance. She paused by the fountain and fished into a pocket of her dress for a coin.

"May I have success," she murmured, clapping her hands together twice for luck. With a flick of her wrist, she tossed a penny into the fountain's depths. The coin clinked against hundreds of other tangible wishes.

The filtered air inside the lobby of the Tech Towers was refreshing after the heat outside. Auri flapped the edge of her jacket, cooling her face. The marble floor stretched past twenty security kiosks and ended in a row of elevators at the building's rear. Only two kiosks were lit green with accompanying security guards. Thankfully, there were no entrance lines today, though a holo above the elevators declared the first three floors to be at maximum capacity or closed for maintenance.

Auri led Birdie to the closest female security guard. The guard grinned at Birdie, turning to pull a dog treat from a glass container on her counter.

"Can I give this to her?" she asked.

"Sure." Auri smiled at the petite guard. The woman had dark hair pulled into a low bun and a spattering of freckles across her nose. "Thanks."

The guard offered the treat to Birdie, who glanced at Auri for permission. "Go ahead," Auri said. The treat vanished between Birdie's teeth.

"DISC dog, right?" The guard picked up the barcode scanner beside the treat bin. "I'll take her to the kennels once your ID checks out."

Auri bared her right arm, the barcode like tar against her pale skin. The lines warmed as the guard scanned the mark. She took a moment to read the output on her machine before nodding.

"Great. Try to be back within three hours. We aren't allowed to take the dogs out for feeding or anything else."

"Do I need to go through that?" She pointed to the two pillars at the end of the station. Already her body tensed, recalling the blast of the alarm.

The guard glanced at the other officer, a guy lounging in a chair by his station. His eyes were averted toward the ceiling, immersed in whatever his c-tacts showed.

She shook her head. "You're the GIC's adopted daughter. If I can't trust you, I'm in trouble. You don't have any weapons?"

Relief eased her taught muscles. "No weapons." Auri passed the leash to the guard, unable to keep a smile from her face. "I wish you were on duty every time I came to the Towers."

The guard laughed. "I'm just doing my job." She accepted Birdie's leash and smoothed the nametag on her fatigues. "My little brother," she murmured, glancing around before leaning close to Auri. "He's a cyborg too and has a hard time going through security. I can't imagine what it must be like for a woman."

"Some guards are better than others." She bent down and gave Birdie a kiss between the eyes. "See you in a bit," she said to the guard before moving past the station.

A glass elevator took her to the fourth floor. Holo terminals stretched in every direction across a room the size of a small warehouse. On the edges of the space, two enclosed skybridges connected this Tech Tower to its twin. Auri had entered the Tower open to citizens, while the other side was reserved for Tower personnel.

All the holo terminals directly in front of her were empty, and she started toward one by the floor-to-ceiling windows. Two women and a man, all in civvies, clustered around a projection at the back of the room, smiles on their faces. They wore long sleeves so she couldn't see their barcode to learn names or ranks. Years ago, she might have introduced herself. But she'd learned better.

When she'd almost made it to a terminal, someone called, "Hey!"

Auri hesitated.

"Hey, cyborg!"

She slowly turned to see the man from the group waving her over, grinning. Excitement tempered with apprehension at *cyborg* rose within her. At least he hadn't called her a *clank*.

Don't look too eager, she told herself, closing the gap between them with as leisurely a stroll as she could muster.

"Hi," Auri ventured cautiously, sticking out her right hand by reflex. "I'm Auri. You can call me that instead of cyborg."

One woman's gaze flicked to the man as if trying to understand why he'd invited Auri over. The other shot Auri a shy smile.

The man had olive-colored skin with thick black hair just a few centimeters longer than regulation allowed. When his gaze dropped from her face to her offered hand, Auri fought to keep it extended.

The seams of her synthetic skin were usually unnoticeable, but in the florescent light above and subjected to his scrutiny, the connecting lines along her fingers and forearm were glaring. Hideous.

When he still did not shake her hand, she offered her organic one instead, cheek warming. Still, the man's upper lip curled. He studied her hand for a beat too long before giving it a quick shake, fingertips barely touching her skin before pulling back.

Indignation struck Auri like a hot poker between her ribs. She was over fifty percent cyborg. Two of the fingers on the hand he had touched were robotic. He was the one who had called her over in the first place.

"Auri," he murmured as if recalling a memory. "Aurelia Peri. The GIC's adopted daughter. You're the cyborg who killed that Class One Fugitive, aren't you?"

She clenched her teeth. How had news spread so quickly? She didn't even know these people. "No," she snapped. "And the investigation will prove it." She shook her head. "If that's all, I have work to do." With a nod at the other two women, she strode toward the terminal farthest from the group. She felt their gazes burn hot into her back as the snickering started. Auri willed her organic cheek to stop blushing.

With a sigh, she sat down at the terminal. The holo keyboard flickered on and the projector powered up, loading a login menu. She reached to tap the screen only to realize her organic hand was shaking. She clenched it into a tight fist and let out a slow breath. Then another.

After signing in and pulling up the database, she keyed in Tanaka Hiroki's name and date of birth. She knew the broad aspects of his case from Agent Hillsdale's transfer, but the database contained details she hadn't received.

According to the MPB report, at the time of the murders, Tanaka Hiroki had filed for bankruptcy and was days away from losing his home. He had murdered his wife by...

Auri blanched, leaning closer to the screen. He had beaten her and then torn into her with...

With his *teeth*.

They found his daughter's body kilometers away from the house in a cattle pasture, as if she'd been trying to run. Her body had been ravaged by a dull knife or perhaps even sharp fingernails. No sign of teeth marks.

No sign of teeth marks. She rubbed a hand across her face. Never did she imagine she would read that phrase in a report.

And the dried blood on Hiroki's clothes—so much blood—verified that story.

A green map icon hovered next to the case number. Auri tapped it and a 3D rendering of the crime scene appeared.

Bile burned the back of her throat as she swiped at certain areas to zoom in. In the back bedroom, a door had been torn off its hinges, the remnants of a barricade—chairs, a dresser, a ladder—obliterated. On the bed lay the remains of a human body, blood staining the blue duvet black, crimson splashed across the yellow walls. A window was open. According to the reports, authorities discovered the daughter's fingerprints there. She'd been only five years old. They assumed she had escaped Hiroki's rampage against her mother only to be cut down. Officers found Hiroki soon after, hiding in a dilapidated barn near the child's body.

Auri rested her chin in the palm of her hand, fingers tapping a thoughtful beat on her cheek. Hiroki had been malnourished and weak when she cornered him on Babbage three days after his jailbreak and successful theft of a civilian shuttle on Kaido. That short timespan couldn't account for the state of his body.

Weeks of starvation during the dry season on Kaido could.

Hiroki's home had been destroyed, his wife and daughter murdered with ferocity and brutal strength. Strength she would be surprised a starving Hiroki even possessed. Could the wounds on his daughter have come from someone else?

Auri closed out of the 3D rendering and clicked the first keyword associated with Hiroki's case: *cannibalism*.

The holo lit up with a buffering circle as the system searched for other cases with the same keyword. Auri leaned back, arms crossed, confident that the findings would be few.

The buffering circle vanished. Case after case appeared on the projected screen. Auri's eyes widened in horror as she counted them.

Eighteen, nineteen, *twenty*.

There were twenty documented cases over a span of twenty-eight years. And it was possible more went undocumented. She crinkled her nose at Captain Ishida's dismissive attitude earlier. Was it really this common for people to go crazy and become cannibals?

She clicked through the cases, disturbed over the number of suspects who either committed suicide before their trial or proclaimed innocence—even at their execution. She scrolled through the suspects' photos. The only unifying trait was the same crazed look that Hiroki had. A gaunt disbelief shone from their eyes, as if the world had imploded around them.

One man's picture in particular troubled her. His eyes had blinked shut just as the photo was taken, and a lazy officer had not bothered to redo it. The man's hair was overgrown and a scraggly beard covered his face. He fit the outward description of a cannibal stereotype, if there was such a thing, but there was a brokenness in his expression. Guilt? Or loss?

Intrigued, she read further. He was accused of killing approximately one hundred victims—an entire district. She snorted in disbelief. Even using a series of shrapnel bombs, like the investigators believed, murders on that scale took talent and serious planning.

Auri backtracked and skimmed the keywords under the case links. Only the three outer planets were tagged: Kaido, Delfan, and Medea. Kaido was the closest planet to her, located just on the other side of Krugel's Curve. She clicked the planet's keyword combined with cannibalism. The results narrowed to five. Hiroki's attack and the hundred-person killer were both on Kaido and only a district apart, though almost three years separated the murders. Regardless, visiting both would make for a quick investigation.

Auri snagged a floppy, a palm-sized foldable screen used for storing secure information, from the stacks between each monitor. It'd be easier to upload the information to her c-tacts, but security protocols required a tangible copy. She transferred the two case files onto the floppy and then, after a moment of hesitation, all the cannibalism cases. While the holo and floppy synced with one another, she scrolled through the full list.

Her eyes lingered on the ten cases reported from Medea. Her original home, according to the GIC.

A pair of rangers had found her in an abandoned mountain settlement, bleeding out after an animal attack. The GIC happened to be visiting the rangers' outpost when they brought her in. She'd almost died. Multiple times. Seventy percent of her internal organs had been replaced. Auri's right eye, cheek, and jaw all had to be reconstructed. Her right arm had been torn clean off, her leg suffering a compound fracture that resulted in gangrene...

The GIC had taken Auri in as his own, paid for the best medical care, commissioned the fitting of high-end robotic limbs. Then, when she had recovered, learned to speak and walk again, he adopted her. She had been six years old.

She didn't remember anything from before. Not her parents or how she ended up alone, half dead. She only knew one thing: she owed the GIC her life.

A peal of laughter, reminding Auri of the monkeys that populated Rokuton's dense jungle, jerked her from the memory.

She glanced at the group. It had been a woman who laughed. The man had loaded a basic training "fail" montage on his holo, popular among everyone *but* those in basic. On the screen a female recruit dropped into a runner's stance, her expression determined. Around her, other recruits did the same. A whistle blew and the runners took off. Except the female recruit. For all her determination, at the sound of the whistle, she had tripped on an untied shoelace, landing on her face.

Auri grimaced on the female recruit's behalf. Every day she thanked the stars she was out of basic. Very few recruits had positive memories of their training, and every military branch claimed MPB Basic was the easiest. The Marines was more like a death camp. Or so the stories went. The Marines mainly took recruits from students who failed high school entrance exams, so the branch was known to be a little… rougher.

The floppy on her lap chirped, alerting her that the file transfer was complete. She glanced down at the screen only to cry out at the time stamp.

She was late for lunch with the commanding general of the entire Ancora Federation.

CHAPTER SIX

---

10 Aug 3319, 12:55:03
Ancora Galaxy, Planet 02: Isoroku-Patton, Moon:
Yosai, Officer Dining Room

Auri hurtled through the doors of the dining room, side-stepping a startled security guard outside. "I have a meeting with the General-in-Chief," she called on her way past, hoping the guard would recognize her as the GIC's adopted daughter. She'd been here for lunch often enough.

Instead he trailed her inside, finally catching up when she paused to salute a superior officer headed to the bathroom. The guard's gloved hand wrapped around Auri's upper arm. When she turned to look at him, his mouth was frowning underneath a swatch of red razor burn.

"Ma'am, I need to see your barcode before you can enter."

The officer's dining room was half full, high-ranking officials seated at round tables covered with pristine white tablecloths. A few turned to glance at her, but most of them didn't notice, too caught up in matters of state to pay attention to the GIC's adopted daughter here for her weekly lunch. This security guard must've been new.

"I think you'll find she's been invited," a familiar voice said over Auri's shoulder.

She turned, grinning. The General-in-Chief stood before her, hands clasped behind his back at military rest. He wore his uniform, a dark gray jacket and pants, decorated with medals of all sizes and colors. His tanned face was clean-shaven, expression serious save for a twinkle of amusement in his wrinkled eyes.

The security guard went rigid, his hand rising in automatic salute. "Yes, sir." He scurried away, glancing over his shoulder at them every few paces, possibly to ensure the GIC hadn't ordered the man's arrest for accosting his adopted daughter. The man was the leader of the entire Federation, after all.

"I'm late," Auri said with a grimace. "Very late."

The GIC led her back to the table. "Yes, you are. So you'll be stuck with what Tyson ordered for your lunch."

Ty waited for them at their usual table in the back of the room, surrounded by open windows. A hot breeze rifled the gauzy curtains. He stood as they approached and pulled a chair out for her. She sank into it, longing to take off her jacket to cool the sweat running down the center of her back. Instead, she took a sip of icy water and pressed the cold glass against her organic cheek.

"Did you run all the way here?" Ty murmured as the GIC took his seat across from them.

"I had to drop Birdie off at my room. And the transport was delayed."

The GIC folded his hands, the buttons on his sleeves clinking against the empty salad plate. Beside his plate rested his hat. Five stars encircled the front with an eagle in the center. The symbol stood for his rank as the most powerful man in the system.

Though Auri knew Earth had operated with multiple types of governments, Ancora was a stratocracy—a military-run federation. An advisory board, comprised of representatives from

each military branch and the divisions therein, offered sugges-
tions on what actions the GIC should take, but, ultimately, every
decision rested in his hands. The mantle of that responsibility
astounded Auri whenever she thought of it, and she respected
him more than any other person she knew.

"Aurelia," he said, "while we wait for the food, why don't
you tell us about your first mission?" For a moment, the corners
of his mouth pulled tight as if in pain or, worse, disappointment.
The expression vanished with a blink of his hazel eyes.

So he already knew about the swap. She shouldn't have
been surprised.

As much as Auri appreciated the GIC for what he had done
and continued to do for her, she hated these lunches almost as
much as Ty. Rather than a time to catch up, she always felt like
she was being interviewed. The GIC acted so reserved and distant, taking care of her and Ty from afar. The only time he
seemed to show emotion was on her birthday. And even then,
there was a sadness locked behind walls of ceremony.

She longed for the GIC to slouch in his seat, make a joke,
tell them about *his* days. But everything her adopted father did
was classified well above her clearance level, released only on a
need-to-know basis.

Ty coughed beside her, and Auri sat up straighter. She repeated the mission report she'd given Captain Ishida hours
earlier, though the GIC probably already knew everything.

"You had an interesting time," he commented after she finished, glancing over her shoulder at the waiter arriving with
their food. "Maybe you've learned not to swap assignments?"
The question sounded innocuous enough, but Auri's spine went
rigid.

"Y-yes, sir."

When the waiter placed Auri's plate, she bit her lip. A
cheeseburger sat in the center, ringed by an impressive number
of fries. She loved cheeseburgers, so Ty couldn't be faulted for
that. It was also impossible to eat one in a dignified way, which

is what she'd preferred given the important favor she wanted to ask the GIC. She glanced at Ty's plate. Sushi was arranged with edible flowers and splashes of bright sauce. The same meal sat in front of the GIC.

She kicked Ty under the table with her robotic foot, hissing, "Why did you order me a burger when you two have sushi?"

He shrugged as if he didn't know why she was upset. With the sunlight shining on his face, he was the image of angelic innocence. She sighed.

The GIC pressed his palms together and lowered his head. Ty and Auri followed, all three repeating "*Itadakimasu*" to show their thanks for the food.

They ate in silence for a few minutes, only interrupted by the chatter of the other officers and the *clink-clink* of Auri's fork and knife as she cut into her burger.

After bolstering herself with beef and bread, she took a sip of water and looked up. "General, in regards to my case, I'm concerned about the monsters Tanaka Hiroki mentioned."

The GIC's chopsticks paused against his plate.

She plowed ahead despite the burger turning to bricks in her belly. "Captain Ishida said that I should disregard the claims, but I went to the Tech Towers this morning and found twenty related cases. Five on Kaido alone, one of which was close to Hiroki's district."

The GIC lowered his chopsticks, the intricately carved metal catching the light from the chandeliers above. "You're showing initiative even after your case was closed. Well done, Aurelia." He turned to Ty. "What of your missions, son? I've heard positive things from your lieutenant. Maybe an early promotion?"

Ty sat up straighter at the coveted p-word. He cleared his throat to reply, but Auri spoke first.

"Sir—" she began. Ty gave a subtle shake of his head. But she needed to ask her favor before the conversation shifted away from her mission. "Sir, I would like you to order Captain Ishida to let me investigate Tanaka Hiroki's claims."

The GIC's dark brows rose, his forehead wrinkling up to his shaved head. "You're requesting a favor?" He looked meaningfully at Ty before returning to Auri. "You've never asked me to yank on the strings of my subordinate officers." Auri tensed. Had she imagined his emphasis on "you"? She had hoped that Ty's frequent favors would mean the GIC wouldn't begrudge her this one, but she hadn't considered how Ty would react to her request.

In her peripheral vision, Auri watched Ty's face redden. His mouth formed a thin line, but he didn't speak.

The GIC reached across the table to take her hand. She froze at his touch on her organic fingers, startled by the feel of human skin, the warmth and pulse of it. She couldn't remember the last time he had shown fatherly affection. Her fingers tightened on his by reflex.

Ty snorted and pushed away from the table, the majority of his sushi uneaten. "If you'll excuse me, the hypocrisy at this table has upset my stomach." He stomped toward the exit without the required salute or a substitute bow to the man who controlled the fates of seven planets.

"Ty," Auri called, shifting in her chair to follow him, but the GIC tugged on her hand. "Shouldn't someone go after him?" She winced as the doors to the dining room slammed shut. Silence descended on the room. Furtive glances from the other diners strayed to their table before the GIC cleared his throat. The gazes slid away like oil on water. Soon the clink of silverware and polite chatter resumed.

The GIC's mouth was a firm line as he stared over Auri's shoulder at the closed doors. Then he sighed. "Let him be. His behavior today has been embarrassment enough." The GIC gave her fingers a final squeeze before picking up his chopsticks. "Aurelia, what exactly are you asking me? Why is this so important?"

Auri toyed with one of the fries on her plate. She forced her mind away from Ty. "Something about these cannibal cases seems wrong. And when Hiroki mentioned the monsters, what he claimed they did…" Her jaw locked against the words, but the GIC wasn't the captain. He had done nothing but deserve her trust. She worked her mouth open. "I had a hallucination. Of screaming. So much screaming."

His understanding smile didn't make her feel better. "You were involved in a horrific attack as a child. That criminal mentioning the atrocities he committed must've triggered a memory. Unless you think we should send you to a cyborg specialist?"

She shook her head hard enough to send a flash of pain down her neck. "No. I'm fine."

"Good." He popped a piece of sushi into his mouth and chewed deliberately so the silence between them stretched out. He swallowed and then leaned forward, any compassion gone from his face and replaced with cold authority. "Leave this alone, Aurelia. As your general, I am ordering you to do this. Do you understand?"

The warning in his voice wrapped its icy talons around her heart. "Y-yes, sir."

"Good."

They finished their meal in silence, Auri picking at the remnants of her burger, painfully aware of Ty's empty place beside her. The GIC's order stung. Every nerve ending burned with the shame and surprise of it.

He had *never* ordered her to do anything. Her career after high school had been her choice. Other fathers forced their children to follow in their footsteps. Any general, not to mention the GIC, would've been embarrassed that their offspring chose to enter the "cushy" service branch.

Once she explained why the solitary aspect of the DISC taskforce appealed to her—she wouldn't be partnered with people who mistrusted cyborgs—he assented. Ty's decision a year earlier hadn't been so smooth. There were nightly arguments, silent treatments, even threats. No matter how many times Ty declared his reasoning—his mother had been an agent and risen in the ranks faster than any serviceperson in Federation history—the GIC refused to relent. He almost seemed to despise his son for his choice to be like his mother.

But Auri... The GIC always treated her like she was precious, a glass sculpture to be protected. To have him relay such an order fractured a vital part of her.

The GIC pushed away from the table, and she jumped. "Excuse me, Aurelia. I just got an emergency ping. Apparently some drones have malfunctioned on Aurora and damaged one of our transporters. The monotonies of being leader." The last part was said around a chuckle, an attempt to lighten the mood between them.

Auri stood and bowed. "Thank you for lunch."

He grabbed her shoulder as he walked by, whispering, "Don't disappoint me, Aurelia." He pulled back and said with a smile, "I'll see you and Ty again at the Obon Festival in a few days. And the military ball in three weeks! We'll shop for a dress after the festival." Then he was striding away.

She didn't turn to watch him leave. He might've stopped at the entrance to wave to her in their usual tradition, but she wouldn't know. Her body had frozen at his subtle threat.

Don't disappoint me.

The idea of disappointing the GIC, the man who had given her everything, the only one to care for her, to take her in as deformed as she was...

It horrified her. But so did the GIC's strange behavior.

If she continued down this path and investigated Hiroki's claims, would her adoptive father abandon her? Could someone be un-adopted?

Auri's fingers strayed to the tips of her scars, hidden underneath her jacket. The ghostly screaming raked at her ears as she relived the memory of Hiroki stepping off the roof. She watched his body shatter against the water. Again and again and again.

Twenty cases of cannibalism. Twenty lives—plus their victims'—destroyed. They deserved an investigation.

If Auri were honest, her motives were double-edged. She wanted to correct the failure of her first mission. She longed to prove herself worthy of everything the GIC gave her. Even if he didn't approve.

Auri turned away from the half-eaten food on her plate and followed the GIC's path out of the dining room. With her week of leave, she could get to Kaido and back, assuming the orbital transfers aligned in her favor to shorten her ride home.

No one would ever need to know she disobeyed orders.

Unless, of course, she found something.

CAPTAIN'S LOG

Hachigatsu 10, 3319 at 1900

Captain Malachi Vermillion here. Though most of my crew just calls me Cai. I'm not the type to make one of these. A captain's log. Always thought they were for pretentious assh—

[Clears throat]

After being taken out by a rogue traffic drone during our delivery on Aurora and losing consciousness for an hour, Katara insisted I detail the crews' jobs in audio format. By *insisted*, she held a knife to my throat and demanded it.

In fact, [nervous laughter] she's currently holding a knife at my back while I'm recording this.

[Muffled female commentary]

She's not pleased I just said that.

Anyway, slaving away for the Fed is paying off. We got a meeting with the General-in-Chief's secretary after the droid incident. Just an opportunity for him to apologize and avoid negative PR. But still. A meeting with the GIC's secretary is something.

[Voice lowers] It's taken so long to get here. Too long.

[Clicks tongue and sighs] The ship is now enroute to Kaido where we'll celebrate Obon again this year. Being the good cap' that I am, I gave the crew leave to take the shuttles to participate in their own celebrations. [Sighs again] Yet they're all sticking around. For some reason they think I'm going to get myself into trouble.

Considering I'm headed back home…

I probably am.

CHAPTER SEVEN

———

10 Aug 3319, 22:05:59
Ancora Galaxy, Planet 02: Isoroku-Patton, Moon:
Agar, DISC Living Qtrs.

A cucumber vine curled around Auri's bare foot. She disentangled herself without looking down, oblivious to the plant's prickles against her prosthetic skin. The balcony garden surrounded her, plants soaking in the sparse moonlight above. Of all the planets and moons in the Ancora Galaxy, the terra-formed atmosphere on Agar was a perfect environment for food growth. Something Auri took advantage of. Luscious scents of crushed basil and rosemary drifted on the warm evening air. She breathed deep, curling her toes in the dirt, then stepped off the raised garden bed.

Sometimes she wondered what she would do after her two years of required military service. A year had already been spent in basic. Just one more to go. Many people stayed enlisted and rose in the ranks, the sign-on bonus acting as a big incentive. Whenever she stood among the plants she spent hours tending, she wondered if being an agent was what she really wanted.

She cradled a basket in the crook of her elbow. It bounced against her hip as she moved through the rows of vegetables and herbs packed into the four rows of raised beds she'd made herself. She had plenty of MREs, Meals Ready to Eat, for the week-long journey, plus spares for emergencies. But a girl could only handle so much pre-packaged food. Though she never got tired of the hi-chews or puchaos included for dessert.

After filling her basket with tomatoes, herbs, cucumbers, oranges, and plenty of carrots—Birdie's favorite vegetable—she tiptoed back into her room. Her dirty feet left marks on her tiled floor, but she didn't pause to clean them. Instead, she shoved her feet into socks and then into her boots. She was already running behind.

A snuffling, wet nose nudged the vegetable basket and Auri tsked, shooing Birdie away. "Go to bed, Bird. I'm busy."

Birdie obeyed, tail drooping. The dog whined as she plopped onto her futon, eyes watching Auri hurry about the dimly lit room.

"I'm taking you with me, *aho*. Relax." Her MPB issued rucksack was full of clothes, MREs, two canteens, and hygiene packets with just enough room left for her produce and herbs sealed in VPro bags to keep them fresh. Her shuttle supplied a huge tank of drinking water. One less thing for her to worry about.

She pulled the route up on her c-tacts for probably the hundredth time that evening. The lenses over her eyes connected with the planet's grid, displaying the information she needed.

Since her mission wasn't Fed sanctioned and she lacked the funds to pay for the quick travel the slingshots provided, it'd take her four days to reach Kaido, two to get back. Leaving a day for investigating.

As she added her final foodstuffs to the rucksack, she tried not to think about the consequences of her actions. She would miss the annual Obon Festival with the GIC and Ty. She had her excuse pings ready to send, but if she got caught... Worst case scenario she would be court martialed and DD'ed, or dishonorably discharged. DD citizens usually ended up begging on the streets or joining one of the rebel militias throughout the system. The thought made Auri's fingers fumble on the rucksack's flap.

"Look at the positive, Aur," she told herself, tossing her rope braid back over her shoulder before it got caught in the rucksack's zipper. If she uncovered something in her investigation, the GIC might allow her to travel past Krugel's Curve for future missions. And people might finally, *finally* like her. She'd even give Agent Hillsdale credit. Just the thought of not eating alone in the chow hall was enough to banish her worries.

Auri propped her hands on her hips, scrutinizing her rucksack. She had all the essentials, including food and treats for Birdie. It was time to get her poodle ready. She scooped Birdie's working harness from her desk. "Birdie, come h—"

A knock on the door snatched the word from her mouth. She swung around just as the door opened on silent rollers. There was only one person who knew the lock code…

Ty stood before her, illuminated by the hallway light creeping into the room. His gaze darted from her terrified expression to the bulging rucksack on her bed.

"Well, then." He stepped inside and slid the door shut behind him. "What's going on in here? Why is it so dark?" He tapped the wall panel twice, maxing the lights to full brightness.

Auri winced and shielded her eyes with a hand. "I was… Um…" She frowned, crossing her arms over her chest. "What're you doing, just walking in? I could've been undressed."

His gaze made a slow circuit from her head to her feet and back again. She bit her lip against the tickle in her belly. "You're in your uniform. I bet you even sleep in the thing." He smirked. Birdie trotted up to him and sat. When he didn't pet her right away, she barked and pawed at his leg. He gave her the obligatory scratch under the chin.

Auri released an exasperated breath and stomped over to her bed, a guise for hiding the rucksack. Maybe if it wasn't in his line of sight, he'd forget it was there. "I don't sleep in my uniform."

"Oh? What do you sleep in?" He looked up at her, eyes twinkling as he straightened, much to Birdie's chagrin. He laughed at the flush no doubt seeping across Auri's face. "I'm actually here to apologize for how I acted at lunch. Storming off was childish. The GIC always gets under my skin. You know how it is."

She nodded. Ty had spent hours throughout their high school years sprawled on her bed complaining about the GIC. He never called him "Dad" or "*Otō-san*" like the traditionalists did. Not that she did either, but for her things were different.

In a step he was beside her, looking at her bed and the offending bag. "What's the rucksack for?"

Auri didn't bother pointing out that he hadn't technically apologized. "You know what it's for, Ty."

He ran a hand through his blond hair, cropped on the sides but longer on top. The bristles scraped at his fingers. "You're going to investigate those two cases on Kaido. Does Captain Ishida know?"

She shook her head, unwilling to say the words aloud. No, he doesn't.

"*Kuso*, Auri. You know he'll find you out. Are you sure about this?" Despite the concerned tone of his voice, he started adjusting the loose straps on her rucksack. Like he was helping to send her off.

She waved his hands away and worked on the straps herself. "I'm sure. But since you know now, if it doesn't rain this week, would you water my garden?"

"Water your garden? Something's wrong with you." He let out a breath and reached into the voluminous pockets of his civvies' cargo pants. "All day I had this feeling that you'd go through with your crazy plan. I think it's idiotic, but I have something for you." Balanced atop his long fingers was a square box.

Her hands stilled on the straps. She turned to fully face him. "Ty?"

He grabbed one of her palms and lowered the box into it, the material satin-smooth. "Stop gawking and just open it."

Auri held her breath as she lifted the lid. Resting on a bed of white silk was a gladiolus blossom crafted from rose gold, the petals filled in with pink glass. A delicate chain pooled underneath the pendant. She sucked in a gasp, jerking her head up to look at her friend. "This… It's beautiful. But why?"

"I was going to give it to you for your birthday. Gladiolus is the flower for the month of August."

The current of joy barreling through Auri's veins rendered her speechless. Ty had never done anything like this for her. Half the time her birthday "slipped his mind," and she ended up with a last-minute gift like a delivered pizza with *HBD* spelled out in pepperoni.

"Thank you," she choked out. "I love it."

"Let me help you put it on. Turn around." He took the box from her and Auri obligingly turned. She lifted her braid as Ty slipped the chain around her neck. The pendant clinked against one of her uniform buttons. His fingertips brushed the sensitive skin along her neck as he secured the clasp, and she shivered.

"There." Suddenly, Ty's lips were against her ear, his whisper sending a thrill down her spine. "Happy birthday, Aur." He stayed close to her for a deliciously painful moment, one hand on her shoulder, as if breathing in the scent of her. Then he stepped back.

She turned to face Ty, her nerves aflame. "Thank you. Uh, again."

He tilted his head, a smile looping the side of his mouth. "I'm glad you like it."

"I do. I'll never take it off. Like a good luck charm." She clasped her hand over the flower, the metal cool to the touch.

"Good. I'll let you finish packing."

"Right." Yes, packing. That's what she was doing before Ty came in. *Packing*. She walked him to the door and opened it for him.

"Be safe, Aur," he said, offering her the lazy man's salute with two fingers before he left.

She shut the door and leaned against it with a sigh. Happiness burbled in her blood, singing a silent, joyful song. She tucked the necklace underneath her collar. The petals felt like a kiss against her chest.

Ty's teasing about wearing her uniform to bed made her smile as she moved away from the door. She'd debated whether to wear it for her unsanctioned mission or take off in her civvies.

The uniform won. It would earn her immediate sanctuary if she needed aid from a base on Kaido. She'd heard horror stories of soldiers past the Curve being quick with their guns instead of getting close enough to let their c-tacts scan a barcode. She didn't want that happening to her.

After settling Birdie into her working harness, Auri yanked her disc into its strap and settled the rucksack on her back. She still buzzed from the sensation of Ty's breath against her ear. The prickles along her organic skin, the pleasant buzzing of her nerves… She wanted to remember it forever with perfect clarity, to submerge herself in the memory again and again.

But right now she needed to focus on her current mission: sign out her shuttle under false pretenses and make it into free airspace.

"Here we go," she said to Birdie. Auri rolled her shoulders back and strode out the door. A small part of her, ignored by the excitement of what lay ahead, wondered if she'd ever set foot in her tiny room again.

CHAPTER EIGHT

---

14 Aug 3319, 18:17:59
Ancora Galaxy, Krugel's Curve

Auri had listened jealously to fellow students all through elementary, middle, and high school giggling about pulling all-nighters at sleepovers. Now she wanted to send her younger self a scathing ping. All-nighters were for crazy people.

Crazy people and AWOL DISC agents praying their autopilot navigated Krugel's Curve successfully.

Auri's jaw cracked as her lips spread wide in a yawn. She groaned, rubbing at her eyes. She'd been awake for almost twenty-four hours, ever since her Raptor Class vessel entered the asteroid belt. For the first three hours she'd been alert for pirates that, according to rumors in basic, lurked among the rocky debris hunting transport vessels. Krugel's Curve posed enough of a navigation hazard that the Fed didn't send the AC, Air Command, to patrol.

Krugel's Curve had been named after a particularly bloody general-in-chief with a penchant for giving orders, changing his mind, and then punishing anyone who contradicted him. Countless men and women had died, courtesy of his vacillating and open-ended death penalty. He'd been the twenty-first GIC in the

Ancora Federation's history, each serving until they retired. Or, in Krugel's case, were assassinated. Auri's adoptive father had been promoted to GIC twenty-four years ago.

Compared to the Milky Way Galaxy where Earth was located, Ancora Galaxy's settlement was fairly new; the planets in the Federation's solar system only terraformed in the last millennia. Back then, the terraforming had taken twenty-five years to complete its cycle on each planet. Those on the other side of the Curve were even newer. A military expedition of citizens had been launched from the USA and Japan to colonize the system over decades as the planets became safe to inhabit. The colonists were lured by monetary incentive, the promise of adventure, and a better life. It had been a long time since anyone considered Earth or their respective countries home.

Krugel had even banned communication with Earth as one of his final acts as commander, claiming they wanted to steal the Federation's natural resources. When a new GIC had come into office, she had been unable to reestablish communication.

Auri checked her pings for the hundredth time in the last three hours. Today was officially her eighteenth birthday. Despite the beautiful necklace, she hoped Ty would send a birthday message too. The GIC had sent her one earlier in the day, mentioning how he looked forward to their time together for Obon. Guilt hit her hard after reading that.

She supposed she should consider herself lucky. So far, she hadn't received any suspicious questions from the GIC or Captain Ishida, and no one seemed to notice her absence. Maybe not having friends was a good thing.

A proximity warning beeped and a coordinating light flashed on the dashboard, making her jump.

She gave her head a hard shake. "Calm down," she scolded herself as she pulled the sensors up on the touch screen. Her body tensed as she studied the readout, ready to burst into evasive action. Except she was perfectly safe. The warning originated from an asteroid that had gotten too close, despite autopilot's careful navigation.

No pirates, no immediate danger. The lack of sleep was getting to her. She needed a break.

Auri pushed to her feet, snagging a carrot that she'd been half-heartedly munching. Her Raptor Class ship was small, sporting the bare essentials for a DISC agent on routinely short missions. There was a narrow bed built into the wall at the back, a microscopic bathroom. Per regulation, a circular escape pod half the size of her shuttle had been added as a safety feature. Many DISC agents considered them inconvenient since they had no navigation interface and instead ran on pre-installed protocols that flew the escapee to the nearest planet. But what made the Raptor Class ships the most unique in the Federation were the dog kennels.

On the left back end of the ship, beside the hatch leading to the escape pod, was an enormous kennel. The kennel housed a cooling gel mat, a trapdoor for waste that Birdie hated using, and a built-in food/water dispenser. Inside the sturdy cage, the world's most perfect poodle stood on top of her pad, wagging her tail. Auri scratched Birdie's head through the wide-set bars. She'd actually let Birdie out a few times over the course of the trip, very much against the rules, but both of them had gotten bored.

"Lie down," Auri instructed, brandishing the carrot. Birdie dropped to her belly, her tail picking up speed. "Good girl." She shoved the carrot through the bars. Instead of lunging for it, Birdie looked up for permission. "Go ahead." The carrot was locked between Birdie's massive paws in an instant. She gnawed on it, teeth flashing. The poodle's white hair would be stained orange around the muzzle, but Auri didn't mind. She loved watching Birdie enjoy treats.

Static burst through the shuttle's speakers. Auri's head jerked up, her heart wedging itself at the base of her throat.

"Hailin' ship… Raptor Class, A.F.V. 623… uh… 89." The voice crackled with interference but was definitely male, carrying the harsher accent of citizens from the outer rim planets like Delfan or Medea.

Birdie abandoned her carrot to the floor of the kennel, head cocked at the voice. Auri rushed to the dashboard, leaning over her seat to read the sensors. It took her three scans to find the hailing ship. The ship's body was dented and dark gray, almost blending into the asteroids hurtling between them. Suspicion itched at Auri's scalp. Could this ship have been the "asteroid" her shuttle detected earlier?

She licked her dry lips, knowing radio silence was futile. The ship would hail her again. Or worse, try to board. Pirates or not, there was no way she could outrun them. Her shuttle was built for speedy travel, but surrounded by hundreds of ship-destroying asteroids, she didn't trust herself at the controls. Speed beyond what the autopilot provided was impossible. Maybe they were just other travelers, looking for conversation…

"This is A.F.V. 62389. I am on Federation business and cannot be detained."

"Fed business, eh? Well, we just got some iffy life readings and wanted to check in. See if yous and yours were in any distress." Maybe Auri imagined it, or it was the static through the coms, but she could've sworn he sounded on the verge of laughter.

She glowered at the mic fixed into the dashboard. "All is well," she said. "Over and out."

Auri shifted to pull up her sensor readings again when a red warning light flashed, followed by a wailing proximity alert. Something smacked into the shuttle with jarring force.

The shuttle rolled. Auri's feet were swept from under her as the artificial gravity momentarily failed. Her stomach slammed into the top of her pilot's chair, and air burst from her lungs.

The ship jerked to a halt, autopilot righting the controls. Auri hit the floor with a cry. Birdie yelped from inside her kennel, then stood and shook from her head to the tip of her tail. A deep *woof* came from her throat.

Auri wheezed, forcing herself to her feet. The flashing red lights and siren still blasted through the ship. She cursed the engineers. How could anyone function with this chaos?

She'd just reached the console when her ship lurched forward as something pummeled it from behind. Her fingers latched onto the dashboard's edge, keeping herself from sprawling over the sensitive controls. She attempted to send an SOS ping, but an error message flashed in her vision: *grid connection unavailable.*

A loud *thunk* penetrated the hull of the shuttle, sending icy fingers dancing across Auri's spine. She spun around at another *thunk.* Enormous harpoons had dug themselves into the sides of her shuttle. The metal tips and three attached prongs gleamed in the red emergency lights.

"*Chikusho,*" she hissed. These weapons were a pirate's favorite tool. By penetrating the hull, their victims couldn't disengage the harpoons without depressurizing the ship.

"I'm going to be boarded," she said aloud, anchoring herself with the terrifying words.

Surrender was always an option. One regulation of the pirate code stated if an attacked party surrendered, the pirates might let their victims live.

But Auri didn't go for maybes. And she didn't submit to pirates.

The warning alarms dimmed as more static came through the speakers. "Everything okay over there?" the man from the other ship asked through laughter.

Auri darted for her rucksack, shoved under the dashboard during the ship's roll. She flung it over a shoulder, shouting into the mic, "Telling you it's my birthday wouldn't keep you from boarding, would it?" Her voice dripped with disdain.

She didn't wait to hear the reply, if there would be one. Her disc and its harness had ended up wedged under the door to the bathroom. She dropped the rucksack in the escape hatch before freeing her disc and securing the straps over her shoulders and back. Having the weapon eased some of the panic building in her chest.

"It's going to be okay," Auri murmured to Birdie, whose ears lay flat against her skull, head jerking toward every sound. No doubt the poodle could sense her partner's unease. Auri fumbled with the kennel's latch. The metal caught, slicing the skin of her finger. A drop of blood splashed onto the floor. Meters away, the airlock doors groaned and clanged as the pirates locked on for boarding.

Auri cursed again. She wouldn't have time to free Birdie and get them both in the tiny escape pod. She would have to fight and hope for a chance to get into the pod later. Her limited boarding training ran through her head as she wrestled with the latch. A hard kick with her boot shoved the bar open. The door swung forward, and Birdie hunched, ready to leap from the kennel's confines.

"Stay," Auri croaked, pressing her fingertips against Birdie's wet nose. "You're going to be my surprise."

The doors at the back of her ship creaked as the pirates hacked the controls. Whatever had hit her ship in the rear had damaged the opening mechanisms. She gritted her teeth, toes curled in her boots. Her ship's anti-breach protocol should engage, bottle-necking the entrance. It *should*.

Auri whipped her disc free. It expanded as deadly electricity crackled around the edge.

The doors screeched to a halt, the opening barely a meter wide. The sound of gunshots dropped Auri to her knees, hiding behind the protection of her disc. Something pinged against the metal. She felt the impact all the way through her robotic arm.

She peered around the edge and waited for someone to run through the cover fire. A man squeezed past the gap, a long blasting gun strapped across his shoulder. The weapon worked both for staff fighting and long-range targets.

The pirate had just stepped onto her ship when she hurled her disc. It slammed into the man's chest, lightning crackling through his body. He dropped, the disc flying back into Auri's outstretched hand as her c-tacts automatically activated its return feature.

The disc's battery levels flashed a panic-inducing fifty percent in her peripherals and she swallowed a bolt of fear. The voltage had been turned up to maximum, killing the pirate on impact and draining half the disc's battery.

"*Kuso*," Auri hissed through clenched teeth.

Through her c-tacts, she lowered the disc's voltage to shock and darted forward as the next pirate rushed through. Man or woman, she didn't notice or care. She slammed the flat of the disc against the pirate's chest, shoving them against the wall, their long taser pinned against them.

She attempted to dodge a kick, but it glanced across her robotic leg. Auri grabbed a laser knife from her belt. The pirate blocked the blow with a free arm, sending the knife clattering to the floor. A woman, Auri distantly registered as she activated the lightning on her disc once more. It pulsed through the woman's body with less intensity than before. The woman slumped with a groan.

The disc's battery flashed a thirty percent. Any lower and the voltage would feel like an annoying static shock. A depleted battery took eighty seconds to recharge. Her last resort was to activate the disc's curved blades. They were brutal and bloody, but right now she didn't care. She just wanted to survive.

Something yanked on the back of Auri's braid, towing her to the floor. She landed atop the first pirate's corpse as another man leered over her.

This pirate clutched a magnetic coilgun, known for their agonizing barbed metal bullets, in both hands, the barrel aimed at her face. She moved to bring her disc up, but quick reflexes brought his foot stomping on her bicep, pinning her disc arm to the floor.

"Birdie, gun!" Auri shouted.

The pirate's head jerked up at the sound of a dog snarling. Birdie launched herself across the shuttle, jaws spread. She latched onto the man's throat, forcing him to the floor. A wet gurgling cry escaped his lips as Birdie shook. Crimson stained her white muzzle, blood dribbling down her neck. He went still.

Two more pirates shoved through the door, a man and woman. Auri had already released her disc by the time the man aimed his gun at Birdie, finger curling against the trigger.

The impact snapped his wrist back against his arm. He screamed, dropping the gun. The disc swirled back toward Auri, her hand outstretched to catch it and attack the next pirate.

The bang of pulsed laserfire exploded through the small shuttle. Auri stiffened, ready for the pain and blood following impact. Instead, a fist-sized blaster beam struck the disc, sending the disc off course. The edge slammed into the wall above Birdie's kennel and stuck. Auri tried to recall it, but the disc barely loosened a centimeter.

The woman shifted to point the gun at Auri. A wicked scar ran the length of her forehead, down her nose and chin, disappearing into her high-necked tank top.

"I'm a-thinking it's time you surrendered," she suggested with an icy grin. "Refuse and I'll shoot you now and shove the whole damn pirate code up a rat's pink ass. I just hired these men, and I hate wasting my time and money almost more than I hate the Fed."

Auri gritted her teeth. At least this crew abided by the code. So far. Maybe she could still get out of this alive. She glanced around, biting back a curse as the female pirate she'd stunned with her disc rose groggily to her feet, joined by the man whose wrist she had broken. Three against two. With guns figured into the equation, there was only one way this catastrophe could end.

Auri raised her hands, sinking to her knees. "I surrender."

Birdie dropped to her haunches, training overruling the instinct to fight. She whimpered, the sound slashing Auri's heart to ribbons.

"I surrender," she repeated, despising the bitter taste of the words. "I surrender."

CHAPTER NINE

---

14 Aug 3319, 19:00:08
Ancora Galaxy, Outskirts of Krugel's Curve

"'ll be damned," muttered the woman with the gun. "For the fight you put up, the inside of your boat is the saddest piece of junk I've seen." She glanced at the remnants of her crew and, Auri noticed with satisfaction, frowned. The woman caught Auri's gaze on her and shrugged as if unbothered. "There's more where they came from."

Auri and Birdie had killed a quarter of the boarding pirate crew and disabled another. The man still whimpered over his broken wrist. Only the two women seemed fine, though Auri reminded herself the number of pirates aboard the ship was a mystery.

"Graham, search this miserable lump of metal," the woman commanded, crinkling her scarred nose. "Better pray to whatever listening gods there's something of value here since you demanded we stop."

Graham clenched his jaw but was quick to obey, holding his injured wrist tight against his body. He proceeded to toss the mattress of her bed to the floor, rip apart the leather of the pilot's chair, and clamber down into the escape pod, emerging with her rucksack. He dumped the contents of the bag onto the floor, eyes searching for anything valuable. Unless the pirates were after MREs and fresh vegetables, they'd be disappointed.

Meanwhile, the two women watched Auri. The scarred woman, likely the captain, kept her gun trained on Auri's forehead. Auri attempted to scan the pirates' barcodes, but they all wore black leather cuffs around the skin where the code would've been.

A snorting laugh from the other woman made Auri grit her teeth. She had knelt to rifle through the MREs with tattooed fingers. Her braided hair slithered over her shoulders like snakes as she stood.

"There's nothin' of value. Unless you count this." She waved the MREs for emphasis. "Waste of time. Wouldn't you agree, *G*?"

The captain raised one brow at Graham. "I told you this was one of those bounty hunter boats. They never carry anything worth boarding over."

Auri bristled at *bounty hunter* but kept silent. If they detached the staff of their harpoons and left the spikes, she might be able to fly the ship to Kaido. It would be dicey if the autopilot was damaged, but at least she'd be alive. The last thing she wanted to do was annoy—

Her plans shattered as she noticed Graham eyeing her with growing interest. He cradled his wrist tight to his chest, the joint a swollen mass of flesh. As he drew closer, his gaze fixed on her earring.

Auri felt as if the floor had dropped out from under her. *No, no, no...*

"I see somethin' of value," he drawled, voice twanging with a familiar accent.

The man on the radio. It had been him.

As if he could read the terror in Auri's eyes, a sneer spread across a face she might have otherwise described as handsome. He sauntered up to her, catching the dangling metal flower with a finger. She flinched at his closeness. "It looks like real gold. Maybe even a speck a' diamond. Worth a few hundred creds at least." He leaned in close as he examined it, the scent of engine fuel a cloud around him.

"No." Auri heard her voice from faraway as if it didn't belong to her. The raw submission, the fear she heard in it, repulsed her. "Please. I have credits. I'll transfer them all to you."

"So the Fed can track us?" The woman crossed her arms. "Nah." She inclined her head at Auri's disc, still trapped in the shuttle wall. "That worth somethin'?"

The captain shook her head. "Not to us. Can't even be melted down. But grab the dagger, Kei. I left mine in some sod's gut on our last boarding."

Kei hurried to obey.

"Graham, get the piece of *kuso* already," the captain snapped. "And hope some Medea hawker finds value in it."

Graham grinned at Auri with anticipation and leaned forward. He grabbed the earring in his good hand—

And ripped it out.

Pain seared through Auri's ear and seemed to lance down her neck. She bit her cheek to suppress a scream. Tears burned her eye, and hot blood oozed down her jaw and collarbone, staining the white bow on her uniform. Birdie growled low in her throat, claws scraping along the floor.

"Stay," Auri rasped, praying Birdie obeyed. The dog didn't move, but the growl continued to rumble in her chest. The captain eyed Birdie but didn't shift her gun away from Auri.

Graham dangled the earring in front of her. Chunks of skin and clotted blood stuck to the delicate chain. "For my wrist." He flicked her torn ear as he stepped away. She hissed.

The captain lowered the gun and called over her shoulder. "Yo, *busu*, get in here and get these corpses on ice. We'll hit up the organ stall."

The Japanese insult made Auri hold her breath. *Busu* was what Ty had named his DISC dog. The necklace hidden under her collar seemed to burn her skin. Was the chain visible? She'd already lost the most important thing to her, other than Birdie. The thought of losing Ty's necklace too…

Two more crew members, both men, squeezed through the door. It was obvious why they'd stayed out of the initial assault. They both cradled a broken arm apiece and sported facial cuts that gave the impression they'd been on the wrong side of an explosion. Together they hauled the bodies through the doors while Kei picked through the MREs.

The captain's attention shifted to Birdie. She ran her fingers along her scar while clicking her tongue. Finally, she shrugged. "Kei, get the dog. We might be able to sell it for something. The hide at least."

"No!" Auri hurled herself at the captain. She slammed into the woman, and they crashed to the floor. The gun spiraled out of reach. Auri slammed her robotic fist into the woman's face. Bone cracked against her knuckles.

The click of a hammer being cocked reached Auri's ears. A coilgun. She opened her mouth to give Birdie an attack command.

Something flashed in the captain's hand, and Auri leapt back, but too late. The laser knife cut deep into her synthetic forearm, grating against the metal bone hidden underneath. Auri cried out in surprise as the wires sparked. An alert shot across her vision, the cyborg half of her brain reporting the malfunction.

She fell back, the fingers of her robotic hand twitching as she struggled to move them. She barely registered the gun Kei had trained on her, the pirate's eyes wide in panic.

"Clank." Kei spat at the floor in front of Auri. "I'll put a bullet in your brain."

"Don't touch her." The captain shoved herself upright, spitting crimson out of her mouth. The gun was back in her hand.

"She's mine." She staggered over to Auri, the woman's face so close she could smell the sweat on her skin. "Normally I take your kind to the Market. Your parts sell for a pretty piece of cred. But no one—*no one*—hits me. You can keep your bitch." Globs of blood and saliva sprayed across Auri's face as the woman spat on her. "Suck space air, clank." The captain raised the handle of the gun and slammed it into the side of Auri's head.

Pain blasted through her skull. Dots exploded across her vision, multiple alerts flashing and disappearing, flashing and disappearing. She blinked. The pirates' forms swam as they turned to go. The door shut behind them with a clang. Suddenly Birdie was at Auri's side, against orders, whining and licking at her face.

Sensory inputs came in waves of intense feeling and then blackness. Cold. Something cold pressed against her cheek. She realized with sluggish alarm that she had hit the floor.

When? When had she fallen over? She tried to open her eyes, but her right eye was sealed shut by something sticky. Her fingers trembled as she brought them to her temple. Blood smeared her skin. So much blood. The urge to vomit spasmed her stomach.

The shuttle shuddered. A metallic scream sliced through the walls. It took Auri too long to realize what was happening. The harpoons…

"Warning, hull breach," a female voice said over the shuttle's speakers. "Oxygen levels, eighty-five percent... Seventy percent..."

Auri wanted to lie down, close her eyes, and open her lungs to the emptiness of space. What was the point anymore?

Birdie's bark sent another wave of nausea through her. *Birdie*. Auri had to get Birdie out. She swallowed hard, shoving herself up with an arm, cradling the malfunctioning one to her stomach.

"Oxygen levels fifty-two percent."

The world swirled. Only Birdie's warm bulk at her side kept Auri moving. She staggered against the wall where the emergency hatch was located. Her sweat-soaked fingers slipped on the latch twice before the door swung open. A five-rung ladder led into the pod, seats and safety belts built into its spherical walls with plenty of emergency supply kits for them both. The floor below the seats was empty and beveled out. Going inside would be like jumping into a giant salad bowl. The thought made Auri giggle and duck her head.

Her eyes caught on a tiny square of flexi-glass a few meters away: the floppy with all the cannibal cases stored on it, considered useless by Kei.

"Gentle retrieve." She pointed at the storage device. Birdie scooped the tiny piece of tech into her jaws, teeth gripping the glass with just enough pressure. "Now jump," she rasped. "Jump, Birdie." She swayed against the wall, gaze focusing and unfocusing.

Birdie stepped back before running forward and leaping into the hatch opening.

"Oxygen levels thirty percent."

Auri moved to follow when her eyes locked on her disc, still trapped in the wall above the kennel. She licked her lips, the taste of salt and copper making her gag. The future had suddenly turned into an unknown black hole. Her plans torn to shreds, her body broken. The only thing she had to hold on to was her identity as a DISC agent.

She pushed off the wall and collapsed against the kennel. The edge of the disc gleamed, the matte metal splashed with the illusion of blood from the emergency lights. She tugged on the handle underneath. A wave of dizziness left her dry heaving.

"Oxygen levels twenty percent."

The buzz of thousands of bees droned in her ears. Laughter burst from her mouth, doubling her over. *Kuso.* The part of her brain that still functioned registered the symptoms with horror. *Move, Auri. Move now!*

She reached up again. Gritting her teeth, she anchored herself against the kennel and pulled on the disc's handle with all her remaining strength. The uncontrollable laughter weakened her muscles, but the disc shifted a centimeter. Then another. Suddenly, it slid free, almost dislocating Auri's arm with the force.

"Oxygen levels five percent."

Birdie's frantic barking reached Auri's ears. *I'm coming.* She wasn't sure if she'd said the words aloud or not. She battled a thick fog toward the sound. When she felt the open space of the hatch she let out a whimper and fell inside, hoping Birdie moved out of the way. The hard floor of the pod bit into her back, but it was a faraway pain compared to the cacophony in her head. She forced herself up again, knowing the oxygen down here wouldn't hold as long as the hatch door remained ajar.

Above, the final warning trilled: "Oxygen depleted. Oxygen depleted."

She'd fallen at the base of the rung ladder. A few meters above her head was a button the size of her palm. Underneath it an open panel bristled with damaged wires. Auri prayed the pirates hadn't filched anything vital from the pod.

She arced up and slammed her organic hand against the button. The open hatch above her slid closed with a click. The walls hummed as the sphere powered on. Fresh, breathable air streamed in.

"Nearest planet," a computerized voice announced, the tech less fancy than the shuttle's, "Kaido. Arrival in five hours, two minutes, thirteen seconds." The pod's vibrations increased, chattering the teeth in Auri's clenched jaw as it dropped from the belly of the shuttle, hurtling through space.

Auri fought against the tentacles of darkness pulling her under as she collapsed. Birdie, trembling, curled up against her. She let out a whine, interrupted by a stress-induced yawn.

"I love you," Auri wheezed, resting her chin on Birdie's head. "I love you."

The tentacles dragged Auri down, down, down into an inky black sea.

CHAPTER TEN

---

15 Aug 3319, 08:12:33
Ancora Galaxy, Planet 05: Kaido,
Arrowhead Badlands

Something rough and wet raked across Auri's face. It smelled disgustingly of fish and carrot. She groaned, raising a hand to knock it away.

Except the fingers attached to the hand refused to move.

The wrist wouldn't bend.

She crashed into full consciousness with a start, eyes tearing open. They stung, as if Birdie's tongue had loosened a seal.

The poodle stood over her, whining and pacing in a circle. Auri knew that dance well.

She sat up, and the world promptly exploded.

Lights flashed behind her eyes and a wave of queasiness made a cold sweat break out on her skin. She doubled over, locking her head between her knees until her vision steadied.

It took three attempts to stand. Once she was on her feet, some of the pirouetting black spots retreated. Error messages continued to flood the corners of her c-tacts, all warnings from her cyborg parts. She blinked them away, already too aware that something was terribly wrong.

The escape pod had landed on its side, the ceiling hatch now a circular door level with the ground. Birdie led the way over to it, favoring a hind leg. Concern lanced through Auri, but bending for a closer examination brought the black dots back.

"I'll take a look when we get outside," she whispered to Birdie. Her throat felt like she'd swallowed a handful of glass shards. She found the door control button, now on the floor, and stamped down on it.

The hatch hissed as it swung open. Sunlight burst into the tiny pod, making Auri squint. Hot air ruffled the sweaty curls around her face, bringing the smells of dirt and carrion. The stench did little to ease her stomach.

Birdie shot out of the pod and vanished into the planetscape beyond. Auri moved at a slower pace, using her hand to brace herself against the rounded side as she staggered outside. Her boots landed on hard-packed earth. She cradled her destroyed robotic arm and scrutinized the world around her, eyes scrunched against the sun's glare.

A few meters away, Birdie relieved herself behind a scrubby tree. Ridged, grassless hills rose from the earth in every direction. *Badlands*, she realized. Her high school planet geography teacher had said Kaido, or the Western Planet, had more desert-like badlands than arable earth. Cattle ranches populated the arid planet, districts small and scarce. She connected her c-tacts to Kaido's grid to determine her exact location.

Sudden nausea brought her to her knees, and she vomited. Pain lanced her skull with each heave, centering on her scalp where the captain struck her. Tears streamed down her cheeks, drying before they hit the ground.

When her stomach had emptied itself, she rolled away to lean against the escape pod. The sun-warmed metal soothed the sore muscles in her back. Her sweat-soaked jacket clung to her, but she was too exhausted to take it off.

Birdie trotted back, the limp already improving with use. In the bright sunlight, Auri grimaced at the scarlet staining the poodle's muzzle. She blinked away the memory of Birdie tearing out the pirate's throat.

At the thought of the pirates, loss hit her anew. She reached up to probe her shredded ear. Dull pain throbbed along the skin, but the blood had dried into a crusty scab. She was missing a centimeter-sized chunk of flesh.

Her robotic arm was worse. The wound was hideous, the skin peeling away in ribbons, the gash revealing the ugly secret parts of her. The fingers curled in on themselves, and attempting to move them resulted in the pinky giving the barest twitch. How would she be able to function with just one hand? And trying to access the grid again brought her nausea barreling back. She immediately stopped, taking deep breaths to regain control over her stomach.

The direness of her situation crowded around her. Invisible spectators shouted their disapproval, proclaiming her failures to the empty badlands, laughing at her stupidity and utter uselessness.

"Shut up!" she shouted at the personified doubts. Birdie's ears quirked back at the sudden noise. *Shut up, shut up, shut up* echoed through the landscape, bouncing off rock and stone.

She let out a slow breath. "Think, Auri. Think." The sound of her hoarse voice grounded her. She continued to talk aloud, to work through a plan. "The pod has an SOS signal I can activate. And there should be emergency supply kits." Her tongue stuck to the roof of her mouth as she spoke, a sign of approaching dehydration. "Water first."

Auri was relieved when the dizziness didn't hit as hard when she stood. Vomiting must've helped. She still moved like a zombie, shuffling back into the pod. Emergency supplies were tucked under each of the four seats, totaling twelve MREs and four full canteens of water, plus an empty tactical backpack and limited medical supplies. The backpack was about half the size of her rucksack, so it would take some finagling to get everything to fit. With just her and Birdie, the supplies would last two days, more if she rationed.

Auri poured water for Birdie, using a square supply container as a makeshift bowl. The poodle guzzled while Auri sipped from the canteen more slowly. The water tasted stale and hot but soothed her parched throat. After quenching her thirst, she used two antiseptic wipes and gauze to clean the gash on her forehead and the missing chunk of her ear. Rather than be subjected to the atrocity of her robotic arm, she wrapped the remaining gauze around the wound. Feeling a smidgen more confident and more like a human being, she stood to tackle the next problem.

The escape pod lacked a dashboard or any manual controls, but it did have a shoebox-sized wall screen. The screen had limited use, but she knew from training it contained a GPS and emergency broadcast signal.

She tapped it.

Nothing.

She tapped it again.

Still nothing.

Hysteria crowded out any coherent thoughts in her brain. If she couldn't find her location, she would wander Kaido until she ran out of water.

Auri slammed her palm against the screen. "Please!"

The symbol of the Ancora Federation flickered onto the black screen. The rising sun interlaced with an eagle soaring, a ribbon gripped in its beak reading "res novae animus" was the most beautiful sight in the world.

She sobbed in relief. The logo blinked out, replaced by a map of the solar system, depicting eight planets, even uninhabitable Roanleigh. The screen buffered as it found her location, zooming in on the planet Kaido and then its individual districts. A red dot flashed her current location: Arrowhead Badlands.

Before she studied the map further, she tapped the bottom icon on the screen labeled "Emer. B. Signal." Red letters popped up immediately: OPTION UNAVAILABLE.

"*Kuso.*" She gritted her teeth. Okay. That's what the pirates had taken. They sold for a decent price. No big deal. At least the map was functional.

Auri dragged her finger across the screen, searching for the bright yellow dots that symbolized districts or the black ones that marked military bases. Three klicks southeast was a tiny district with a bisecting road that led to the nearest base. *Nearest* being a relative term. From the district, the base was over ten klicks away. With the battered shape of her body, she'd be lucky to make the walk to base in four hours. The district was a better target. She could do that in an hour or so.

Auri ignored the crowing remarks from her fearful and hopeless inner voice and focused on the route she needed to take to reach the district. Something about the name was familiar, but it was all she could do to get her muddled brain to focus on the map.

With the map fixed in her mind, she gathered her supplies. The tactical bag bulged three times its flattened size once she shoved everything inside it. She had to use her knee to force the belabored zipper closed. The only thing missing from the emergency supplies that she would kill a pirate for was a compass. She vaguely remembered a fifteen-minute lecture during monsoon season when PT was cancelled. Something about using the sun to gauge direction? But she didn't have time to wait around for dawn with a stick. She'd have to trust her intuition.

After fortifying herself and Birdie with a chicken noodle soup MRE, the pair set off. Auri sucked on a strawberry hi-chew candy as she walked, both to keep her mouth moist and her mind engaged. Every so often she checked the sun's location, just in case she needed to find her way back to the pod.

As meters turned into kilometers and the food and water worked through her system, Auri's muggy mind started to clear.

In another circumstance, the natural beauty of the badlands would've left her breathless. Now she jumped at the movement of every tumbleweed, suspicious shadow, or skittering lizard. The pirate attack had awoken a primal fear that couldn't be quenched by hollow reassurances. Lurking at the back of her mind was the torturous question: Did Auri not have the wits to survive a mission past Krugel's Curve, like the GIC believed?

And worse, what if she died out here proving him right?

CHAPTER ELEVEN

---

15 Aug 3319, 10:35:02
Ancora Galaxy, Planet 05: Kaido,
Uma District

It took two hours to reach the district. She'd been forced to rest every twenty minutes to catch her breath and rest screaming muscles. The sun had seared her cheekbone and nose so badly it hurt to squint or smile. She didn't need a mirror to know the burns were pink and raw and would probably peel. Birdie whined every time they left the spotty shade of half-dead trees. The dog's short white hair did little to shield her fair skin, but the working harness gave her some protection at least.

From atop a low hill, Auri got her first look at the district. The homes and shops were clustered in a square layout. From this far away, the buildings seemed unoccupied. No children played in the streets, no men or women hurried along with errands to run or jobs to do. Not even any stray dogs roamed about. It was as if everyone had just packed up and left. Something was very, very wrong.

Movement at the corner of her eye made her turn. Over fifty *teru teru bozu* swung from the branches of a shrubby tree on the district's outskirts, their little ghostly-looking bodies suspended upside down. Legend claimed that hanging *teru teru bozu* could stop the rain. Or, by hanging them upside down, rain would come.

She'd tried the trick as a kid during monsoon season on Rokuton, but it hadn't worked. Despite the sweat turned to itchy salt on her skin and her beleaguered state, the sight of the little figures made her smile. She stopped before the tree to take a breath. It wasn't until a breeze sent the *teru teru bozu* dancing that her eyes widened.

The reverse side of their off-white fabric was stained with flecks of dried blood.

A chill scuttled down her spine. "What is this place?" she asked the dancing figures, reaching out to still one's dance.

A stained, lopsided sign behind the tree answered her question.

Uma District
Population: 101

Suddenly Auri knew why the name seemed familiar. This settlement had been struck by a cannibal attack. The case file claimed that a single man decimated the district's entire population, using shrapnel bombs to maim or kill and then feasting on the bodies.

She'd intended to travel here from the beginning.

The drone of approaching engines made her spin around. A mid-sized transport vessel approached from the opposite direction and descended toward the open center of the district. Birdie growled low in her throat, lowering her head. Auri ducked under the tree and held a hand up to shield her eyes. The transport ship was shaped like a falcon, wings spread wide. Which is where it got its name. All Falcon Class ships were government sanctioned, usually responsible for carrying supplies from the outer planets to Babbage, Aurora, Rokuton, and Attica. These people would help her. The thought of shelter from the sun, a shower, a fresh change of clothes... She almost moaned aloud.

Even still, she wasn't supposed to be here and didn't relish the crew's reaction when she introduced her cyborg self. So she entered the town cautiously, keeping the landing ship in her line of sight.

A dirt street split the settlement in half, the hard-packed earth lined with self-filtering and self-distributing rainwater collection bins. The sleek metal seemed at odds with the "old Earth west" vibe of the surrounding buildings. Loose pebbles skittered under her feet as the ship touched down. Auri ducked behind a pharmacy, her back pressed against rough wooden shingles. She wanted to scope out the crew before she begged for help.

Auri and Birdie stuck to side alleys, the main street always to their right. The settlement was small but seemed a tight-knit community. The homes themselves were nearly identical, sharing the same rectangularly narrow, single-story design, likely only holding two bedrooms at most. Even if she wanted to, Auri would be hard-pressed to squeeze through the tight gap between each home.

Voices reached Auri as she stopped behind a house facing the square. This home was even more dilapidated than the others, siding coming off in chunks where some animal had made a nest. Succulent stumps occupied its window boxes, now barely recognizable as once-living plants. The back door had been smashed in and the smell of rotten meat wafted out. Auri clapped a hand over her nose and mouth. She pressed herself against the side of the house, far away from the nest. Birdie waited at her back, her nose twitching as she fought a sneeze.

"Retreat," Auri hissed before the poodle gave away their position. If the smell drifting from the house was bad for her human nose, she couldn't imagine how intense it was for Birdie.

The poodle didn't hesitate; she trotted three houses back and laid in the shade.

Auri turned her attention to the crew lounging about the exit ramp of the ship.

There were only three people: one man, one woman, and a young girl with an umbrella. The girl looked to be around eleven years old, her head shaved bald. The man and woman sat on the ramp's end, their legs stretched out before them.

"Why does he do this every year?" the woman asked. Her beautiful copper skin seemed to soak in the sunlight. Her hair was long, the left side tied in a myriad of braids.

The man shook his head, his blond hair and pale skin a contrast to the woman's. "Don't ask me. I always thought he was a weird one. Blame his blood type. Me, I'd avoid Uma like a vengeful lover with the spots."

The woman's lips quirked in a rueful smirk. "Ever had a vengeful lover with the spots?"

"Wouldn't you like to know."

The girl turned toward Auri suddenly, her shaved head cocked under the bright yellow umbrella. She wore a traditional *yukata* dress, her bare feet poking out of the hem.

Auri froze. Something about the girl's eyes seemed off. She couldn't be sure from this distance, but the shape and the way they reflected the light—

The girl's gaze narrowed.

Auri scrambled back, knocking her cyborg elbow into the side of the house. The synthetic skin tore, revealing flecks of metal underneath. Great. As she eased away from the building, her heart prepared to gallop straight out of her chest. She held her breath, listening, but the girl didn't audibly alert anyone or approach.

Something felt off about the group, and Auri wanted more intel before waltzing up and asking for help. She turned to the poodle, who was rubbing her back into the dirt. Auri rolled her eyes.

"Come," she whispered to Birdie. "Come here."

Birdie groaned as if it all was a great inconvenience and trotted over.

The two followed another road a meter back from the main street that ran parallel to the ship. Auri intended to circle the vessel and come at it from the back. She could check out the rest of the district and maybe learn something more about the ship and its crew.

She passed a crumbling stone church on the outskirts, all the stained-glass windows shattered. Dead trees lined the exterior of the broken picket fence that enclosed the building. A lopsided gate, suspended by a single hinge, opened into the cemetery. Tombstones stretched out in every direction, arranged in neat lines like a miniature army prepared for war. There had to be almost a hundred people buried here.

The district's entire population.

A man knelt before a tombstone near the dilapidated fence. His hands were tight fists at his sides, muscles tensed through the long-sleeved black thermal he wore.

Today was Obon, she realized. A small part of her knew she wouldn't be able to send her "I can't make the Festival" ping to the GIC. But the danger of her current situation lessened her fear of being court martialed. Whoever these people were, they had flown to Uma District so this man could pay respects to a deceased family member.

She would love to question this man about what he knew about the attack.

He raised a towel from a basin of water and rang out the excess. Droplets rained into the small bowl. He used the damp cloth to wipe away the dust and grime from the tombstone until it shone. Each stroke was slow, deliberate, aching with tenderness and care.

Auri found herself mesmerized by the motion. Who lay underneath the earth? What kind of individual deserved such a deep love?

Loneliness hissed a biting truth into her ear: no one would mourn Aurelia Peri the way this man mourned. Not even the GIC or Ty. Their lives would go on as normal, as if she were a passing rainstorm on a sunny day. Quickly overlooked and forgotten once the earth dried.

The crunch of boot heels on dirt brought Auri back to the present. The man stood, the cleaning supplies gathered in his arms. He'd stabbed a single falcon feather into the dirt before the gravestone. Though she couldn't see the dates, the name stood out in deep grooves: *KESTREL TREATIS.*

The man turned, gaze locking with Auri's. He dropped the supplies. His hand darted for one of the three coilguns Auri now noticed: two fixed at his waist and one in a thigh holster. The barrel of one was trained on Auri just as her fingers wrapped around the grip of her disc. She cursed the slower, clumsier nature of her organic arm. She'd never used it to handle the disc before, trusting the faster reflexes of her robotic arm to give her an advantage. She now saw the folly of that dependency.

And so, for the second time in less than twenty-four hours, a weapon was aimed at her face.

CHAPTER TWELVE

---

15 Aug 3319, 10:50:40
Ancora Galaxy, Planet 05: Kaido,
Uma District

"Who are you?" the man asked, frowning as his eyes skimmed Auri's bedraggled appearance. Could he tell she was a DISC agent? If she commissioned his aid, would he transport her back to the nearest military base as law required?

His voice carried a slight twang she recognized from the holos based on Kaido, marking him as a native. Dark hair had been brushed back from his face, cut short on the sides but long on top in the popular style. His nose was terribly crooked. She guessed it had been broken more than once.

"I'll repeat myself," he said, shifting his gun to point at her chest. "Who. Are. You?"

Auri wasn't keen on trusting anyone after the pirate fiasco. "Does it matter?" Her fingers curled tighter around the disc handle, prepared to yank it fr   ee of the straps.

Birdie growled, baring her teeth. Auri's training told her to command the dog to take down the gun, but there were too many dangers. Birdie could easily be shot. Could easily be killed.

Ty's repeated warnings about her dog surfaced. Her annoyance had felt justified at the time, but he was right. She did treat Birdie like a friend, not the weapon and asset she was meant to be. Refusing to command her to go for the gun was a disservice to Birdie and a disservice to the hours they'd trained together. But Auri couldn't imagine what she would do if something happened to her dog.

"Since I can tell you plan to hurl that weapon at me"—the man gestured to the disc at her back—"I definitely think who you are matters."

Auri cleared her throat but didn't release her grip on the disc. "I was attacked by pirates. I landed nearby and was hoping to find some shelter or help in this district, but..." She trailed off, the abandoned settlement finishing the sentence for her.

The man nodded in understanding. His grip on the gun was lax, but Auri suspected if she even twitched, she'd have a bullet in her chest. "You wouldn't be the first to be the victim of piracy," he said. "Though most people traveling to the rim take precautions."

Auri's eyes ran over his arms, the sleeves of his shirt shoved up to his elbow, a wrist-length glove on his left hand. His left arm was completely covered with spirals of tattooed letters. On the right he wore a black cuff over the spot where his barcode should be, just like the pirates had. The meager contents of her stomach turned to lead. Why would a lawful citizen want to hide their barcode? Unless they *weren't* lawful...

She could throw her disc before he fired. Break his wrist or at least get the weapon pointed somewhere other than her chest. She'd been commended for her quick reactions back in basic, but her head hadn't been cracked open then.

Her sweaty fingers slipped on the metal handle as her grip shifted. She tensed, moving to attack.

Birdie yelped in pain.

Auri whirled around. The dog lay curled on the ground. A small, green-feathered dart stuck out of her haunches.

"Who—?" She raised her disc just as something sharp buried itself in her neck. The pain was barely a pinprick before numbness swept her body. Auri blinked once and suddenly she was on the ground. The man with the gun knelt in front of her. His hand moved toward her neck, but she couldn't feel if he touched her.

"What did you inject her with?" he called over his shoulder. His hand eased away from her neck to reveal a dart identical to Birdie's pinched between his thumb and forefinger.

Open-toed sandals baring midnight skin walked into her line of sight. She couldn't turn to see his face, but the heady scent of tobacco drifted over her as the man approached. His voice was deep and melodious with a smoker's huskiness. "A mild sedative. But I can shoot her again if you—"

"I was in the middle of questioning her. She looks like a Fed agent. What am I supposed to do now, *busu*?" The man raised Auri's injured arm and unwound the gauze. Her panic felt as if it belonged to someone else. It was concerning in a logical way, but the emotional response was absent. Disbelief flickered across his face.

She blinked. When she opened her eyes again, shadows hovered at the edges of her vision like an inverted star.

"—just leave her. The wild dogs can finish her off," the second man was saying with a laugh.

"No." The first was adamant, the word a command. At the very edge of her vision, she could see her disc in his hands. One of her organic fingers twitched the tiniest amount in answer to the longing in her chest to possess her weapon. "She might be useful in other ways. I'll—"

"Wait, she's still conscious. Her clank components must interfere with the sedative's effectiveness. I doubt she'll remember this conversation, but I would guard your tongue."

"You know how I feel about that word." The first man rose, her disc still in one hand. He seemed to fade. "Get... the doctor... over here. I'll need help moving her. She's pretty beat up."

Birdie, Auri tried to say, *don't forget my dog*.

"*Cyborg* components, then. But this is stupidity," the other man said. "You're risking yourself and..."

Despite her panic over Birdie being left, something snapped inside Auri. The tether that kept her conscious unraveled. Her eyelids fluttered in a final blink.

CAPTAIN'S LOG
Hachigatsu 15, 3319 at 1500

[Clears throat, chair squeaks, taps fingers on dash] New development: we have a hostage. Ferris is furious with Castor for using a dangerous sedative on a Fed agent. *Furious* for Ferris means spouting off the negative attributes of Castor's blood type.

He's lucky if Castor doesn't put a laxative in his dinner. Though Ferris has never struggled in the luck department. The annoying bastard.

We're headed to the north side of Kaido so some of the crew can attend an Obon festival. Katara and I are staying behind. She's not pleased, judging from the new knife hole I have in the kitchen wall. But we need to keep an eye on the agent.

The agent. She might be the key to everything. This is the luckiest I've gotten in a long time. [humorless chuckle] Ferris must finally be rubbing off on me.

Though I could be playing with laser fire. The fear in her eyes when she looked at me... My time of anonymity might be over. I'll find out the truth when she wakes up.

[Takes a shaky breath]

I really hate Obon.

CHAPTER THIRTEEN

---

15 Aug 3319, 18:12:06
Ancora Galaxy, Planet 05: Kaido, Free Airspace

Auri's consciousness returned in a rush. Her eyes snapped open. Above her stretched a slate-gray metal ceiling. She rolled her head to the side, the movement requiring all her concentration.

When her vision refocused, she realized she lay on a bed inset into a wall. The room around her held two bolted-down hospital gurneys and an array of glass cabinetry. She shifted to sit up, but thick straps above her chest and on her wrists and ankles held her to the mattress.

Panic. She should be panicking right now, but she only felt peaceful and sleepy. Squeezing her eyes shut, she struggled to remember what events had led to this moment. The pirates and the crash-landing on Kaido were clear. So was her death march through the badlands to Uma District. She had arrived there, seen a ship, and run into a man. Then...

Someone shot Birdie with a tranquilizer.

They must've shot Auri too. That explained the memory loss and grogginess.

A flash of movement made her head jerk up. Two men stood outside the infirmary, talking. She couldn't hear their voices through the glass that took up half the opposing wall, but she vaguely recognized one of them.

A blond man shook his head, frowning as he rubbed a hand over a manicured beard. The other turned to look at her.

Auri found herself suddenly back on Kaido, the heat of the sun a crackling fire on her exposed skin. The man raised a gun. *"Who are you?"*

She blinked and the memory faded. Through the glass, the man still watched her. He said something to the blond one and then turned toward the door of the infirmary. The blond man shook his head and walked away.

The tips of Auri's toes and fingers tingled. Her drug-induced peaceful feeling started to deteriorate, replaced by anger and suspicion.

"Where am I?" she asked as the man entered. The question came out slurred, as if she'd been on a *saké* binge.

The man grabbed a rolling stool from a built-in desk and wheeled it over to her. He sat down, elbows resting on his knees. His eyes met hers, and Auri couldn't help but stare. It was as if someone had dripped colors into his irises, splotches of hazel here and brown there. They were startling.

He ran his gloved hand over his stubble-covered jaw. Auri's tangled memory of him smoothed out, strand by strand. He still wore the tight pants and black thermal from earlier but had added a jacket. If he was in the same clothes, not much time had passed. At least not an entire day. That was a relief.

The man steepled his fingers against his lips. "You answer one of mine, and I'll answer one of yours. I'll go first."

Auri opened her mouth to object, her organic hand tightening into a fist. The last of the confusion cleared from her head. "I—"

"And no lies. So, who are you?"

Auri glowered. She didn't want to listen to this man or obey his rules. He'd kidnapped her, for stars' sake. But she desperately needed answers. Like where Birdie was. She'd play his game, but the truth? Not happening.

"My name is Aurelia. I was on my way to visit family on Medea for Obon." She cleared her throat. "Pirates attacked my shuttle and I crash landed on Kaido. I think I told you that already, but I can't be sure considering I've been *drugged*."

"You? Visit Medea?" The man laughed, sitting up straight. "Where do you think the space pirates come from?"

She opened her mouth to ask what he meant but then closed it. Chances were he'd be the cheeky type to consider that her question. "It's true, whether you want to believe it or not." Technically, she had family on Medea… once.

"Where is my dog?" There was a desperate edge to her question, but she didn't care.

The man's sarcastic demeanor softened somewhat. "She's asleep in our kitchen's pantry. She's safe."

"I want to see her." Auri tried to sit up again, straining against the straps. "Let me go."

"No."

She froze at the harsh tone. He sounded just like the pirate captain. What would he do to her, tied up as she was? Even worse, what had he done to her while she'd been unconscious?

Help. She needed to get help. Contact Ty to tell him where she was. She reached for the ever-present grid. The ship had to have one she could connect to if the planet's was unavailable.

Dizziness slammed into her. A gong clanged in her ears, echoing again and again. Her bones vibrated with the sound, her jaw locking shut. She collapsed back against the bed, groaning, eyes squeezed closed.

"I'll tell you what's wrong with you in exchange for another answer." He must've taken her nausea-filled silence as affirmation, for he continued, "If you're just visiting family, why did you have this in your tactical bag?"

She opened her eyes, vision clearing after a few blinks. From a jacket pocket, he revealed her floppy. He had turned it on, and its file contents burned bright on the screen. The cases taunted her, laughing at her failed attempts at subterfuge.

Auri remained silent, fist clenched. No wonder the GIC and Captain Ishida refused to let her past Krugel's Curve. She was useless. The entire mission had been doomed from the beginning. Just one mistake after another.

The man shrugged. "Your silence is better than the ridiculous lie about your family." He stood, headed toward the door.

"Okay!" Auri scowled up at the ceiling and wished she hadn't worn her uniform. "I'm a DISC agent, but I *am* visiting family. What's wrong with me? Why can't I access the grid?"

He paused, his back to her, one gloved hand on the door's handle. "The DISC taskforce. Disciplinary Interstellar Statute Command." He returned to the stool. "Technically, that's two questions, but to show my goodwill I'll answer both.

"Your arm's been damaged, both the circuitry and the barcode function. You won't be able to move it until it's repaired. As for your head, my medic says that you've suffered a concussion. Because your grid access was wired into your brain instead of your c-tacts, it's been disconnected. There's no permanent damage and an experienced tech will be able to repair both issues. We put synthetic skin on your ear. You were also given an IV of fluids." He waited a beat to let her process the news.

The coil of dread in her stomach loosened. Everything they'd done while she had been unconscious was for her health. Not only that, but the broken cyborg parts of her could be fixed.

"What are you really doing here?" he continued. "These files are all related." He waved the floppy for emphasis. "You were in Uma District, the exact location where one of these cases occurred. Did your captain send you? Are you looking for someone?"

His barrage of questions sent her head spinning. "What? No. I... I really am visiting family. Those files were related to an old case. I was just carrying them."

He studied her, eyes searching, probing for the truth. Auri's organic skin itched under his scrutiny. She had no idea what she looked like, but she could feel the rub of gauze on her forehead and the smear of gel on her sunburn.

"This is a waste of time." The man stood up again. "My ship will reach Medea tomorrow afternoon. I can drop you off on the moon Tanoki. From there you can hop a transporter planetside. But I assume you already knew that. Since you're so adamant about visiting your *family*." His eyes twinkled, though with mirth, suspicion, or sadism, Auri couldn't tell.

Without giving her another option like, say, letting her go *now*, he left, sliding the infirmary door shut behind him.

It took Auri fifteen minutes to free herself from the straps. If it hadn't been for ten-year-old Ty wondering if she could dislocate her robotic limbs, she'd still be bound to the bed.

Now she tiptoed across the infirmary toward a mirror on the opposing wall. She still wore her uniform, blood and all, but her shoes had been removed. That fact wasn't too disturbing—most ships didn't allow shoes in living quarters—but it would make her escape more difficult.

The reflection in the square mirror made her grimace. Gauze wrapped her temples, obscuring her forehead. Underneath the white bandage, where the pirate captain had hit her, a purple-green bruise ran across her brow, looped over her eye, and bled down her temple. Dark smudges smeared the skin under her eye. The braid she'd plaited back on her shuttle before the attack had become red tangles bunched around her head like one of the many tumbleweeds on Kaido.

No wonder the man hadn't believed what she said. She looked half-crazed. If things were different, if she hadn't been attacked by pirates, she might've trusted him to take her to Tanoki.

But she *had* been attacked by pirates. And she certainly didn't trust him.

Outside the infirmary was a large living area. Shelves filled with odds and ends lined one side. A low table hunched in the center of the room with couches pushed against the walls. Blankets of all colors and fabrics lay strewn about the floor, some folded and some not. The space looked warm and inviting and was, thankfully, empty. A spiral staircase led to the floor above. To her left a short hallway stopped at a large sliding door made of old-fashioned rice paper. She set off in that direction.

Her socks slipped on the faux hardwood floor as she skidded to a stop before the sliding door. She curled her fingers around the door handle and pressed an ear against it. The rough paper scratched her cheek. Silence engulfed whatever space lay beyond. In fact, the entire ship seemed to radiate quiet. Almost suspiciously so.

Auri slid the door open a crack, peering into an enormous cargo room. Boxes were stacked around the perimeter, the metal floor reflecting the bright lights set into the ceiling. Two sets of stairs, one on either side of the door, led to the catwalk above. A footwear storage shelf was inset into the wall beside her. Slippers and shoes occupied the individual slots.

When Auri recognized her boots, she darted into the cargo room and tugged them on, not bothering with the laces. She longed to hunt down her disc but knew she'd gotten lucky enough obtaining shoes.

Across from where she stood, a huge mechanical door barricaded the ship against the outside world. The door itself was closed, but a small glass window had been constructed at eye-level.

She scurried to the window, curling one hand around her face to look out. "*Kuso*," she swore.

Endless night sky stretched beyond, the darkness spotted with bright stars. The ship wasn't still grounded on Kaido like she assumed.

They were in space.

"Lost?"

Auri whirled around at the female voice. A copper-skinned woman, the same one from Kaido, stood in the doorway, arms crossed.

CHAPTER FOURTEEN

---

16 Aug 3319, 10:55:22
Ancora Galaxy, 3,000 klicks off Tanoki Moon,
Planet 07: Medea

Muffled voices drew Auri out of a light sleep. She groaned, massaging the small of her back as she sat up. After being caught in the cargo room, Auri had been unceremoniously marched into a kitchen and locked in the pantry with Birdie. Around her were bins of dehydrated food, sacks of potatoes and rice, and haphazard towers of clean dishes and cookware.

Birdie uncurled from her position at Auri's feet. The dog stretched, her tongue unfurling in a yawn. Auri found herself yawning too. Tears sprang up in her eye and she blinked them away.

The voices rose. One distinctively male and familiar. The pantry's thick door rendered the words unintelligible, but the sharp tone hinted at an argument. Auri shifted to press her ear against the wood, the cuff on her wrist pulled taut where it was attached to a twenty-five-kilo tub of rice.

"You're all to stay out of her way." The deep voice got louder, as if the speaker were moving toward the door. "Now get out of here."

The lock clicked as someone on the other side unhooked it. She scrambled backward as the pantry door slid open.

The man with the mesmerizing eyes stood before her in the same jacket, zipped up to his neck. He eyed her with one brow raised. Neither of them moved. He seemed to be waiting for her to speak. When she didn't, he knelt in front of her to undo the bindings around her ankles as well as the cuff at her wrist. Birdie sat a silent observer, though the sides of her lips were up, baring her teeth. Judging by the man's steady hands, he didn't seem to mind the canine threat at his back.

Once freed, the man led Auri out of the pantry and into the kitchen. She rubbed her sore wrist against her side. The scent of breakfast lingered in the air: bacon, eggs, and ripe strawberries. Her stomach grumbled, but the man didn't seem to notice. To her left, an enormous dining room table with seven chairs sat vacant.

He led her through the kitchen and down a long hallway lined with doors but not a crew member in sight. Birdie pranced alongside Auri, eager to be out of the pantry. Even still, the dog didn't take her eyes off the man.

"Where are we going?" Auri asked, abandoning her silent bravado in favor of self-preservation.

He halted before the last door and turned to look at her. "Hear anything interesting?"

Her brows furrowed. "What?"

"When you were eavesdropping." He leaned forward, almost conspiratorially. Birdie growled.

"You're holding me captive." Auri refused to step back. "Of course I eavesdropped. Where is the rest of your crew?"

"Far away from you." He slid open the door, revealing a decent-sized bathroom.

She was overcome with the urge to rip off her uniform here in the hallway. The stench, dirt, and blood coating its fibers suddenly seemed too much. Birdie whined, making her personal needs known.

"There's a change of clothes in there," he said. "My doctor says you can't get your head wound or your arm wet." The man gestured into the bathroom. "A small tray is in there for your dog to relieve herself. Clean up after her. I'll be back for you in an hour or so. Oh. And *don't. Leave*." He said the last two words slowly, annunciating the threat that lurked there. There was an edge of nerves in the tightness around his mouth. What was he hiding?

"*Arigato*." Auri gave him a shallow bow. Considering she'd tried to escape last night, the last thing he needed to do was let her bathe. She'd been surprised she hadn't been tossed out the airlock. "I…" She hesitated, searching for the best words. "I tried to leave last night because I don't know what you want. If you'd just tell me why you're helping me, maybe…" Maybe what? She didn't know. She let the sentence dangle, waiting for his reaction.

He rubbed a finger under the glove on his hand. "If you'd tell me the truth about the files on your floppy, maybe we could come to an understanding."

That was a secret she wasn't willing to trade. Before she told anyone else about the subtle connections between the cases on her floppy, she wanted to have concrete facts. She respected the GIC and his officers too much for rumors to be spread about them throughout the galaxy. Besides, she barely knew this man.

When she didn't respond, he turned and walked away. Auri stepped into the bathroom and shut the door behind her, engaging the lock one-handed.

Birdie wasn't pleased about her waste requirements. Even when Auri commanded her to go, the dog hesitated, the whites of her eyes showing in a painfully pitiful expression. In the end, like a good DISC aid, Birdie obeyed.

Auri stripped out of her grimy clothes with reckless glee. The entire bathroom was tiled, with a handheld shower nozzle built into one wall. The tub next to it had a waterproof touchscreen for controls. Three sinks and a toilet comprised the rest of the space. She wondered if this bathroom belonged to the crew. And if so, where they were all hiding.

She bathed in the traditional way: showering first and then soaking in the tub. The shower was awkward as she had to keep her arm and forehead dry, but she groaned as her sore body sunk deep into the warm water of the bath. Her robotic arm dangled outside, safe from the dangers of mixing liquid and electricity.

Until Birdie tried to jump into the tub.

"No!" Auri cried through laughter, shoving the dog away. Though she would've loved to clean the blood-matted curls, poodle hair dried notoriously slow, and she didn't have a drier. Not to mention she would need two usable hands.

Once Birdie grudgingly curled up on the floor by the tub, Auri slid into the water up to her nose. Crimson strands of hair floated on the water's surface, eddying this way and that. The gladiolus pendant nestled in the hollow of her throat under the water. She blew a burst of bubbles, and they popped against her nose.

Medea was the farthest habitable planet from Krugel's Curve, a notorious hotspot for criminals, gangs, and anyone interested in escaping the Fed's watch. Hence the man's suspicion at her destination, though she knew there had to be regular people, families, who lived there. Everyone couldn't be a criminal. There were still military bases in the more remote areas. Once she got off the transport from Tanoki, she would get to one. And then?

She had only one day left before she was supposed to report to Captain Ishida for her next assignment, if there was one. There was no way she would make it back to Rokuton in time.

Indecision played tug-of-war in her heart. Seeing Uma District for herself hadn't given her any clear answers. What should she do next? Keep investigating? Or fess up to disobeying orders and going AWOL?

The ship gave a rough jolt as if its forward trajectory had slowed, then stopped. Movement resumed again, making the bathwater slosh gently against Auri's chin. There was a final jerk and the entire craft stilled. They must've landed on Tanoki.

Auri forced herself from the tub and into the clothes left out for her: a pair of cargo pants and a gray, high-necked tank with a cartoon cat face on it. The pants were a little small in the hips and the tank too big in the chest. Auri wondered if they belonged to the woman from earlier.

She looked down at the tank once she'd wriggled into it and grimaced. The webbing of scars along her shoulder stood out in sharp contrast against the gray top. She bit her lip, glancing at her dirtied uniform jacket. Blood stained one shoulder and sleeve. Dirt clung to the fabric, not to mention splotches of dried vomit and rank body odor.

Auri ran a finger over the ridge of one scar jutting across her skin. Putting on her jacket, as much as she longed to hide the scars, was idiotic. Not to mention disgusting. Besides, why should she care what that man thought of her? She gritted her teeth and looked away from her disfigured flesh.

A sling had been left for her robotic arm, which she made awkward use of. Since she lacked two hands to braid her hair, she combed it out as best she could. The curls dampened the back of her borrowed tank, making the material stick to her skin.

For a moment, she considered barricading herself in the bathroom and never coming out. The scent of lavender still hung in the air from her bathwater and shampoo. But another growl from her stomach nixed that idea. If the man was kind enough to let her bathe, maybe he would also give her breakfast. That thought was enough to slide her feet into a pair of slippers and unlock the door.

To her surprise, the man hadn't returned. Instead, a girl leaned against the wall across the hall. She wore a traditional *yukata* with a sunflower pattern across the bright fabric. Like the man and woman, she also bore a black cuff over her barcode. After a moment of hazy recollection, Auri recognized her as the bald girl on Kaido.

Up close, the girl's eyes looked similar to Auri's: not quite right. They didn't house light sensors like all robotic optics required, but hers were still… different. Less human somehow. Like everything the girl saw was processed in binary code and fed into a machine.

Like the girl is a droid. The thought made Auri shiver. But there was no way she could be. Droids—humanoid robots—had been banned on Earth after their code malfunction, and even hundreds of years later, no one wanted to make those same mistakes. Sleep deprivation was messing with Auri's head.

The girl pushed off the wall, her bare feet silent on the wood floor.

"Um, hello," Auri said, splaying a hand across her shoulder to cover her scars. She glanced at Birdie to judge her canine partner's reaction. The dog's tail was low, but it twitched in a tentative wag.

The girl's face remained expressionless, but she answered, "Hello, *Onee-chan*."

The term made Auri's forehead crinkle. *Onee-chan* meant big sister. "I'm not—"

"Marin!" The man hurried down the hall, black slippers swishing against the wood floor. "What are you doing?" He ignored Auri, wrapping an arm around the girl's shoulders and towing her away. Auri caught his whispered words, "I said I didn't want the Fed to see the crew. That includes you."

After a hushed conversation, the man shooed Marin away. Marin glanced back at Auri before she walked off, turning left at the end of the hall and vanishing from sight.

The man returned to Auri's side. He eyed her hand, still splayed across her shoulder.

"Do the clothes fit?" he asked.

"Yes, thank you." She clenched her jaw and forced her hand back to her side. The scars seemed to burn on her skin as the man's gaze flicked over them.

When his stoic expression didn't change, the embarrassment whirling inside her stilled. As much as she claimed not to care what he, or his crew, thought of her scars, she'd expected a reaction. Disgust, surprise, pity. Curiosity, even. Not this uncaring stare. For an instant, she wondered why she spent so much time hiding her deformities back home.

Then her fingers fluttered back to her shoulder.

"This way." He escorted her to the kitchen, where a solitary plate bursting with bacon, eggs, and fruit waited for her. She sat at the table, salivating at the beautiful sight. The man took a seat across from her.

"*Itadakimasu*," she said and scooped up a pair of disposable chopsticks. Auri alternated between feeding Birdie and feeding herself. Her concerns over her scars disappeared under the onslaught of delicious flavor. Even the man's multi-colored scrutiny didn't suppress her appetite. She'd devoured half the plate's contents before he finally spoke.

"While you were in the bath, we touched down on Tanoki."

Auri choked down a chunk of eggs. "Is this where you threaten me?"

"No. You're free to go after you eat. Oh, and here's this." He slid her floppy across the table.

Her eyes widened. She never expected to get it back. Afraid he might change his mind, she snagged the tech and secured it in a pocket of the borrowed cargo pants.

"Am I really free to go?" She sipped at her hot green tea with what she hoped appeared to be uncaring bravery. Not suspicious anxiety.

"You are." He leaned back, stretching his arms overhead. "It might be hard for you to find your way without connecting to the grid, but you're a DISC agent. You all are born with an infallible sense of direction, right?"

106 · EMILY LAYNE

Auri lowered the round mug to the tabletop. When she mapped out her plan in the bath, she hadn't factored in lack of directions. For every citizen, the grid was a constant companion. Remembering that she couldn't connect to it made her organic skin icy. How would she locate a transport on Tanoki? How would she even reach a military base on Medea?

"Your friend from last night could escort you to the transports," he offered with a shrug.

The woman's face rose up in Auri's memory: the danger in the curve of her muscles, the playful malice in her eyes. *Friend* was the last word Auri would use to describe her.

"She could even escort you to your family. For an extra fee." He glanced at her, brows raised.

She frowned. Usually credits were transferred via the grid, but if the intended party was less than ten meters away, they could be transferred off-grid. She'd just never had a reason to do so.

"Right. Does my 'friend' have a name?" she asked. "Do you?" She was getting tired of thinking of him as *the man*. If she needed to rely on *the woman* to guide her around a criminal's haven, Auri deserved to know her name.

He hesitated. "You can call her Katara."

"And you?"

"Malachi."

"Malachi." It was an old-fashioned name and tasted sharp on her tongue. "How much would it cost for Katara to escort me to the transport shuttle on Tanoki?" As much as she needed a guide on Medea, she *didn't* need one of Malachi's crew members obtaining proof of the "family" ruse.

They spent a few minutes haggling over the price. She agreed to pay him half now and half when she arrived safely at the transport. The cost was steep and drained more than half of her monetary reserves. But what else could she do?

Malachi sent her his account information and some of her suspicion lessened. The pirates hadn't wanted her credits. Malachi accepting them was proof that he acted as a real Fed supply transporter, right? Maybe people on the rim covered their barcodes with cuffs to protect their personal information from strangers.

"What about my disc?" she asked once money changed accounts.

"It's waiting for you in the cargo hold along with your shoes. You'll get both when you leave."

"Good." Auri flexed the fingers of her hand, recommitting to practicing using the disc with it instead of her robotic arm. At this point, she would just be happy to hold the weapon again.

Malachi led Auri and Birdie out of the kitchen and into the upper balcony area of the cargo room. Katara stood in the center of it, Auri's disc and its holster tucked under an arm. Auri shot a wry look at Malachi as they walked down the steps side by side.

"You already told her to take me?" she asked, covering her scarred shoulder with a hand as they got closer to Katara. "You didn't know I'd say yes."

Malachi didn't reply, but she was surprised to see him smirk.

He crossed to Katara while Auri awkwardly shoved on her boots with one hand. He whispered something into Katara's ear, which made her sigh in annoyance. The woman wore an outfit similar to Auri's, except she had added a cropped jacket and fingerless gloves. Her hair was still styled in the same undercut and multiple braids.

Katara turned from Malachi to stare at Auri, her eyes a solemn mask. It reminded Auri of high clearance MPB officers. Some people called them Shadow Walkers due to the careful way they moved, as if they existed in a world of murderers and ghosts. Always on guard, always armed for attack.

Auri's toes curled at the thought. But if she was going to have someone lead her through Tanoki, she figured Katara would be the best choice.

Not that she had a choice.

"I have a meeting for a job with a Fed supplier on Tanoki," Malachi said, turning back to her and swapping slippers for shoes. "So I'll walk to the docking gate with you. Then you two are on your own." He gave Katara a pointed look that Auri assumed meant, *Don't eat her alive.* The woman held the disc and harness out.

Auri hesitated. She longed to have her weapon back, but she didn't want to move her hand. Malachi didn't care about her scars, but this woman was beautiful and strong.

"You should wear them proudly," Katara said.

"What?"

Katara just shook the disc in front of Auri like it was a dog treat.

That sparked her indignation. Auri took the disc and fumbled with the harness, attempting to adjust it one-handed.

"Here." Malachi held it out for her so she could ease her arms in. He adjusted his grip so each time she moved his fingers wouldn't brush her bare skin.

Once the holster and disc were settled, he stepped back.

"Wait." Katara slipped off her jacket and held it out. "If she's going to be wearing that weapon, she'll need to cover it up. They won't take kindly to bounty hunters on Tanoki or Medea."

She was getting tired of being called a bounty hunter, the worst insult for a DISC agent. Not that she would refuse the jacket. It would hide her deformed skin.

"I don't understand." Auri shook her head. "Tanoki is part of the Federation. My presence should reassure the people."

Malachi quirked his lips. "Are you sure you've been to Medea, Aurelia?"

"Yes." She glared at him.

"Right."

Again, he helped her slide the jacket on. Auri redid her sling. She hesitated, but then ripped off the velcro *DISC* patches fixed to both sides of Birdie's working harness and slipped them into a jacket pocket.

Katara nodded her approval. Auri found herself strangely warmed by it, though what it meant for the next steps of her journey was anyone's guess.

CHAPTER FIFTEEN

---

16 Aug 3319, 13:56:57
Ancora Galaxy, Planet 07: Medea, Moon: Tanoki,
Dock C456

Tanoki, or the Sunless Moon, certainly earned its name. Outside the ship, an overcast sky hung heavy overhead. The clouds were thick and shifted among one another in a constant state of flux. As a child Auri would've spent hours lying in the grass, guessing their shapes. Except there wasn't any grass to lay on here. Just dirt, metal, and endless stretches of asphalt.

The docking station mirrored the hangar Auri knew from Rokuton, except this one was outdoors and bustled with activity. An enormous spire acted as a control tower, its lights flashing at programmed intervals to protect it from moving ships. Auri stared in amazement at the sheer number of people and different classes of space vessels.

Katara and Malachi led her down the exit ramp onto the crowded main strip, hemming her in on either side with just enough room for Birdie. The scent of ozone and body odor made Auri crinkle her nose.

They followed the crowd toward a massive sign that declared *Tanoki Docking Station C456* in holographic letters. Prices rotated along its length ranging from hour by hour to days and months.

At the sign, Malachi split off without even a goodbye. Auri paused to watch him go, curious about his meeting. A yank on her arm made her turn.

Katara sighed as if guiding Auri was akin to a death sentence. "This way, Little Robot."

Auri scowled at the nickname but didn't bother arguing. She supposed it was better than *clank*, though only marginally.

They walked in silence for a long stretch of time, Katara maneuvering them through packed streets and empty alleys. She moved with a purpose, a confidence Auri envied. Katara seemed so in control of herself, at ease with who she was and her purpose in the world. Her stoic expression practically screamed, "To hell with your opinions. This is who I am."

"Thank you again for the clothes," Auri said when the silence between them became too oppressive. They winded through a small side street lined with four-story apartment buildings. Futon sheets and garments hung from balconies. Some Obon lanterns were still strung across the road. The lanterns here were smaller and homemade, almost crude compared to the ones on Babbage.

"The clothes were a necessity." Katara rolled her shoulders. "Having you walk around naked on Tanoki would only get us the wrong sort of attention." She said the words so deadpan, Auri didn't realize it was a joke until she glanced at the woman and saw her smiling.

"Oh." Auri offered a tight smile of her own. "Right."

Katara turned down a street where a rowdy group of kids chased a soccer ball, shouting insults at one another. "We're taking a shortcut." Katara raised her voice, but Auri still struggled to hear. "Stay close to me. The Fresh Market can be dangerous if you don't watch yourself."

Auri frowned. Fresh Market? That didn't sound so bad. She pictured vendors offering assortments of vegetables and fruits. Maybe even homemade soaps and perfumes. It sounded like a place she would love to stroll through on a sunny day, a basket crooked in one arm.

Auri followed Katara as she took a right turn. The dirty but well-kept street transformed into something from her nightmares.

Body parts floating in glass preservation vats sat on stained tablecloths. Assorted weaponry and malicious-looking torture devices lay side by side. Even human beings were auctioned off on a large stage, giving themselves away to the highest bidder. The smell of fresh blood and decaying meat curdled the air. It, combined with the stench of the crowd, made Auri's throat constrict.

The Market's clientele hid their barcodes beneath cuffs of varying colors and sizes. Some even concealed their faces underneath hoods or masks. Birdie bared her teeth at each person she passed, drawing closer to Auri.

Then they strode under a sign that made Auri's eyes widen in understanding: Flesh Market. A sour taste tainted her mouth. How could a place like this exist in the Ancora Federation? In the early decades of the Fed's founding, Tanoki existed as an MPB base that oversaw all operations on Medea. Due to citizen unrest and multiple assassinations, the base had been abandoned. She'd expected some debauchery. But she never thought the lack of law enforcement on the moon would turn into... *this*.

Katara glanced over and must've seen Auri's horrified expression. "They look more dangerous than they are," she promised even as she shortened the gap between them. "Keep your dog close if you don't want her to vanish. And don't let anyone see that sliced up robotic piece of yours." She gestured to Auri's arm in its sling. "That's worth more credits than you can imagine."

"They would take my…?" She couldn't finish the sentence, gaze darting to the surrounding crowd. No one seemed to pay her special attention. They were too intent on haggling for supplies or avoiding eye contact with every passerby.

Katara shrugged.

Auri wanted to run back to the ship. It was one thing to be hated for what she was. Another to have to worry someone might take her apart like a cheap doll. But to then be sold, piecemeal, in an open market?

They hurried past a booth where a vendor was hawking jewelry and shouting his black market prices at the top of his lungs. Birdie sniffed the air and stopped. A low growl rumbled in her throat.

"Birdie?" Auri backtracked and looked around, trying to pinpoint what snagged the dog's attention. "What's—?" A guttural laugh made Auri turn, the motion stiff and disjointed.

A familiar form lounged against the jewelry stall. Graham, one of the pirates who attacked her, chatted with the vendor's other customers. His left hand was tucked into a sling, the wrist and palm wrapped in thick gauze. In the other, held overhead so his onlookers could stare, dangled Auri's earring.

"You!" She knocked the crowd aside and rammed the pirate with her shoulder, shoving him against the stall's support beam. The entire table and mechanical awning shook. A few items tumbled to the ground as a hush swept over the onlookers, heads turning in her direction.

Graham stared at her for a beat, like he couldn't determine who she was. When a slow smile spread across his lips, Auri knew he remembered.

"Return my earring," she hissed, barely resisting the impulse to rake her fingernails across his smug face. "Or I'll break your other wrist." Beside her, Birdie snarled in agreement, hackles rising. The dog sunk low, prepared to pounce.

Katara was at Auri's side in a blur of speed, catching Auri's wrist as she reached for the hidden disc.

"That is quite enough." The woman's grip was iron, the edges of her fingerless gloves scraping against Auri's skin.

"This man has something that belongs to me." She tried to yank her arm free, but Katara only tightened her grip. The bones in Auri's wrist shrieked their discomfort. Graham's infuriating grin curled higher in pleasure. The sight sent daggers of hate through her chest.

Katara yanked Auri back, away from Graham. The woman's mouth pressed close to Auri's ear as she whispered, "Take a look around, Little Robot. Surrender. *Now.*"

Auri's gaze scanned the crowd, finding weapon after weapon, some pointed at her, others halfway slid from sheaths or holsters. The group near Graham openly pointed laser pistols at her. Even the vendor held an extended taser, the tip sparking.

"I…" She let Katara drag her away, stunned. What kind of place was this, where everyone came to the defense of the thief?

"Katara," she pleaded. "That earring is all I have left from my family. I need it back." Even as the words left her lips, she followed Katara back into the crowd, Birdie at her heels.

"You mean the family you're visiting?" Katara asked with raised brows.

Auri tensed, realizing her mistake. She fumbled for a lie. "It was my mother's. She died a long time ago."

"Uh-huh." Katara didn't look convinced. "Keep walking."

Tears burned Auri's organic eye as Graham and the earring disappeared into the mass of bodies. She'd lost the keepsake all over again.

Within a few meters, Katara had guided Auri out of the final Flesh Market stalls. The street dead-ended at the ramshackle remains of multi-story MPB barracks. They took a sharp right turn and Katara stopped.

She crossed her arms, openly studying Auri with pursed lips. "What fool is training DISC agents these days?"

Auri scrubbed at her tear-stained face. "I'm not a fool. If someone stole something from you, I doubt you'd hesitate getting it back."

Katara's expression turned distant. "True," she murmured. She glanced at Auri once more before her eyes darted upward in the typical ping-sending pose.

Auri dug her fingers into the curls at the base of Birdie's shoulders, just above her working harness. The dog licked at the inside of her wrist.

"The transport hangar is over there." Katara's voice made Auri look up. The woman pointed to a squat building at the end of the street. A few people were headed inside, backpacks or grocery bags slung over their shoulders or in hand. "The transport only goes from Tanoki to Medea and back. A new one arrives every thirty minutes… most of the time. I think you can handle that." Her tilted head contradicted the faith in the statement. "I'll take the rest of the credits now."

Auri obliged without comment. Katara could've helped in the Flesh Market. With that speed she displayed when interceding, she had the training of a fighter, and certainly the body of one. But the woman only cared about one thing: money. That was fine. The sooner Auri got on that transport and to a base on Medea, the better.

When *transfer complete* flashed on Auri's c-tacts, Katara turned and strode away, waving her hand once over her head in farewell.

"Come on, Bird." Auri maneuvered through the crowd into the hangar.

The interior wasn't air conditioned or as clean as the one on Rokuton, but it was as easy to navigate as Katara promised. Within twenty minutes, Auri sat on a shuttle with Birdie a statue at her feet. The transport resembled a long metal tube with plastic seating that was only half full.

Everyone around her stared into empty air, likely checking their pings or watching invisible holos. She felt naked without access to the grid. Could the other passengers tell? That she was vulnerable in the basest way? She toyed with a loose thread on the sling holding her injured arm.

An old woman wearing a long cotton dress and combat boots eased into the seat beside Auri. "Hello." She smiled, revealing crooked teeth.

Auri started. Back home almost everyone avoided sitting next to her on transports, even if they were overcrowded. They chose to stand instead. "Uh, hello." She returned the smile tentatively.

The woman groaned as she sank deeper into the hard plastic chair. "Hopefully this transport makes it planetside without needing repairs. Last time my trip was delayed by two hours, and I missed my train to Varity."

"Are repairs often needed?" Auri asked, eyeing the surrounding ship with growing concern.

"Every other ride for the most part. The Fed don't spend its limited resources out here on vagabonds and thieves. But we might get lucky this time." The elderly woman said with a broad smile.

Only then did Auri notice the seams in her face. Whoever performed the surgery did a mediocre job, aging the synthetic skin so it somewhat blended with the organic. But the line bisecting her face was still there, even more obvious than Auri's.

Looking closer, Auri noticed that the organic versus robotic sides weren't matched. The robotic parts were bulky and square while the organic side was oval-shaped and delicate.

"You're..." Auri murmured. "You're a cyborg." She knew the comment was borderline rude, but she rarely met someone like her.

The woman shrugged. "*Shouganai.*" *What can you do?* "May I pet your dog?"

"Sure. Birdie"—she pointed at the woman—"current friendly." The term meant she wasn't a threat at the moment but wasn't someone the dog should always trust.

The woman scratched the hair underneath the collar of the working harness. Birdie's foot smacked the transport floor in delight.

Auri watched the woman with curiosity. She never thought about her robotic parts that way. As *shouganai*. Did the elderly lady face the same prejudice on the rim? The pirates' reaction to Auri's exposed wiring had been severe. Severe enough to want to put her down.

She couldn't help but ask, "Do people like you?"

The elderly woman cackled. "I never cared to notice if they did or not." She leaned closer to Auri, "We got a second chance at life, you and I. That scares people, makes them jealous. The rumor that the GIC spies through our metal parts is just an excuse. If he did that, I'd be trapped in Attica instead of on this piece-of-junk transport. And the danger of that robot code infection? We got human brains, don't we?"

The woman fished inside her enormous purse, pulling out a many-times-patched drawstring bag. "Cookie?"

CHAPTER SIXTEEN

---

16 Aug 3319, 15:26:51
Ancora Galaxy, Planet 07: Medea, Transporter
Terminal #021A

Auri stepped off the transport shuttle into cool air. A crowded terminal that smelled of sickly sweet urine stretched ahead to the left and right. Groups of people waited on benches or leaned against walls, perking up as the arriving transport disembarked.

She squeezed through the press of exiting bodies and retreated to stand beside an out-of-the-way hologram advertising chewing gum. In her cargo pocket was the old woman's fabric bag of cookies. They'd chatted together for the length of the trip from Tanoki to Medea, which had ended up being an hour. The shuttle hadn't needed repairs, thankfully, but takeoff had been delayed by someone who had snuck a chicken onboard. Domesticated pets were allowed. Farm animals required a special waiver.

When they parted ways, the woman, needing to exit through a handicap ramp, had given Auri her "secret recipe" cookies. Auri munched on one now. They were green with chocolate chips and coconut flakes mixed in. The breakfast on Malachi's ship felt like decades ago.

Auri watched the transport empty, picking around chocolate to offer Birdie bits of cookie. Everyone kept their heads down, moving with purpose. No one laughed or chatted to one another. There weren't even any children traveling with their parents. The thought of approaching someone to ask for help set bees loose in her stomach.

She tentatively reached for the grid, but a sharp pain pulsed in her head like a pinched nerve. She stumbled sideways and knocked into a short, plump woman.

The woman leapt back, brandishing a knife with a buzzing blue electric blade. "Back off."

"*Sumimasen*," Auri bowed, hands raised. "I just got dizzy. Do… do you know where a local military base is?"

"A base? No." The woman glanced over her shoulder before glaring at Auri. "No, I don't. Look over there." She pointed to something behind Auri before she hurried toward the terminal's doors.

Auri turned away from the emptying shuttle toward two full-length screens installed on a wall. It wasn't surprising she hadn't recognized what they were. Though glowing letters spelled out "ormation center," the "inf" had gone out and no one had bothered to recharge them.

Hairline cracks skittered out from one of the screens in a spiderweb, as if someone or something heavy had slammed into it over and over. The other, Auri realized with mounting dread, wouldn't load anything past the *Welcome to Medea! Transporter Terminal #021A* screen.

So much for that. She would need to ask for help. Again. Hopefully not everyone would be as on guard as that woman earlier.

"Hey, there," a gritty voice made Auri turn. "Ya lost?"

A man in the light blue fatigues of the Air Command stood a few meters behind her, hands in pockets. Hope flooded her veins. She had to keep herself from running up to the officer, sobbing.

But as she studied him, that hope turned to suspicion. The man's fatigues were horribly wrinkled and a size too small. He did have the short hair and clean shave typical of AC officers, but his skin was rough from sun exposure and rife with pock-marks. Tanoki and Medea hadn't seemed the most cared for places; maybe it was the same with the AC stationed here.

"Hello," Auri said, curling her fingers in Birdie's hair.

"They've been broken for at least a decade." He gestured to the screens with a shake of his head, eyes sunken into his skull as though he had suffered malnutrition as a child. Not an oddity on Medea. The Fed was supposed to deliver extra food stuffs and medical supplies to Medea, Delfan, and Kaido, the planets where crops didn't grow as abundantly, but Auri had heard it was never enough.

"Are you from the AC?" Auri asked. "Or are you familiar with the local MPB?"

"Are you looking for a base?"

She nodded, noticing he didn't answer the question. "I am. The closest one that has a ship to take me past Krugel's Curve." She didn't want to reveal she was a DISC agent until she knew for sure that this man was an officer. Even then...

He clucked his tongue. "There's a local FOB you could try." He crossed his arms. "Stupid question, but why aren't you using the grid to get yourself to a base?"

She hesitated. "I had a malfunction. I lost access to it."

"Ah. I figured you were one of those cyborgs." He gestured to one of his human eyes. "Maybe they'll like you." His jaw tightened as if that last statement slipped off his tongue by acci-dent.

"Like me?" She shook her head. "What is that supposed to mean?"

He cleared his throat. "The officers there. They're not the nicest sort and might be… uninterested in cyborgs. Unlike me. I don't mind those parts of yours. Makes things more *interesting*."

Auri hoped the grimace she felt didn't show on her face. "Oh."

He scratched the back of his head with the hand that held his hat. "Now this is what you need to do…"

The officer listed each step to get to the base. It was a fair distance out of the terminal and past the train's final stop, but she knew Medea's bases tended to be large and far apart. She thanked him and, at the last minute, fished her final cookie out of the bag and gave it to him.

Surprise showed in his raised brows. His mouth formed a thin line as if he wanted to tell her something. Instead he held up the cookie in a salute and wandered off, bound for the next transport as it roared into the terminal.

Auri followed the officer's directions out of the station and down the street to an underground train. So far so good. It wasn't until she found herself leaving the final train stop and following a road that turned to gravel and then unmarked dirt that she started to worry. The officer had suggested she take a taxi for this portion of the trip, but taxis required identification. Auri's barcode was destroyed, and that meant she had to do everything on foot.

It was late afternoon when Auri first felt the buzz of someone's stare. But looking back at the barren dirt expanse, she was alone. Over the next hour, she felt the eyes again and again. Eventually she'd written the feeling off as exhaustion and hunger and focused on the next step to the base.

By now, Medea's early night had descended. Only the stars and full moon provided her any solace. But considering the moon above her was packed with cut-throats and criminals selling human anatomy, she didn't feel very comforted.

Over the rise of yet another hill, scant moonlight illuminated the outline of a massive row of buildings. They were all curved into the dirt, like a cylinder had been sliced in half and set on the ground. Relief washed over her. She recognized the area from basic as a Forward Operating Base, or FOB. They existed to support tactical operations through airfields and emergency hospitals. A tall fence encircled the FOB's perimeter with giant roadblocks positioned at various openings where an entry guard would typically stand.

Almost as immediately the relief fizzled, and concern dampened the palm of her hand. No light escaped from any of the many windows. Soldiers didn't patrol the grounds. The place looked abandoned.

The tread of a boot on loose stone made Auri tense and whirl around. Nothing. A growl rumbled in Birdie's chest. She raised her nose and sniffed the air. Her tail wagged once, almost in recognition. Though not the pleasant kind.

Whether or not Auri was followed earlier, now she was definitely not alone. She broke into a brisk jog down the small hill. The base was a hundred meters out. Birdie kept pace, claws digging grooves into the hard-packed dirt.

The roar of an engine overhead made Auri glance skyward. A ship zoomed past her, headed for the base. "Yes!" She doubled her speed, hope giving her a renewed burst of energy. "C'mon, Birdie! Race you!" Birdie took off, her four legs faster than Auri's two.

Overhead, the ship bypassed the landing strip within the base's confines. It executed a sharp turn and sped back toward Auri. A spotlight activated on the vehicle's belly, illuminating the ground below. Auri slowed to a stop, one hand held up to protect her eyes as the spotlight landed on her.

With the aid of the bright light, she recognized the ship. It was an old Komodo Class. Komodos were enormous vessels, practically indestructible, and once used for transporting soldiers. Most had been decommissioned in exchange for newer models.

She waved her arm overhead, afraid the officers aboard mistook her as a criminal trying to sneak into their base. "Don't shoot. I'm—"

The ship creaked as if a hatch was being opened.

"Get down!"

A hard body slammed into Auri. She hit the ground and rolled to a stop. Something—no, someone straddled her, their cheek brushing her robotic one. She shifted.

Not someone.

A man.

She slid her foot underneath his ankle and thrust up with her hips, knocking him off and hurling herself upright. He rolled over with a surprised gasp as she landed atop him. She yanked out her disc, shredding Katara's jacket in the process. She pressed the edge against the man's neck.

The spotlight searched the ground nearby before landing on them again. Her eyes widened in genuine surprise, her grip on the disc loosening. Malachi lay beneath her, glaring. Beside her, Birdie snarled up at the ship. Only the snarl turned into a whimper. Her tail tucked between her legs and she stepped backward, out of the spotlight.

Auri frowned. She'd never seen Birdie react like that to a ship.

Malachi knocked the disc away from his throat, shoving Auri off him. He leapt to his feet, yanking her up and towing her out of the spotlight.

She sheathed her disc. As much as she didn't trust Malachi, Birdie's response to the ship made her wary.

"We need to get out of here! C'mon!" He grabbed her uninjured wrist, and she allowed him to pull her into a breakneck run. Birdie took off after them, easily matching their speed.

"What are you doing here?" She tried to yank her arm free, but he held it in an iron grip. "Malachi, I don't need you to help me run. I need you to explain. That ship is from this base. They're—"

"That ship isn't from the base." His voice sounded strained when he spoke, as if his vocal chords had frozen around the words. "That ship is full of people who want to eat us alive."

CHAPTER SEVENTEEN

---

16 Aug 3319, 17:58:03
Ancora Galaxy, Planet 07: Medea, FOB #4956
ABANDONED

Malachi's declaration pounded through Auri's head as they scrambled over the roadblocks and through the fence's narrow opening. Behind them, the engines unleashed a deafening roar as the ship landed. The ground trembled with the sudden impact.

Malachi paused long enough to haul the fence's gate closed. He secured it with a magnetic zip tie from his pocket, fingers trembling. Then he and Auri were running again.

They sprinted for the first building. Malachi didn't pause to try the door. He forced it open with a vicious kick. It banged against the wall behind. The inset floor lights flicked on as they entered, dimmed to a weak glow by years of disuse. The scant illumination added to the skittering unease creeping over Auri's skin. Old ATVs were parked in militaristic rows. Enormous crates stamped with "MRE" or "MED" had been stacked in corners and abandoned. Their shadows stretched across the floor, reaching for Auri and Malachi with contorted claws.

Malachi started for a stack of crates at the back, but Auri caught his wrist. She pointed above at a staircase that led to the FOB commander's headquarters, all reinforced glass and a lockable door. He nodded and she led the way.

Their boots clanged on the metal steps as they ran, Birdie's nails click-clacking in time. Auri kept glancing over her shoulder, her imagination created monsters of hulking muscle and crazed eyes.

At the top of the steps, a catwalk led off to the left and right. On the left side was another storage area with stacked cots and blankets. To the right was the office. She raced for it, praying the door had been left unlocked. The knob turned. She shoved it open as the sound of screaming metal echoed outside. The cannibals had reached the fence.

Malachi shoved her into the office. He slammed the door shut and engaged the lock. The lights set into the ceiling flashed on as they detected movement. Auri froze.

The cannibals would be able to see the lights from below. The creatures would know exactly where they were.

Malachi, seeming unconcerned about the light, began shoving everything of significant weight in front of the door: the officer's desk, various boxes. When he got to the old-fashioned filing cabinet, Auri hurried to help him. It landed atop the desk with a clang that made her wince.

He positioned a second, smaller desk, possibly for a secretary, into the corner by the wall. The desk lay on its back, providing a shield against whatever came through the door. Malachi, Auri, and Birdie hunkered down inside it.

"Be as still as possible," Malachi choked out. He hunched uncomfortably close in the small opening, his shoulder tight against hers. "The Bleeders—"

"Bleeders?"

"That's what we call the cannibals." He gave his head a hard shake as if the name didn't matter. "Look, they won't notice the lights in here at first, but the sooner they go off, the better."

"Birdie, stay," she commanded, voice tight. Birdie sank down to curl up against Auri's leg, chin resting on her thigh. The desk would hide any of the dog's unintentional movement from the sensors.

Questions burned Auri's throat, but she held her breath, locking them away until darkness descended.

The room was fairly large for an FOB office, built in a long rectangle with two windows set into one wall. Dust coated everything. The motes danced in the air, disturbed by the movement of the furniture. Her body surged with adrenaline and the fear of an unknown adversary. Beside her, Malachi trembled with each inhale. His breaths were ragged and uneven as if he struggled to control his body.

The lights winked out. She swallowed, keeping as still as possible. His fear disturbed her in a way she struggled to understand.

"Malachi, what is going on? What are Bleeders?" Her ears seemed to vibrate with the intensity of listening for footfalls outside the office.

He clenched his hands into white-knuckled fists. In the moon's light through the windows, his skin gleamed with sweat. "They're monsters hiding inside human flesh."

Auri's breath caught. She was transported back to the sticky humidity of Babbage, rooftop tiles slick under her boots. Tanaka Hiroki stood before her, battered and blood-stained, pleading with her: *they're monsters hiding inside human flesh.*

"What do you mean?"

"They're a ghost story children whisper when the lights go out. A nightmare that steals into the waking hours." His eyes flicked to hers, not daring to move his head. "They hunt humans, Aurelia. And they eat them alive."

Her eyes went wide with disbelief. "Why haven't I heard of them?"

"It's funny you say that, considering your floppy was loaded with their victims."

Visible through the windows of the office, the lights at ground level flicked on, section by section, reflecting on the domed roof. The sight chilled Auri's blood, but Malachi didn't stop talking. Maybe it was to ease his own fear. Maybe because darker thoughts, thoughts he wanted to escape, lurked in the silence.

"You've been hunting them, haven't you?" His lips formed a tight, humorless smile. "And now, they're hunting you."

Goosebumps washed over her organic skin. "M-my first DISC case involved a man who killed his family. He chose to commit suicide rather than be taken into custody. Before he died, he mentioned monsters..." Auri trailed off into silence. The lights in the storage area stayed on as the Bleeders, or whatever they were, moved about. She strained to hear what was happening, terrified to catch the clang of shoes on the metal steps. "How do they exist?"

"Humans are all mismatched fragments of starlight and bone, but you can't have starlight without darkness." His voice dropped to barely a whisper. "Bleeders are all darkness. The Fed covers up their attacks, keeping everyone vulnerable, especially those on the rim. They're stronger than the average human and nearly impossible to kill." He stared at the barricaded door, as if a Bleeder already lurked there. Watching, waiting, ready to devour them.

Auri opened her mouth to argue that the Fed couldn't possibly cover up every attack, then paused. It was technically feasible. The news outlets all answered to the GIC. Would he really stoop so low as to pull the media's strings? Manipulate case files? Bribe officials? Auri didn't want to believe it. Why would he want to hide the Bleeders' existence in the first place?

Malachi cleared his throat. "I have something for you." He slid an object from a pocket of his pants, the desk hiding the motion. Auri squinted in the dim light only to muffle a sob with her clenched teeth. Moonlight glistened on tiny flower petals and a finger-length chain.

Resting in Malachi's palm was her earring.

"How did you get it?" she asked around a throat tight with unshed tears. What kind of man was Malachi? Each time she spoke to him, he revealed something new. Sitting this close to him, seeing the fear in his eyes, made Auri realize he was younger than she first thought. He couldn't be much older than she was.

"Katara sent me a ping." His gaze flicked to the windows that reflected the barren landscape outside. "I had her take you to the Flesh Market to stall for time so I could make my meet and still follow you to Medea."

"But why would you—?"

The clang of boots on the steps made Auri gag on the words. Each sound made her body tense, prepared to run. Malachi dropped the earring into Auri's damp palm as if knowing she needed its reassurance. She closed her fist around it, the design biting into her skin. The pain grounded her. She tucked the earring into a pocket of her borrowed cargo pants.

The footsteps paused outside the office door. *Only one set of footsteps*, the calm part of Auri's brain registered. They could take one Bleeder.

She hoped.

Through the window overlooking the FOB she saw the crest of the creature's shoulder. It didn't look like the ravenous monster she expected from Malachi's warnings. The Bleeder wore a jacket like any human might, though it was stained with dried blood and there were more holes than actual fabric.

The sound of snuffling startled her. It sounded like DISC bloodhounds catching a scent before a hunt.

She blinked.

A shadow hovered at the window. The face was a gaping hole of darkness, as if light didn't dare touch it. And it was staring right at her.

"*Maitta na.*" Malachi yanked Auri upright. The lights flicked on but he didn't seem to care. "It's going to get in. She's not here yet. We need t—"

A massive force barreled into the door. In one blow the lock bent, the frame splintering. Another slam and their barricade of furniture shuddered. On the next barrage, the filing cabinet hit the floor with a bang. The desk scooted back a few centimeters.

"How are they so strong?" she asked, horrified.

"Damned if I know," he hissed.

Auri activated her disc, fingers slick on the handle. "Birdie, enemy," she murmured, pointing at the door, though she doubted the dog needed to be told. Malachi hadn't bothered to pull out one of the many guns strapped to his body. Auri wanted to shout at him but was too afraid to raise her voice.

The door crashed off its hinges under the fourth assault, the desk flipping over itself and breaking in half. The Bleeder stalked into the room.

The lights revealed a scar-ravaged face and stringy hair that clumped in patches. Trickles of blood seeped from its eyes, nose, mouth. Crimson droplets pattered to the floor. The creature snarled, revealing human teeth blackened with decay and clotted blood.

The world blurred. Phantom cries exploded in Auri's skull, drowning out the Bleeder's howl. Pain burned hot in her arm, her face, her ribs. A memory swallowed her, all darkness and shadow apart from a single voice. *"I love you,"* a woman *sobbed in horrible, heaving gasps. "I love you."*

The office folded back around her with mind-crushing suddenness. Auri dry-heaved, vaguely aware of the sound of breaking glass. She staggered against the wall, eyes burning. The Bleeder stepped closer. Malachi stood atop a crate, the remains of a shattered window at his back. He was shouting at her, but she couldn't hear what he was saying. The echo of those horrible screams resounded in her ears.

The Bleeder sniffed the air, once in Malachi's direction, then Auri's. Its body shook with pleasure, a bubble of blood burst from his nose. The creature charged Auri, mouth spread impossibly wide.

Birdie was a blur of white. She leapt onto the Bleeder, digging her claws into his chest, but it flung her off as if she was no more than a wasp.

Auri dodged its taloned hand, and it slammed into the wall, sending plaster and dust flying. She shifted her grip on the disc, increasing the voltage to full capacity and activating the serrated blades. She screamed, an echo of the cacophony of voices in her head and sliced the disc into the monster's exposed back. The disc cut deep into muscle, catching on bone.

The Bleeder stiffened as the lightning crackled through it. But it didn't go down. The creature shook its head, staggering backward, almost falling. A growl emanated low in its throat as its gaze fixed on Auri. It struck.

The creature's massive hand caught her robotic arm, knocking her ten feet back against a wall. If her limb had been bone and muscle, it would've shattered.

An arm looped around her waist, hauling her on top of a crate. The shards from the broken window glistened on the wood. Malachi's eyes met hers, panicked and wild.

"Jump!" he was yelling at her. Two more Bleeders appeared in the doorway. They charged.

"Birdie!" Auri yelled. The poodle was at her side in an instant. Auri didn't hesitate. She jumped through the window, Birdie leaping with her.

CHAPTER EIGHTEEN

16 Aug 3319, 18:23:38
Ancora Galaxy, Planet 07: Medea, FOB #4956
ABANDONED

Auri's robotic knee caught on the hatch opening as she slammed onto the floor of a shuttle. Birdie yelped in pain but was quick to scramble away as Malachi landed in the spot where she had been. Auri rolled to avoid being crushed by his legs. She shifted to her knees, securing her disc into its harness before she accidentally sliced off a finger.

"Go!" Malachi shouted to the pilot, staggering to his feet. He winced and brought a hand to his ribs. "Their ship will be coming in hot now that they have something to hunt."

Auri had just managed to crawl to her feet when the shuttle took off, the force hurling her back as the hatch door closed. She pressed against the far wall and gawked at the pilot. Katara huddled over the controls as Malachi flung himself into the chair beside hers.

He turned back to Auri. "Aurelia, you're going to want to buckle up. This piece of *kuso* might not have fancy thrusters, but she can weave through Medea's canyons even better than the wind."

"You're forgetting who's driving her," Katara said. The lights on the front of the tiny shuttle illuminated a sprawling canyon a klick away. Katara sped right for it.

Auri hurried forward and commanded Birdie into the seat behind Katara. The dog loped up and Auri rushed to loop the seatbelt through the harness one-handed. Birdie's tail wagged as if the insane circumstance was just another joyride back on Rokuton.

"Aurelia, what the hell?" Malachi started, turning to her. The roar of engines made his head snap back to the control panel. A red dot blipped to life a thumb-length from a black speck on the screen. "Katara, kick it up a notch. They've locked on to us."

Auri threw herself into the last available seat. She'd just secured the belt across her chest when the shuttle lurched forward. They plummeted into the canyon in a hurtling nosedive. Auri's hair flew above her head while her stomach performed nauseating flip-flops. She clapped a hand over her mouth to hold back a scream.

The bottom of the canyon approached with dizzying speed. On the dashboard the distance calculator whirred. One hundred meters. Fifty meters. Thirty-five meters.

"Katara!" she shouted. "Pull up! Pull up!"

Katara's grip on the controls went white-knuckled, but her face didn't betray any anxiety. On the proximity screen, the red dot almost encompassed the black one. The Bleeders were practically on top of them.

"Tell me when," Katara whispered.

Ten meters.

Auri could only stare in mute horror. She was about to die. These people were insane!

Three meters, two meters, one...

The dots suddenly separated as the red one pulled back.

"Now!" Malachi shouted.

Katara yanked on the controls. The belly of the shuttle skimmed the bottom of the canyon with a grating force that Auri felt through her boots and up her legs.

Katara swore in English and Japanese as she fought to gain separation between the shuttle and the ground. Sparks flew past the windshield, popping in the darkness. With a final tug on the controls, the shuttle rose and shot toward a rock fissure.

Darkness enveloped the vessel as the cave swallowed them. Auri stared at the proximity detector and the single black dot on the screen. Malachi braced a hand on either side of it, waiting. Katara maneuvered the tiny shuttle around stalactites, gaze straight ahead.

After a minute of heavy silence, Malachi let out a breath. "We're in the clear. Relax, Katara."

She rolled her eyes. "I am relaxed." Her voice betrayed no sign of emotion, but she loosened her fingers on the controls, stretching them as if the bones ached.

Auri waited for her renegade heart to return to the safety of her ribcage before she spoke. Even then, her words sounded raspy and faint. "How far does this cave go? Won't the Bleeders just wait for us?"

Malachi turned around to look at her, hair a tangled mess. His eyes still gleamed with a feral wildness that sent a pulse through her. "This isn't a cave, DISC agent. Medea's canyons are full of manmade tunnels that the Air Command used to practice drills, before the criminals kicked them off their base. This one goes on for a few klicks and will spit us out far away from the canyon. And the Bleeders."

Auri wondered for the first time what branch Malachi had served in. Every citizen was required to spend one year in basic and another in the service. The universal test, the ASVAB, determined an individual's branch based on intellect and potential. This man was obviously smart and level-headed, plus he had knowledge of local training routes. Maybe he'd been in the Air

Command. Somehow, though, that conclusion didn't seem to fit Malachi.

She released a breath and sank into the torn seat cushion at her back. Birdie panted and yawned beside her. "It's okay," Auri soothed, stretching over to smooth an ear that had been bent back.

The darkness around the shuttle was so complete, the tunnel so soundless, that Auri lost track of time. Adrenaline and disbelief still pounded through her veins. Why weren't Bleeders mentioned in basic? Case after case stood out in her mind in sharp detail. Not just the brutal deaths of the victims, but those who had been found guilty of the cannibalistic crimes. According to the files, citizen after citizen had been arrested, by police or DISC agent, and put to death.

Hiroki's final words rose in her mind, ghost-like and haunting: *They should've killed me. Monsters hiding inside human flesh.*

An icy fist clenched around Auri's heart. She sucked in a breath. Hiroki's family, the entire population of Uma District, who knew how many more... They hadn't been killed by unhinged humans after all.

The existence of the Bleeders changed everything. When these monsters roamed the galaxy, why were innocents being executed—murdered—for crimes they so obviously didn't commit? What in the hell was the Federation doing? Did the GIC know?

And the most terrifying question of all: Where did Bleeders come from?

She reached into her cargo pocket and removed the earring. The lighting in the shuttle was dim enough that she couldn't make out the intricate details on the leaf or the flower. Who did this trinket originally belong to? Twice now she'd endured the despair—and the incapacitation—of those bodiless screams. What were they from? A memory? A hallucination?

Her mind felt like it was a swirling void. The tidy little galaxy she'd imagined for herself, already splintered from the Flesh Market, had cracked a bit more at the edges.

"Are you going to tell her?" Katara's voice intruded on Auri's thoughts. "You couldn't have asked for a better opportunity."

She looked up. "Tell me what?" Silly question. There were so many things that she wanted Malachi and Katara to tell her.

Malachi frowned. "You make it sound like I intentionally had Bleeders attack us."

"When that mafia captain directed our Little Robot to the abandoned FOB, you knew what would happen. They only send people out there to disappear. Yet you didn't stop her."

Auri's nose crinkled both at *little robot* and Katara's implication. "You knew that man sent me off to be… to be *eaten* and you didn't stop me?"

Malachi didn't answer at first. He stared out the windshield at the illuminated tunnel as it twisted and backtracked. He let out a slow breath and swung the seat so he faced Auri. He released the harness across his chest. "I didn't know Bleeders were the cause of the disappearances. I had my suspicions, but…"

Auri reached for her own harness, anger a hot pressure under her skin, but his next words stopped her.

"You needed to see Bleeders for yourself or you wouldn't help me."

Her brows furrowed. "Help you?"

He leaned forward, fingers clasped together as if he was praying for her understanding. "Aurelia, Bleeders are a whispered threat on the rim, a story. People disappear all the time and the Fed doesn't blink an eye. No one on the other side of Krugel's Curve has even heard of them. But before tonight, I've watched them kill, devour, and decimate."

He swallowed hard, rubbing a hand over his eyes. "For years I've been searching for proof of their existence. The Fed covers up every single attack and I've been…" His fingers knotted into tight fists. He let out a slow breath and met her eyes. "And I need to know why. Two years ago I got close. I discovered the existence of files containing the truth about the Bleeders. Unaltered police reports, why Roanleigh's terraforming failed and how it relates to where the Bleeders come from… But the files are restricted and protected against any remote access."

"Roanleigh? How could that have anything to do with Bleeders? And what does that have to do with me?" Auri asked, voice small. The maniacal glint in Malachi's eye had intensified as he spoke. He seemed obsessed with his mission of revealing the truth. Almost to the point of insanity. Then she remembered the gravestone back on Kaido. For him, the Bleeders' attacks were personal.

"I don't know how Roanleigh's terraforming is related. But the files will give me the answers I need. The only way to retrieve the files is to access them at their source, the storage facility on Harlequin, Aurora's moon. I never thought I stood a chance of getting in… Until I met you."

Auri's eyes widened in understanding. The lush moon Harlequin had a single building: the Spire, a maximum security vault where every shred of information created by the Federation was stored. The Tech Towers, a set located on almost every planet and habitable moon throughout the galaxy, pulled their data from the vault. But only to a point. The Fed—the GIC himself—occasionally restricted access to certain files. Those classified as restricted could only be retrieved by physically entering the vault.

And only one person was allowed access: the General-in-Chief.

Years ago, the GIC had broken countless protocols and taken her inside.

The day had been warm and sunny. She'd just turned seven years old and was about to be released from the hospital after a year relearning everything that made her human. The GIC ordered a tech officer to program her barcode with the special security clearance.

"I want you to understand the seriousness of what I've done," the GIC said to Auri. "The responsibility and trust that comes with it. That's why I've taken you here." Then he took her down into the icy depths of the Spire.

The basement itself was a massive warehouse of darkness, so big Auri couldn't see the boundaries of it. Bulbs set into the floor along pre-determined pathways were the only source of light, and they only lit the path ahead, not the rest of the room. The ceiling itself almost seemed to disappear into the darkness above. She shifted closer to the GIC.

He had chuckled and placed a hand atop her head. "Information comes to the vault in all shapes and sizes. The room is big enough to accommodate the grandest of ships to the smallest of floppys and the equipment needed to process it into a storable format. Nothing to fear down here."

Auri nodded but didn't dare move away. The warehouse-type room was empty except for a wall at the far end with a metal sliding door and barcode scanner fixed next to it. Beyond it waited the vault. It still stood out in childlike detail in her mind.

Inside the vault was a forest of floor-to-ceiling server towers that a user could plug into. An enormous screen hung in the center of the space with a small control panel underneath. The GIC fiddled with it as she stood beside him. She'd been amazed by the beauty of the vault, the way the obsidian server towers shone as electricity and information pulsed through them.

The GIC loaded a personnel file on the screen and told her to look.

She recognized her picture, but it took her long minutes to read the information below it. When she did, she dropped to the ground at the GIC's feet in a submissive bow, her forehead pressed against the chilly floor. Tears leaked from her organic eye as she sobbed, "Thank you, sir. Thank you for adopting me."

Auri frowned at the memory and ran her fingers over the tattered barcode on her forearm, still nestled in its sling. She shook her head at Malachi. "I had access to the vault once, but they removed it as soon as I left."

"I believe that the information is still there. Each GIC has a unique code that isn't changed until he retires or dies. I want to try to reactivate yours."

The pieces of Malachi's plan shifted into place, all except one detail. "My barcode is destroyed. How did you know who I was? How did you know the GIC took me into the vault?"

This time Katara answered. "I recognized you. Malachi thought you were an agent who might give us better intel on the Fed." She pushed a button that set the shuttle on autopilot but didn't turn to face Auri. "I saw your face on a short news clip about a mission on Babbage. It was a small story, but you're the GIC's adopted daughter, so you received about five seconds of momentary fame. Or infamy, it seemed."

The drones by The Avenue... Auri had thought they were more interested in Tanaka Hiroki's suicide than her. Apparently, she was wrong.

About so many things.

"When Malachi first brought you in," Katara continued. "We checked out the dormant capabilities in your torn barcode." She paused for a beat. "I was like you, once." She pulled something from a strap on her belt and flipped it. The object was black, the frame shaped like a rectangle with the bottom piece missing, a metal grip positioned toward the top.

"Like every Ancoran," she said, "I served my two years in the military. But instead of joining a typical branch, the MPB recruited me and I became a Dispatcher." She caught the object around the grip. A black laser blade shot out from the top, about as long as Auri's hand.

Auri leaned forward in admiration. She had never seen anything like the weapon. She knew only vague details about the MPB trained assassins; the Dispatcher division was the most secretive of all the sub-branches of the MPB.

"They named me after my weapon of choice, the katar, and unleashed me on renegade citizens." She continued flipping the weapon—the katar—around with practiced ease like it was an extension of her soul. "One day they sent me after a man who had escaped Fed custody and was spreading negative propaganda. They wanted him dead without fuss. Just before I was going to kill him, he started telling his story. I spared his life, left the Dispatchers, and decided to join his crew on a temporary basis." With a flick of her wrist, the blade blinked out and she sheathed the weapon back into her belt. She looked over at Malachi. "But I always complete what I start. So I'll still kill him someday."

"Luckily for me, someday wasn't today," Malachi said with a serious tone.

Auri's eyes widened. "What about your story convinced her?" How did he even trust her to be on his crew knowing she still planned to shove her katar in his back whenever she felt the slightest inclination?

"That's not important." Malachi waved her question away. "Will you work with us, Aurelia? Will you help us find the truth?"

Auri didn't answer. Going solo to delve into suspicious cases was one thing. Joining a crew intent on breaking into a secure government facility? If caught, she would be worse than court-martialed.

She would be executed.

Even more terrible than both punishments was the knowledge that she would be betraying the GIC. He had healed her, opened his home to her, and supported her.

Could she turn on him?

The Bleeder's snarl echoed in her ears as if the creature lurked just behind her, its clotted blood oozing onto her shoulder. When Auri brought the cannibal cases to the GIC, he'd had the opportunity to tell her the truth. Instead, he used his position to command her to acquiesce to his and Captain Ishida's lies.

So many people had died. Auri had nearly been killed over a threat that the Fed was desperate to cover up.

And she wanted to know why.

She rolled her shoulders back, turning her spine into iron, her resolution to steel. "Malachi."

"Yes?"

She sucked in a breath, meeting his eyes. "If we're going to be working together, I'd like you to call me Auri."

CHAPTER NINETEEN

---

16 Aug 3319, 23:11:34
Ancora Galaxy, Planet 07: Medea,
Free Airspace

The shuttle slowed as it approached Malachi's ship. They skimmed underneath, the headlights illuminating the name painted on the side: *F.T.S. Kestrel*. Auri almost smiled. Naming a Falcon Class vessel after a falcon breed bordered on ironic. Until she remembered the one other place she saw the name.

Kestrel was carved into the gravestone on Kaido. Whoever Malachi lost there—lover, sister, or friend—still haunted him.

Auri glanced at the man, his profile illuminated by the running lights of the *Kestrel*'s middle. He stared ahead, watching Katara dock the shuttle. There was an aura of brokenness about Malachi, but strength too. As if he'd fitted the pieces of himself back together, sealing the cracks with determination and a desperate need for the truth. No wonder she'd thought he was older when they first met. Life had aged him prematurely, given him scars that no boy could bear. So he'd been forced to grow up. Kind of like her.

He glanced back at Auri, and she offered him a small smile. He nodded in return before turning around.

Katara docked the shuttle and cut the power. Minutes later, the four of them exited the tiny craft into the cargo room. New crates were stacked in the center, stamped with the label *DE-LIVERY: Babbage, FRAGILE*. Auri paused just outside the shuttle doors to cover a yawn. It was long past midnight on Medea, and all she wanted to do was curl up in bed.

Except she didn't have a bed.

She hesitated to catch up with the others. Malachi and Katara were already swapping their shoes for slippers.

"Do I have to sleep on the sack of potatoes?" She didn't think she could take another night in the pantry.

To her surprise, Malachi chuckled. "You're part of the crew now, Auri. We're like family."

Family. Warmth swept through her. She squatted to plant a kiss between Birdie's eyes to hide the loony grin spreading across her face and hurried over to take off her boots.

They strolled down a short hallway before turning right as the kitchen came into view. This corridor was where Malachi took her to bathe earlier. It seemed like a lifetime ago.

Malachi stopped at the first rice paper door on the right side. Meanwhile, Katara knelt in front of the third door down on the left. She picked up a green stem littered with tiny purple buds. Auri recognized the plant as a Limonium flower. It looked oddly delicate in Katara's muscled and scarred hands.

"Will the man ever give up?" she growled. She kicked her door open with a foot and stomped inside. But as she shut the door, a small smile bloomed on the assassin's face as she brought the flower to her nose. A secret smile she probably didn't intend for anyone to see.

Auri glanced at Malachi with raised brows. He just shook his head. "In case you were wondering, I strongly discourage onboard romances. Too messy." He gestured to the door they stood in front of. "This is your room."

She decided not to ask any more questions about the flower—she was definitely not interested in onboard romances—and slid open the door. It was a simple space with a small bed in one corner and an empty bookshelf in the other. A *kotatsu*, a low table with a built-in heater underneath and blanket lining the edges, sat in the center of the room. Near the door was an open closet with a few shelves and hangers. Clothes already occupied the space. Even her dirtied uniform that she'd abandoned in the bathroom lay off to the side, sealed in an odor-proof laundry bag.

She turned back to Malachi. "You knew I'd agree to help."

"I hoped." He crossed his arms. "Besides, you were already helping by investigating, you just didn't know it." He hesitated, then added, "Thank you, Auri." With a final nod, he retreated from the room, shutting the door behind him.

Auri changed out of her dirty clothes into a set of sweatpants. She then spent the next half hour attempting to sleep. Birdie had shoved herself under the *kotatsu*, with just her snout and tail sticking out from under the blanket. The sight reminded Auri so much of her tiny room back home, she couldn't help but ache for the familiarity of those faraway four walls.

Since a *kotatsu* was only used in cold weather, the presence of the table had confused her, but as time passed, she understood. The corridor was located inside the wing of the *Kestrel*, which meant limited heat.

After an hour passed and Auri was still awake, she threw off her covers and turned on the *kotatsu*'s heater. She rifled through her closet, not bothering to turn on the light. After a few false alarms, she finally found her floppy and settled in front of the *kotatsu*. Birdie groaned as Auri slid her legs under the table and bunched the blankets around her lap.

"You shouldn't be under there anyway," she muttered, stroking the dog's soft fur with her toes. The floppy's screen glistened in the light creeping under the crack in her door. She flicked through the cases, studying the attack on Uma District more closely. She frowned at the picture of the suspect, pinching the screen to zoom in. The more she looked at the image, the more familiar the facial features became, half obscured by a beard and a tangled mass of hair. A terrifying truth whispered in the back of her mind, but she refused to listen to it.

Malachi could not be this man. She scrolled down to the suspect's personal information and froze. *Peter Treatis*. She stared out the small window across from her. Treatis was Kestrel's last name too.

Frost crept over the corners of the window where space stretched in an endless horizon. The infinite blackness reached for her, tantalizing—yet terrifying—with its limitless possibilities. Out there somewhere, Bleeders wreaked havoc and ruined lives. Staring out into the void made her wonder how many of the monsters were out there. Just that one ship? Fifty ships? A hundred? More?

Her imagination concocted an entire army of Bleeders descending on the system, devouring humans like cows did grass. Until nothing but blood and corpses and desolation consumed every planet.

She shook her head and brought her gaze back to the screen. Malachi must've known the Treatis family. Maybe he grew up in a nearby district and Kestrel had been…

Someone special.

Auri scrolled to the very bottom of the case, her grip on the floppy white-knuckled. Peter's trial had been quick and decisive, his execution date set for 20 Jan 3316.

He was already dead.

A chill seeped into Auri's bones that the *kotatsu* couldn't fight off. When Malachi visited Uma District, did he just mourn Kestrel's death? Or did he also mourn the wrongful death of her brother?

Auri fell onto her side, pressing her cheek against the chilly faux wood floor. There were too many secrets in play, too many mysteries for her to unravel. She needed to sleep and not dwell on the lives she couldn't have saved.

Sliding open her bedroom door, she peered into the hallway. All the doors on her wing were shut. She tiptoed into the bathroom to splash cold water on her face. The bruising on her face had worsened, the colors melding together like a half-mixed palette of paint. The stitch tape glistened, a line of red marring the skin underneath where the gun had split it. The wound would leave a scar. Just another addition to her Frankenstein appearance.

She left the bathroom. Halfway inside her bedroom, a muffled whimper made her pause. *Birdie*, she thought, but an all-too-human grunt followed it, emanating from the corridor across from her. The noise reverberated through her with painful recognition. Those were the echoes of someone suffering through a nightmare.

By the time she had sneaked across the hall and reached the entrance to the corridor opposite, the sounds quieted.

She bit her lip, dancing from foot to foot. What was she thinking? Auri didn't know who cried out in fear. She hadn't met the entire crew yet, and though she'd agreed to help, she doubted Malachi would be pleased with her poking around.

With one last glance over her shoulder, Auri crept back into her room and shut the door. Soon after, she fell into her own nightmares of blood, teeth, and slashing claws.

CHAPTER TWENTY

---

17 Aug 3319, 07:28:02
Ancora Galaxy, Planet 07: Medea,
Free Airspace

The smell of frying bacon woke Auri from a deep sleep. She dressed in a mental fog, her nose ordering her out of her room. All she'd eaten since breakfast the day before was a few cookies.

Birdie already stood by the door, ready to go. Auri eyed the dog's working harness. Birdie had been wearing it since they set off from Rokuton days ago. They were relatively safe now. Maybe it was time to give the poodle a break.

"Stay," Auri instructed as she bent to unstrap the harness. Once the velcro came free, Birdie shook, pausing only to scratch at her side.

Auri padded into the kitchen on her supplied slippers, wearing another pair of cargo pants and a t-shirt with the kanji symbol for cat across the chest. The top was too short for her long torso and showed her belly when she raised her arms, but it covered her scars, unlike the other tank tops in the closet.

Birdie trotted beside her, nose quivering as she sniffed the air. The dog's tail wagged with enthusiasm.

Auri turned a corner into the kitchen. The space was a bustle of activity. A dark-skinned man stood behind an island countertop with an oven and stovetop set into it. He flipped frying bacon with a pair of chopsticks, his braided white hair held back by a thick band.

In the dining area Katara lounged in a chair beside a blond man Auri recognized from the infirmary.

"It has a meaning," he was saying to her. "The Limonium. It means *I miss you.*"

Katara rolled her eyes. "Only a Chair Command doctor would have time to look up flower meanings. What a waste of time."

He smirked. "I wouldn't call it a waste of time." He held up his hands. "I'll stop leaving them outside your door if you want…"

"I didn't say that." She cleared her throat and fiddled with the hem of her jacket. "But whatever you want. I don't care."

The doctor leaned back, head supported by his hands, a self-satisfied smile on his face. "Sure you don't."

Katara turned toward Auri, who quickly looked away. She didn't want to be caught eavesdropping, especially on a possibly unrequited love.

The captain was busy setting out an eclectic collection of plates and glasses. Marin, the pale bald girl Auri already met, shadowed him, laying intricate chopsticks beside each place.

Malachi set the last plate and looked up at Auri. His eyes were bloodshot and purple smudged the skin underneath. The cries from last night echoed in the back of her mind.

"Everyone," he raised his voice to be heard over the sound of bacon sizzling. "If we could all have a seat, I want to introduce an interim member of our crew."

The man in front of the stovetop raised three fingers and yawned. "Almost done."

Auri vaguely recognized the voice but couldn't grasp from where. A cold hand on her arm made her look down. Marin stood there, wearing another *yukata*. The fabric of this dress was patterned with a thousand tiny blue swallows, wings spread across pink fabric.

"Your seat is over here," the girl said, pointing to the last chair on the right side of the table.

"Oh, thank you," Auri replied as Marin guided her to the seat. Marin's fingertips skimmed each chair as she walked, almost as if she counted the places.

Atop Auri's plate rested a pair of beautiful chopsticks. Carved *sakura* blossoms grew from metal vines, twirling and twisting around the top. Different styled chopsticks accompanied each place-setting. At the head of the table, beside her, the utensils were shaped like twigs, but smoothed and curved to make for an easy grip. Malachi took a seat there and ran a thumb over the realistically painted metal. He noticed her scrutiny with a twitch of a smile.

"I pick chopsticks for every crew member," he explained as he scooted his chair closer to the table. "Yesterday I saw those and thought they would fit you."

"I…" Auri ran her fingers over the lifelike flowers. "Thank you."

He shrugged.

Marin shuffled into the chair beside Auri. Her chopsticks were shaped like the motherboard of a computer. Marin's hands skimmed over her plate, searching for the utensils while her eyes stared straight ahead. Auri's lips parted in realization. This girl was blind.

The cook hefted the frying pan of bacon over to the table and plopped it onto a warmer. After two trips, the table was lined with fried eggs, rice, bacon, and buttered toast.

The cook seated himself beside Marin, leaving two seats empty: one next to Malachi and one at the opposite end of the table. Auri wondered if the crew had assigned seats.

Malachi clapped his hands together and the rest of the crew followed, each muttering, "*Itadakimasu*." Dishes were passed around, and Auri had to restrain herself from staring at Marin. The girl easily passed the bowls to Auri, though without taking food herself. Birdie acted like she had never eaten before, letting out plaintive whines as each item passed over her head.

"You'll get some soon," Auri chided her. Birdie curled up on the floor, her head resting on Auri's foot.

Once everyone's plate was full and Birdie was happily munching on eggs and bacon, Malachi cleared his throat. "I thought breakfast would be the best time for introductions."

Auri studied the crew gathered at the table. The cook was a mystery, but the doctor seemed nice enough. When she looked at him, he gave her a broad smile, teeth white against his blond beard. The cook focused on his breakfast, guzzling green tea as if it were a caffeine shot.

"No *kuso* remarks," Malachi warned, slicing a fried egg in half with the edge of his chopstick. "But I want us to go around the table and introduce ourselves, even those of us Auri already knows. I'll start." He twirled his chopsticks in one hand, calluses flashing on the palm not covered by a glove. "I'm Malachi Vermillion. Captain and the ship's engineer. Twenty-two-years-old, so you could consider me a prodigy." Katara snorted at that, but Malachi pretended not to hear her. "I spend more time in the engine room than on the bridge." He flexed his gloved hand at her. "*Kestrel* tends to run hot."

The doctor spoke next, balancing a chopstick on a forefinger. His were a replica of surgical needles with the kanji for *prick* engraved on them. Her brows drew together. An odd choice.

"I'm Ferris Quark," he began. "Ship's doctor and all-around good guy." He winked at Aurelia. "Not sure why Cai felt the need to throw age in. It's just a number, ay?" He raised his brows at the white-haired cook, who rolled his eyes.

"Morning people," the cook groaned. He drained another cup of tea. "May your next lover curse you with the spots, Ferris."

"I'm twenty-four and ship's doctor. And apparently a prick." He waved his chopsticks, "Thanks, Cai. Very funny. These are new. Where's my real pair?"

Malachi raised his brows. "I wasn't aware you had a pair."

Katara choked on the green tea she'd been sipping.

"What a disappointment for you, Katara," the cook muttered around a mouthful of rice.

Katara's laughter dried up. She bared her teeth. "Say it again, I dare you. Ferris's balls have nothing to do with me."

"If we could stop discussing testicles," Marin murmured, "I would appreciate it. I am a child, after all."

"Fair enough," Ferris said with a laugh. "Sorry, Marin. Though you should blame Cai." He looked to Auri. "We're old friends... of sorts. We banter."

"Bicker is more like it," Malachi grumbled. "But the *Kestrel* needs a doctor and, as much as I hate to compliment him, Ferris is the best around."

"I won't argue." Ferris slurped up the remnants of a runny egg. "Auri, what's your blood type?"

Auri frowned. Maybe as the doctor he would need to know it in case something happened? "AB. Why?"

He rubbed at his beard. "*Kawarimono*. Eccentric. You're dual-natured and complicated. Also rare. Just like Cai. Who would've thought, two ABs on the same ship. What an intense relationship you'll have."

An awkward silence settled around the table. Heat rushed up to Auri's organic cheek. A doctor who believed in the Japanese blood types. She really was on the rim.

"Well done making things weird, Ferris," Katara said, raising her chopsticks. The points were sharpened to gleaming tips and the tops were shaped like sword hilts. "I'm Katara and my age is none of your business." She shot Malachi a side-eye. "Don't betray us, Little Robot. Or I'll come after you."

Auri's grip tightened on her chopsticks. "I don't plan on it."

"She's a B and I'm an O," Ferris whispered conspiratorially, leaning over his almost empty plate. "It makes our future the most harmonious possible. Though you might not be able to tell by her prickly exterior."

"Who said we had a future." Katara rolled her eyes. "And I like being prickly."

Auri couldn't help but smile. Ferris had a way of making her feel like she'd known him for years instead of minutes. Plus, he didn't hide his emotions—or interests. There was something endearing about that. And safe.

The cook was next. Auri leaned around Marin to get a better look at him. His brown eyes flicked over her in a lazy assessment as he yawned again. The ring finger on his left hand was entwined with a thin tattooed chain that snaked all the way up to the tip of the digit. "I'm Castor Vale, the cook on the ship. I am not a morning person, but Captain insists on full-crew breakfasts."

Castor Vale. The name struck a chord in Auri's memory. Years ago, when she was still in middle school, a court case went viral. A young man from Delfan was charged as the Blood Letter, a notorious criminal who murdered public officials with ricin, an organ-stopping poison. Castor Vale's face, with fewer creases at the corners of his eyes and jet black hair instead of white, had been plastered over screens and holos for months. Until he was acquitted after an error in the holo-transferred evidence.

The rice turned to ash in her mouth. "Y-you're Castor Vale?" She'd been eating food prepared by a suspected poison master. Some poisons took many doses to take effect. Had he also prepared the breakfast she had eaten yesterday?

Castor smirked and his full lips parted to reveal perfectly white teeth. "See, Cap, I'm still famous past the Curve."

OF STARLIGHT AND BONE · 153

Malachi sipped at his green tea, the mug tiny in his hands. "Castor's turned his *alleged* love of mixing poisons into a love of mixing spices. Right, Castor?" He gave the man a pointed look as if even he sometimes doubted the cook's intentions.

"Alleged? I was never found guilty." He laughed, but at Malachi's grimace, Castor held up a hand. "Cook's honor. No poisons." He looked at Auri and smiled, deepening a single dimple in his left cheek. Seemed like he was completely awake now. "How do you like your rice, though? I like to add a bit of *salt.*"

A joke. It had to be. Everyone scooped spoonfuls from the same bowl. "It's fantastic," Auri said, determined not to let Castor's teasing unnerve her.

"A blood types," Ferris said. "Can't live with them, can't live without them."

Marin sighed as if everyone's behavior was embarrassingly childish. "Is it my turn?"

"Yes," Castor said, his tone softening.

Marin shifted until her gaze met Auri's. A chill rippled down her spine. How did the girl do that?

"My name is Marin," she said. "I'm blind. I'm also the pilot."

"The... the..." Auri clapped a hand over her mouth. She whirled on Malachi. "You have a possible poisoner for a cook and Marin's a pilot?" She glanced at Ferris, wondering if he would interject a blood type. He stayed oddly quiet, gaze on his own now-empty plate.

Malachi frowned, eyes flashing with disappointment. "You of all people should understand that the way you look doesn't define what you can do."

The truth stung. She had fallen into the same trap her MPB colleagues did, judging people based on outward appearances. But could he really blame her?

"Don't be so overprotective, Akki-tan," Marin chided Malachi. Her attention shifted to Auri. "What he means is that I can talk to machines, to the ship. She tells me what lies ahead, and I tell her where we need to go."

Auri struggled to comprehend. A human capable of communicating with machines?

As if she'd read her mind, Marin added, "I'm not as human as I might look. Or as young."

"How old are you?" Auri couldn't help but ask.

"This body correlates to that of a ten-year-old" was Marin's strange reply.

"What does—" Auri started to ask, but Malachi cleared his throat.

Tension radiated off the *Kestrel*'s captain akin to the overprotectiveness of a big brother. He spoke, abruptly ending Auri's chance to question Marin further. "Marin's a little complicated. All you need to know is that she's our pilot and she does a better job than any man or woman with perfect vision."

Well, there was no arguing with that. Besides, what would Auri do? Demand another pilot? Change her mind? No. She would have to trust Malachi's judgment—whatever that was worth. And Marin's uncanny abilities. Maybe she was a type of advanced cyborg Auri hadn't heard of?

Ferris broke the second awkward silence. "Mind introducing yourself?" he asked Auri.

She forced a smile. "Right. I'm Aurelia Peri, but you can call me Auri. I'm a DISC agent and this is my dog, Birdie. She's very friendly, but only pet her when her harness is off or I give you direct permission. Otherwise, she's working and won't like it if you play with her."

Auri realized that she had given this exact speech to a class of kindergarteners when they'd toured the barracks. Her organic cheek flushed.

Malachi leaned forward, elbows braced on the table. "Auri has agreed to help break into the vault on Harlequin. Let's talk strategy." Hearing the words aloud made Auri's stomach churn.

Katara put down her chopsticks and tapped the center of the table. The wood morphed into a screen. Schematics of the Spire spun to life in crystal-clear detail. Auri didn't want to know how they'd obtained the blueprints.

"The military ball is in a little under two weeks." Katara zoomed the schematics to the top floor of the Spire, very familiar to Auri after attending the annual ball with her father for over a decade. Her heart twitched at the thought of going dress shopping with him, which they usually did after Obon.

"We've all been to the Spire at least once for our own military balls, so the layout is familiar. The plan is simple. We distract the guards and security tech, Little Robot opens the doors, and the hacker pulls up the intel for us." The screen zoomed out of the top floor and down into the basement. "Where are we on finding a hacker, Malachi?"

"That's a good place to start the brainstorming," Malachi said, adjusting the glove on one hand. "Anyone have recommendations? The hacker needs to be someone we can trust. The information stored in the vault could destroy lives, and I only want the files relating to the Bleeders."

Thoughtful looks met his question. Auri didn't bother trying to come up with a hacker. She didn't know any.

While the crew discussed options, her thoughts drifted to Ty. She fingered the gladiolus charm. The memory of his hot breath against her ear made her body warm. What was he doing now? She should've arrived back on Rokuton today. Would he worry when she didn't show?

She hoped so.

"You know who we need," Castor said, his tone resolute as he stared at Malachi. "We need *her*."

Malachi shook his head. "As much as I'd enjoy having her on my crew again, it's too complicated."

"Why?" he demanded.

"Castor," Katara warned.

When Malachi responded, his tone was conciliatory, but from where she sat, Auri could see a gleam of approval in his eyes. "Because bringing her in would create a whole different mess of problems."

"Like her falling for you again?"

A muscle ticked in Malachi's jaw. "Excuse me?"

Katara groaned and rolled her head back to look at the ceiling. "Not this again."

Ferris leaned forward as if eager for the drama.

"I want to see her as little as you do," Castor said. "But now we need her help. Besides," his voice softened, "where they've sentenced her... She's not going to last long."

"Castor—" Malachi started.

"She could've turned you and Marin away when you begged for help, but she didn't. She created new lives for the both of you. And now you won't rescue her? Because she came on to you last year and I broke your nose?"

"That does have something to do with it." Malachi rubbed at the crooked appendage. "Though that's not all and you know it."

He snorted. "You're not the man I thought you were. Your quest for the truth has tarnished you. Or you're just a coward."

Castor's words hung in the air, casting a pallor over the room. Was awkwardness a normal part of the crew-mandated breakfasts? And insubordination? Never had she witnessed a lower-ranking officer speak to a captain like that.

Birdie, oblivious to the tension, scratched at Auri's leg with a paw. Auri tossed a slice of bacon onto the floor without looking down.

Marin was the first to speak. "Akki-tan, you know we owe it to her."

Malachi sighed, rubbing his temples. Minutes passed before he spoke, though no doubt he felt the crews' eyes on him. "Fine," he groaned, meeting everyone's gaze in turn. "We'll break her out."

Break her out. The words echoed in Auri's brain. Realization slid over her like grease atop water.

"We don't have much time," Ferris said, gaze off-focus as he used his c-tacts. "Court docket reads she was sentenced yesterday. She has an execution date set for the twenty-seventh— that's basically a week from now."

Castor swore under his breath.

Malachi shook his head. "Doesn't change anything. We were already on a tight deadline with the military ball around the corner. What's the difference if we make it a bit tighter?"

Auri shook her head, fingernails digging into her palms. "You can't be serious." She looked around the table. "You want to break someone out of Attica? The prison planet constantly monitored by satellites with no breathable atmosphere?"

Silence. Then Ferris nodded. "That's about right."

CHAPTER TWENTY-ONE

---

17 Aug 3319, 07:52:23
Ancora Galaxy, Planet 07: Medea,
Free Airspace

"I did not agree to this," Auri said, dropping her chopsticks. They clinked against her plate. "Breaking into Attica is idiocy. And breaking out? It's impossible." The planet was called the Heat for both the temperature and the massive weapon cache. Not only that, but she knew a few guards stationed on the planet. Running into them… The thought made her tense as unpleasant memories crowded the back of her mind.

Malachi cleared his throat and folded his hands on the table. "Actually, someone has escaped Attica from maximum security holdings."

"Death row," she breathed. "Who? Who escaped?"

He hesitated.

"I did," Marin said beside her. "Well, Akki-tan and I did."

"I don't believe it." She forced a laugh to bat away the unease fluttering in her chest. "I toured the prison in basic. Maximum security is underground. There is no way out."

The suspect from Uma District's case flashed in her mind. *20 Jan 2316.* The execution date felt like it was burned onto her forehead.

"That's where you're wrong." Malachi shifted in his seat. "There's a flaw in the design. Marin discovered it after talking to the walls. She got us out."

In any other circumstance, a girl talking to the walls of a prison would've made Auri laugh. But not here. Not now.

Malachi looked to Marin. "When you're finished here, I want you to set a course for Delfan."

Marin nodded.

Questions dangled from the tip of Auri's tongue, but one was foremost: *Why were you and Marin on death row?*

She doubted Malachi would give a truthful answer. Could she still work with the crew knowing Malachi and Marin were escaped fugitives?

To her surprise, her resolve didn't buckle. The existence of the Bleeders altered everything she thought true, changed what might have seem like clear-cut decisions just a few days ago. The Fed wasn't the perfect government she once believed it to be. Those in the cannibalism cases had been wrongly sent to Attica and sentenced to death. Perhaps other innocents met the same fate. She'd become a DISC agent to help people. Not assist in their murders.

"Getting into Attica," Katara muttered, "is the easy part. Getting out is the challenge, even if we have two cocky fugitives sitting at our table. We'll be leaving with an extra body."

"What did she do?" Auri asked before someone else spoke. "Why is this hacker in Attica?" Accepting Malachi and Marin was one thing. If Auri broke a hacker out of the Heat, she wanted to ensure she wasn't setting a crazed criminal loose.

Castor was the one to answer. "Tsuna is a Mercy Hacker. She takes up the causes of the innocent and the poor. She's usually careful, but she has weaknesses for abused women. Rumors claim they sent a turncoat in to trick her, and that now she's being held on level zero, maximum security, like Malachi and Marin were."

"I want that confirmed," Malachi said. Castor nodded.

Auri absorbed Castor's statement. If Tsuna helped Marin and Malachi years ago, she must've deemed them innocent as well. Not that a stranger's beliefs held much sway.

"You've seen planets on the rim," Ferris said to Auri. "I grew up on Kaido with Cai. A relatively nice planet this side of the Curve. Sure, we had one or two hungry seasons. But even I had no idea how people on the rim—Delfan and Medea—lived. I doubt you were aware of it either. People like Tsuna are protectors. Can you really be guilty of a crime when you're protecting the innocent?"

Auri frowned, his words creating more ethical questions she didn't want to ponder. Birdie shifted underneath the table as if sensing the discomfort of her partner. Auri had already taken one step down this path. Turning back now would be pointless.

She met Malachi's gaze. "I'll help with Attica." She wouldn't be breaking into the prison alone. The crew would be there. If she ran into *them*, she would have back up. For once. "We can't get caught. This can't go public. No news drones, no alarms."

"I'm not sure about you, but when I break someone out of prison," Malachi said, "I don't get caught. And we won't." The dangerous thrill in his voice made a chill go down Auri's spine. She couldn't decide if the sensation felt pleasant or not.

Marin slid away from the table, leaving her dishes behind. The chair made a soft scratching sound against the wood floor.

"Now that our little robot has made up her mind"—Katara swiped away the schematics of the Spire to reveal a map of the solar system—"we need to find a place to stay that is close to both Attica and Aurora. Any ideas?"

Marin nodded. "I have a place where we can go. It is well hidden on Rokuton."

Everyone looked to Malachi. His expression had turned grave. "Are you sure you want to go back there?"

"Yes." Marin's voice sounded sure, but the fingers of her right hand twitched over and over, almost like a nervous tic. Or a tech malfunction. How cyborg was she? And why didn't her eyes have sensors like Auri's?

Malachi nodded at Katara. "There you have it." He looked back at Marin. "Keep our original course for Delfan. I'll meet you on the bridge."

Auri wondered what was on Delfan that would help with their prison break, but Marin's hand twitching stilled. She stepped away from the table and hurried off, her bare feet making soft *pitter-pat* sounds on the floor. She didn't hold out her hands to gauge her surroundings or even use a cane.

"How can Marin walk around the ship like that?" Auri found herself asking once the girl left. "She doesn't use anything to guide her."

"She can see the layout of the ship through her feet," Katara answered, standing up and collecting her and Ferris's dishes. "That's why she doesn't wear shoes."

"Oh." She really must be some kind of specialty cyborg. No way in the stars could Auri manage a feat like that.

"Don't think about it too hard," Ferris advised. "I don't."

The ship groaned around them as it broke away from the gravitational pull of Medea. Malachi rolled his shoulders. "I can work on getting us a job on Attica. I might have to pull some favors, but it's doable. That gives us an excuse to enter the prison. Now we need to figure out the rest."

Auri stared at him in disbelief. It took prestige in the Federation to receive transport jobs to Attica. Trust and a good record were necessities. She couldn't believe that an escaped convict had managed both. Maybe Tsuna had played a hand in creating a squeaky-clean identity for him and Marin—before she'd been arrested.

Malachi glanced at her. "We've delivered food stuffs to Attica before. I have a contact on Delfan that will be able to get me the job. Though the one I took on Medea will have to be swapped, which I don't like for my reputation..." He trailed off, gaze going far away, likely composing a ping to the shipment's owner.

Now the course to Delfan made sense. Auri studied Malachi anew. He always seemed to be one step ahead. She couldn't shake the feeling that she had marionette strings sewed into her back, and the ship's captain acted as puppeteer.

As the others concocted a plan to break into the prison and escape with Tsuna, Auri stayed silent, attentive but aware she had nothing to contribute. She scratched Birdie behind the ears and allowed herself to relax for the first time in days.

When the plan was finalized and prodded over and over to check for holes, it was nearly two hours later. Malachi stretched his arms overhead. "Any questions?"

Auri laid her massacred robotic arm on the table. "Maybe not directly relevant, but how are we going to fix this? The guards on Attica will want me identified. And I'll need my barcode for the Spire."

He nodded. "There's a tech doctor I know on Delfan."

"I want my access to the grid fixed too."

He sighed as if she'd just made things a hundred times more complicated. Katara let out a low whistle, but Auri didn't back down. She stared at him and waited.

He watched her, eyes seeming to take in every detail of her face, as if memorizing it. Or reading it.

"Okay," he said. "We'll get you back on the grid too. But, Auri," he lowered his voice, "no contacting anyone outside this crew."

"Sure," she lied. She understood Malachi's concern, but she needed to talk to her best friend. No doubt Ty had sent her millions of pings by now. He might even want to help after she told him what she discovered. Ty had never respected the GIC. And maybe, with her being gone for so long, he might have realized how much she meant to him. Maybe she'd get to be in a picture on his wall.

"If we're done," Castor said, standing. "I have cleaning to do and lunch to prepare. What's everyone say to some fresh crab sushi?"

Ferris's mouth popped open. Auri expected him to start drooling at any moment. It would make her own salivating more acceptable.

"Oh, good." Castor chuckled. "Glad no one was too interested because they didn't have any fresh crab on Medea."

"You're a *busu*," Ferris groaned as he stood. "Next time you need to be stitched up, don't come to me."

"Enjoy the travel day, everyone." Malachi stood as well, headed toward the large steel doors at the end of the dining area. "Auri, can you come with me?" He opened the doors and disappeared inside, leaving one ajar. Auri followed, Birdie trotting at her side.

The door was surprisingly heavy, and Auri had to use the entirety of her weight to close it. An engine room encompassed the other side. The space was enormous, taking up two floors. Malachi swung down from the metal catwalk onto the one beneath, a wrench in one hand.

In the center of the rectangular two-floor walkway, an engine rotated. It spun clockwise in a slow roll, the ship not moving at full speed. Wires and circuitry crisscrossed all over the seed-shaped piece of machinery. Auri stared at it in amazement. She'd never seen one laid bare like this. Typically, they were covered with a protective, temperature-cooling steel case.

Auri followed Malachi down but took a set of stairs instead. She caught up to him as he examined an enormous toolbox at the base of the spinning engine. The heat on this level was stifling, the rotations creating a warm breeze.

"What is it?" she asked. "Or did you ask me in here just to show me your engine?"

He turned to face her with a sly smile, tossing a screwdriver end over end. "Funny. I wanted to thank you for not asking about what put me and Marin in Attica."

She swallowed back her surprise. "Well, I guess you didn't ask me how I became a cyborg."

"True. The rest of the crew doesn't even know the full story, but I'm sure by now they understand the gist of it." He started to turn back to the toolbox but stopped. "One day, if I tell you mine, will you tell me yours?"

Auri stuck out her pinkie, a motion she'd seen giggling girls do in the back of classrooms. Malachi blinked then smiled. He entwined his pinkie with hers.

"It's a promise," she said. The curl of his finger around hers made her nose crinkle in pleasure. No wonder girls did this when they made promises. It felt like the world existed just for the two of them in that moment.

Malachi stared at her for a beat longer before he turned to Birdie. He held out a hand for the dog to sniff, but she growled low in her throat. "Ouch, dog." He tossed the screwdriver into the toolbox with a clang. "Dogs are supposed to be great judges of character. I wonder what that says about me."

"Malachi," Auri began. "You seem very perceptive. Like knowing I would help you after the Bleeders attacked us. You already decided to free Tsuna, didn't you? Why make Castor fight for it?"

"You noticed that?"

She just nodded. When you spent a lot of time observing people, you picked up on the things people said—and the things they didn't.

"I see." He regarded her for a beat. "The truth is…" He scooped up the toolkit, muscles bulging through the pushed-up sleeves of a white thermal shirt. "Castor has always had a complicated relationship with Tsuna. I won't go into details, but he needed to be the one to want to break her out. Not me." He jerked his head toward the spiral staircase and Auri followed him up. "Sometimes people don't know what they want," he continued, his back to her as they climbed, "until you tell them they can't have it."

"You hold a lot of strings," she murmured under her breath.

He stopped so suddenly, she bumped into his back, the material of his shirt damp with sweat. His eyes met hers, the wildness in them roaring to life. "I hold all the strings, Aurelia. All except one. And you're going to help me get it."

"The intel on the Bleeders," she whispered.

He bent over her, one arm on the railing. "Exactly."

She stared up at him. "Is the crew really your family, as you said? Or are they just a means to an end?"

He shifted toward her, the gloved hand on the railing coming up toward her face… Only to fall away. "Nothing is black and white in the world." He pulled back. "It's time you start looking at things with a little color."

He clomped up the rest of the steps, leaving Auri to stare after him. Her heart was a drum in her ears. She felt threatened and exhilarated at the same time.

The engine room door slammed with Malachi's departure. The noise brought Auri back to the present. She looked down at Birdie, whose ears had tilted back at the sound.

"That's that then." She sighed. "Let's see about finding someone to help me give you a bath."

CAPTAIN'S LOG
Hachigatsu 17, 3319 at 1300

[Chair squeaks]

[Speaks in hushed whisper] I almost got myself and Auri killed last night. When that Bleeder came into the office, I panicked. My mind went right back to Kaido and the way Kestrel...

[Fist slams against metal]

[Hiss of pain]

Chikushou. I need to get over it. The memories, everything. I need to focus on my mission.

[Dry chuckle]

Treating this log like a diary isn't going to help. Curse Katara and her ideas.

We're enroute to Delfan to get Auri's body repaired and pick up the food crates for the job on Attica. My contact came through, finally. We're switching jobs—I'm taking hers on Attica, she's taking mine on Babbage. The swap will cost me some much needed income and fresh produce, but it will be worth it, instant food and all. Can't say the crew will be happy.

I'm not sure what to think of Auri. That DISC agent is a contradiction. She sees so much yet so little. Sweet sincerity is in every smile, but she's steeped in dark secrets even she doesn't understand. I can't help but wonder what kind of dangerous creature I've invited on my ship.

[Sighs]

There is a concern that the *Kestrel* is being followed. The other ship is far off. More than fifty klicks, almost beyond our sensors. Marin only mentioned it because she said it made *Kestrel* feel uneasy. And she only says that about Bleeder ships.

Could it still be the Komodo Class from Medea? I know more about Bleeders than anyone, and stalking prey across space when easier meals are available? It doesn't make sense.

But things stopped making sense when I met Agent Aurelia Peri.

CHAPTER TWENTY-TWO

---

18 Aug 3319, 19:43:03
Ancora Galaxy, Planet 06: Delfan,
Revolution District

The comforting hum of electricity warmed Auri's synthetic skin. She felt her circuits reconnect as a diagnostic screen loaded in front of her closed lids.

She couldn't open her eyes—that didn't worry her.

Her heart was a rock in her chest—that didn't disturb her.

She'd endured each terrifying sensation every two years as doctors replaced some robotic part to keep up with her rapid growth. In the beginning, waking up trapped in a dead body frightened her.

Now it felt almost normal.

Instead of focusing on the shell caging her soul, she fixated on the systems activating, the diagnostic screen as the percentages increased.

Four minutes.

She had four minutes until she could open her eyes, until her heart began to beat, until her lungs expanded with air.

The diagnostic percentage climbed. Into the seventies, into the eighties, nineties.

That's when sound reached her. One minute left.

"Is she okay?" Malachi's accent was impossible to mistake.

"She will be in fifty seconds." This low tenor belonged to the man she'd met before she went under. A tech doctor on the planet Delfan. She hadn't wanted to trust him to fiddle inside her head, to fix the secret parts of her. And she still wouldn't trust him until she was awake and all systems were functional.

"She's so pale."

"Her heart isn't beating, but don't be concerned. Aurelia's gone through this many times. I'll send a bolt of power to kick-start her robotic parts. Then they'll be able to use her body's natural energy as fuel."

"She's brave."

"They all are." He paused then added pointedly, "As are you."

Malachi scoffed. "Don't get emotional on me, Doc."

A shot of pure electricity slammed into Auri's heart. She felt herself spasm, sensation returning to tingling limbs. Her heart gave one hard thud. Then another. Her lungs expanded, shallow at first. Then her chest rose in a deep breath.

She opened her eyes.

There was a moment of pure serenity without the trappings of human emotions. The doctor stood over her, shining a light in her eyes. He nodded at the reaction and moved to pick up a handheld tablet. It connected to Auri's skull via a thin wire. Malachi stood beside him, arms crossed, watching each movement the doctor made.

Her humanity rushed back with a slew of questions and feeling.

How long had Malachi been in the OR? Through the entire procedure? Did he watch as the doctor removed the flap of synthetic skin at the base of her skull? Did he grimace as the doctor inserted a surgery drone into her brain to repair damaged cells?

The thought made Auri sick, though she had nothing to throw up. She'd fasted twelve hours prior. Tears pricked at her eye. She knew the feelings barreling through her were an after-effect of the procedure, but she couldn't help feeling so...

So inhuman. So ugly.

She was a monster.

The doctor moved away and Malachi's face filled her vision. "Welcome back," he said. She felt his finger brush a tear from her organic cheek.

Kuso. Now he had seen her cry.

She opened her mouth to speak, but only a gargled sound came out. Too early for vocal chords.

"I didn't stay to watch," Malachi said as if he could read her thoughts. "But I wanted to be here when you woke up. Marin... Marin suggested it."

That brought fresh tears trickling out of Auri's eye. No one but doctors had ever been with her when she regained consciousness. She'd always battled the debilitating emotions alone and coped with the shame of her scraped-together body.

"Th-thank you," she said, her voice scratchy but closer to its usual pitch.

He looked up as the doctor came bustling back.

"Aurelia," the doctor said. "How are you feeling? A little emotional? Overwhelmed?"

She glanced at Malachi before nodding. "I kn-know that's normal th-though." So was the stutter, unfortunately.

"Of course. You probably know more than me about the procedure." He grinned at her, the wrinkles around his mouth a roadmap to years of other smiles.

The doctor was an older man, probably nearing his late sixties. His pale skin contrasted with dark black irises, but his eyes were kind. He turned her head to the side and eased the cord from the back of her skull.

"Give yourself a little time, and you'll be fully operational. You should automatically connect to Delfan's grid in a few seconds. Afterwards, I'll have you do some practice movements to make sure everything's reconnected properly."

For a backwater doctor, he was surprisingly professional. She'd had serious concerns upon entering the humble surgery room inhabited by a doctor wearing a patched surgical coat. The man even wore tiny spectacles, something Auri hadn't seen on her side of the system, where corrective eye surgery was commonplace.

But the doctor had followed every protocol that the Fed's official cyber-surgeons did. And, if Auri were honest, he had been much kinder throughout the process. The Fed surgeons never bothered to explain the procedures, just poked and prodded her while spouting techno-jargon to be recorded on their tablets.

Silence settled over the room, interrupted by the clank and clink of the doctor as he cleaned and stored his tools. Malachi slid a stool up to Auri's bed and perched atop it. His lips spread in a yawn that he covered with a gloved hand. Rather than the smudges under his eyes vanishing after sleeping, they had darkened. She wondered if he was the one she heard last night and the night before, whimpering in the lonely hours before dawn.

She felt her c-tacts latch onto Delfan's grid. Screens exploded in her vision: sites she'd been following, weather updates, the Fed's daily news bulletins that went out to every citizen, and pings. So. Many. Pings.

Auri grimaced as she struggled to filter through them. After mentally swiping away the other screens, she focused on her inbox. The GIC's name ranked first, followed by Captain Ishida. Between the two of them there were twenty-five messages: five from the captain and twenty from the GIC. Nothing from Ty.

Maybe they hadn't loaded yet.

She opened Ty's message folder, cold pricking the tips of her organic fingers and sending ice daggers into her heart. The last message was one that he had sent the day of her first DISC mission: *Mind grabbing me some takoyaki?*

Ty hadn't sent her a birthday message, a hello, or even panicked pings saying how worried he was. Her eagerness to connect to the grid and contact him withered and died.

She didn't bother opening the pings from the GIC or the captain. Their most recent messages were bolded in their folders.

From the GIC: *Attempted to contact you for days. Where are...*

From the captain: *You are to report for duty today. GIC...*

By opening the pings, both men would know she read their messages. She didn't need to read what they sent to know that when she got home, she'd be in trouble.

"Lots of pings from your friends to sort through?" Malachi asked beside her.

She swiped away her inbox until her vision was clear. "Yeah... Lots of pings." The words rang false to her own ears. No doubt Malachi saw straight through her lie.

The floor rumbled as if the surface of Delfan attempted to shake off a pesky bug. When they had arrived on the planet, Ferris had teased Auri that the planet might not like her and try to kick her off. She thought he'd been joking until Malachi explained that mining across the surface and deep into the core caused Delfan to have countless minor—and major—earthquakes. She didn't know how people could live here in a constant state of *will today be the day my home is destroyed?*

But just like with the inhospitable heat and dryness on Kaido, people had adapted to their planet's dangers. All the buildings were one story with flexible walls and support beams. Not to mention most of the furniture and equipment in the cyber-doctor's operating room had been bolted to the floor.

She looked down at her robotic arm. The synthetic skin was smooth, her barcode a dark black. She ran her fingers over the area, checking for any bubbles or rough spots. The synthetic was even and perfectly applied. It must've cost the cyber-doctor, and therefore Malachi, a lot of money. She made a fist, the sheer pleasure of being able to bend her fingers brightening her melancholy mood.

The doctor came around for final checks. He had her sit up, blink, bend her fingers. Once he cleared her, he gestured toward the door. "Some of our children are outside having a bonfire tonight. Your crew is out there. Both of you are welcome to join them after—"

"After I pay you," Malachi said, standing with a grunt. He bowed his head, eyes moving as he transferred the payment. "*Arigato*. Thanks for your help, Doc."

The doctor bowed in kind. "I appreciate the credits, Captain Malachi." He turned to Auri as she slid her feet into a pair of waiting slippers. "And thank you for trusting me. I know doctors on the rim don't have the best reputations."

She felt her organic cheek warm. "You've put an end to the rumors, at least as far as I'm concerned."

The doctor walked them out of the operating room into a waiting area. At the door, Auri swapped her borrowed slippers for her boots. Malachi did the same.

The two of them stepped outside. The scent of cooking meat made her stomach growl. Day had passed into night while she dozed in surgery. The sky overhead was a swath of blackness, the horizon lit with the haze of mining drills still at work. Low air quality accounted for the lack of stars and the rasping, dry sensation in the back of her throat.

At least twenty children clustered around an enormous bonfire a safe distance from the clinic. Some of them held sticks, roasting yams or chunks of meat. Others sat in groups, warming their hands against Delfan's nighttime chill.

All of them, even the youngest who toddled as if she hadn't been walking long, were cyborgs. Unlike Auri, none of their robotic parts were covered with synthetic skin. In fact, many wore rudimentary pieces.

Meters away, Birdie lay on her back, two little girls rubbing her belly. One of the girls was missing both arms, the robotic fingers only half articulate. The other girl's metallic leg gleamed in the firelight.

Auri stopped midstride, grabbing Malachi's arm. "Malachi, what did the doctor mean when he said that these were 'our children'?"

"They're orphans, taken in by the doc and his wife." The firelight deepened the shadows under his eyes. "We first met when I was still enlisted. He runs this orphanage for severely injured kids whose parents were killed in earthquakes or mining accidents. The Fed provides a small stipend, but it's not enough to give them fully functional limbs."

Auri rubbed her newly repaired robotic arm. What trick of fate allowed her to be given so much and these children so little? Why had the GIC picked her instead of one of them?

"Hello!" A boy no older than twelve ran up to them, two steaming yams clutched in each robotic hand. He bowed and held out the food. "Want to join us?"

Malachi took one. He tossed his yam into the air to cool it before catching it, wincing at the temperature. "*Arigato*, Thomas. Did you make these yourself?"

Thomas ducked his head but failed to hide the flicker of guilt. "I stole them from my sister. She doesn't mind though. She's busy playing with *Wan-chan*."

"The dog? Right." Malachi ruffled Thomas's blond hair. "How about we double check?" He gave his yam back to the boy who sighed.

As Auri approached, Birdie flipped onto all fours, abandoning the girls to bound up to her. The dog's tail churned up a small breeze. She plopped to her bottom in front of Auri, tongue lolling out the side of the dog's mouth. Birdie's white curls were covered in red dust, making her earlier bath pointless.

"Having fun?" Auri asked, bending down to run her fingers along Birdie's back. It felt marvelous to use both hands again. Birdie shifted to sniff at the new synthetic skin.

One of the little girls, Thomas's sister judging by the matching cropped blonde hair, hobbled over.

"Can we not play with her anymore?" she asked, her lower lip protruding in a pout. When the girl's gaze landed on Thomas, a frown split her face. "Hey! Those are mine."

"You left them by the fire!" Thomas tucked the yams into the armpits of his patch-worked shirt. "They almost burned."

"I was playing."

"Hey," Malachi said, interrupting the feud. "You can each have a yam—if you still want one after Thomas has stuck them in his armpits. Auri and I will make our own."

The girl crinkled her nose but finally held out a hand. "Give me one. I'll peel off the skin so it isn't gross."

Thomas hesitated but obeyed after a nudge from Malachi.

The two kids stood in sullen silence, neither one biting into their yam.

Across the way, the rest of the crew clustered around the fire. Katara and Ferris had a little girl with a robotic jaw positioned between them. Marin huddled by herself, her hands pressed against the dirt, gaze unfocused. Castor had volunteered to help Malachi's contact load the foodstuffs for Attica, claiming he hated kids. He'd taken the *Kestrel* off to another district on Delfan.

"Have you two heard of the hippopotamus word game?" Malachi's question brought Auri's attention back to the brother and sister.

They shook their heads.

Malachi glanced over his shoulder. "Don't say this around your guardians, but…" He leaned forward. "Say *kaba* five times fast."

Thomas and his sister launched into the challenge. On the fourth *kaba*, Auri realized the word game and smiled. So did the kids. Thomas grinned in impish glee while his sister's mouth opened in a small o.

"When you say it fast *kaba* sounds like… That's a bad word," she scolded, though her eyes twinkled in a way that promised she would pass the game on to her friends. "C'mon, Thomas. Let's go warm these up again."

The two hurried off, whispering *kaba* to each other as fast as they could.

Malachi and Auri followed at a slower pace, Birdie bringing up the rear.

"How did you know about the *kaba* game?" Auri asked.

He tilted his head as he looked at her, hands shoved into his jacket pockets. "You've never heard of it? Every kid knows that game. Even the ones before the Curve. It's a timeless way to say *baka* without getting in trouble."

"Not every kid," she muttered. When he didn't reply, she glanced up. The firelight reflecting in his strange eyes made her step back. In the softness around his mouth, the crinkle of his eyes… Pity lurked there.

Malachi pitied her.

She turned. "I'm going to get a yam to roast." Before he could reply, she hurried away.

The food table was sunken in the middle and the remaining vegetables had rolled into the center. She grabbed a wooden poker and two yams.

Auri chose a spot unoccupied by the children but away from the smoke. She hunkered down, Birdie beside her. The heat felt delicious against her organic skin. She relished the sensation, closing her eyes and breathing deep. Malachi hadn't meant to hurt her. But the emotions from her surgery still pressed tight against her skin. She felt like bursting into tears, like she didn't deserve even a shred of kindness.

"It's sad."

Auri opened her eyes to see Marin standing next to her. She sat down, her feet a little too close to the fire, toes curled tight

"What's sad?" Auri asked, rotating the yams.

"Watching people want something they can't have."

At first Auri's gaze went to Malachi. He stood on the other side of the fire, smiling at the playing children. Then she shifted to Katara and Ferris a few meters off. The expression on the assassin's face was impossible to read, but Ferris's was lined with a sadness when he looked at her. He forced a smile and nudged Katara with his shoulder, saying something as if to cheer her up. Katara nodded and spoke to the cyborg girl, pointing up to the sky.

Ferris's emotions told her all she needed to know about Katara's feelings.

"Katara wants a baby?" Auri asked.

"The Dispatchers don't allow babies."

She faced Marin, almost losing a yam to the roaring fire. "What do you mean? She's not a Dispatcher anymore."

The girl looked at Auri. "She doesn't have a uterus. The women don't learn it's removed until later."

The blunt way Marin spoke made Auri grimace. She looked at Katara anew. While she couldn't imagine the assassin actually having a baby, her right to have one shouldn't have been taken away. "The Fed wouldn't do that."

"Don't be so naïve, *Onee-chan*."

It was almost comical, the words coming from someone so young. "Why do you call me that?" Auri asked. "Are you a cyborg?"

Marin pushed to her feet. She held a stick in one hand. "You'll learn soon. Akki-tan?" she called as she stood. "Where are you?" She slipped away, using her stick to guide her to Malachi's side.

The smell of burning potato yanked Auri's attention back to her yams. The skin had curled and blackened. She tugged her poker out with a frustrated cry. Upon examination, the insides were still soft and bright orange. She broke one in half and blew to cool it.

Birdie stared up at her with sad eyes, scratching at her leg with a paw.

Auri sighed. "You've already had plenty of food, I'm sure." Still, she allowed a chunk of her yam to chill before plopping it in front of the dog. "You're so spoiled."

She rested her arms on her knees and tilted her face up toward the sky. With her eyes closed, the fire's blaze felt like warm sunlight on her skin. If she used her imagination, she could pretend she was back on her balcony, surrounded by her green plants instead of a planet made of dirt and stitched together by machinery.

Normally, she could tuck painful memories away. Snare them in cages at the back of her mind. But the surgery shattered the locks. All her worries and fears and hopes and dreams swarmed together in an endless tornado.

What would it have been like if she grew up here instead of Rokuton? A place where no one cornered her in secluded hallways. A place to laugh with friends instead of cry alone over cruel boys who beat her robotic parts because their blows never left bruises.

She had never said anything about the bullies. She didn't even tell Ty. Auri felt like she deserved their anger after the Cyborg Bomber. The criminal walked into a military base, weapons hidden within steel cavities, and murdered countless soldiers. That day, the bullies had lost a parent or sibling. Their ringleader, Indie, lost his entire family.

Somehow, the GIC learned of the attacks. The boys were expelled, drafted into the Marines, and sent to work on Attica after basic, one of the worst job assignments in the MPB.

The very prison the *Kestrel* and her crew would visit in a few days. But there were hundreds of guards stationed on the Heat. The chance she ran into her childhood tormentors was so low, she shouldn't let the possibility bother her. Auri needed to stop worrying. She would need to be strong regardless of who she encountered. She would need to be ready. But tonight?

A single tear escaped her eye and pattered onto the dirt. She lowered her head and let more fall.

CHΛPTER
TWENTY-THREE

The muggy heat of Rokuton sent sweat rolling down Auri's back. She tugged at the jacket covering her tank top. Around her, members of the crew peered into the jungle. They looked hot but comfortable in the clothes they'd picked. None of them wore jackets.

She swallowed hard and considered removing hers. Her hand even reached for the collar to yank it off, but she stopped when her fingertips brushed the mottled scars. Her hand fell back to her side.

She'd thought that at least this planet would be familiar, unlike Kaido and those on the rim. After all, she spent an entire year of her life navigating the lush rainforest of the Fed's main military base in basic.

But when she clattered down the exit ramp on the *Kestrel*, the surrounding rainforest was anything but familiar. This section burst with plant life and, judging by the chatter above, animal life as well. Trees and shoots of green stretched in every direction, blocking the cloudy blue sky. The Rokuton she knew was overgrown in places, but always maintained.

Leaving Birdie aboard had been a good call. The dog was obedient, though after the three days they spent at the orphanage on Delfan and then the subsequent four days flying to Rokuton, Birdie had picked up some not-so-desirable behaviors for a DISC dog. Like begging for food and groaning when Auri gave a command the dog didn't feel like doing. She still did it. But with a definite attitude. Auri was partly to blame. She had allowed Birdie to wander around without her working harness on—the longest the dog had been without it in her entire life. The two of them needed to get back to their usual roles.

The dense jungles of Rokuton, however, was not the place to do it.

"Now I remember why I never visited after I was discharged," Castor said as he stomped past her. Sweat slicked his skin and dripped down his neck. He wiped at it with a silk kerchief before tucking it into a pocket of his pants. The cook usually wore billowing button-down shirts, the sleeves rolled up, but today had opted for a tight tank top. Auri was shocked to see muscles rippling under his skin.

The rest of the crew was behind him, each in their "warm weather" gear. Even Malachi was wearing a tank top instead of his usual thermal shirts. The tattoos she'd seen on his forearm coiled up his bicep and bled onto his chest.

"I don't mind the heat," Ferris said. "Better than shambling through snow. There's a reason why no one lives on Roanleigh. Well, other than the nuclear atmosphere." He peered behind them. "Where's our lovely tour guide? Ah, Marin! You ready?"

Marin stood just inside the open cargo doors. She wore a pure white *yukata*, her feet still bare. Her left hand twitched at her side, the fingers moving in a jerky snap that looked more robotic than human. "I am," she said, grabbing the appendage with her other hand to try to still it.

Malachi's mouth thinned in a concerned frown, but he didn't speak. Curiosity prickled at Auri's toes. For days she wondered what Marin's hideout was and why it caused such nervousness in Malachi.

"Let's get moving then," Katara said with a roll of her shoulders. "We don't have long until sunset."

Marin led them a short distance away from the ship and paused in the middle of a break in the vegetation. "Wait," she said. The grip on her twitching hand tightened. She took a slow breath. "We're here."

Monkeys gossiped in the trees above and insects darted to-and-fro, their wings droning. Auri waved away a group of hungry mosquitos.

Katara smacked her shoulder, grimacing at the smooshed blood-sucker in her palm. None of the bugs seemed to bother Ferris. He reached out to slap Malachi's forehead, but the captain danced out of the way with a scowl.

Thought I saw a bug, Ferris mouthed with a grin.

Malachi raised his fist in a rude gesture. Katara rolled her eyes.

"How old are you supposed to be? Five?" Castor muttered. "I need to find a new crew."

The playful bickering seemed to ease the tension in the air. Marin's twitching hand stilled. She let out a slow breath and knelt, damp earth and moss staining the hem of her *yukata*. She shoved her hand deep into the soil. At first, nothing happened, but then she twisted something and pulled on a hidden handle. The ground trembled under their feet as a hatch emerged. Clumps of earth tumbled off it as the doors slid apart, the opening spanning the length of a grown man. A flight of steps led down into thick darkness.

"Marin." Ferris was the first to speak. He craned to look down the steps, as if a better angle would reveal what lay below. "What is this place?"

"It's where I grew up," she said. "We can open the hangar from the inside. This way."

A short hallway extended from the bottom of the stairs. Sconces along the walls flickered on in a staggered wave. Everything in the space was styled in shades of gray: the walls, the tiled floor, the ceiling. Their footsteps echoed around them, intensifying the heavy silence. Auri had the uncomfortable sensation that she'd been shoved inside a metal coffin, the air inside cool yet stale as if the space hadn't been used in a very, very long time. Castor's body had gone rigid and he kept looking behind him at the opening to the world above. Auri didn't blame him for wanting to turn back. She swallowed hard.

The corridor ended in a single metal door. Marin yanked it open to reveal a larger room beyond. An enormous, rough-hewn crystal speared the center of the floor. It came to life as they entered, light emanating from its core to illuminate the entire space.

Rows upon rows of medical beds stretched across the room. Restraint straps hung from the pristine mattresses, dangling against the floor as if their occupants had recently fled. Shelves across from the beds housed sharp medical equipment, some shoved in drawers, and others laid out, while everything was covered with dust.

Along the right wall, four sliding doors were sealed shut. Katara's examination showed them to be bedrooms and a filled food pantry, most of the foodstuffs long expired. The last one led to an empty hangar.

The hairs on the back of Auri's neck rose as she looked around. A shadow haunted this place, as if great atrocities had been committed.

"Please explore," Marin said, shattering the oppressive silence. She'd wandered away from everyone else. Her back pressed against a single door on the opposite side of the space. A door Katara had yet to open. "Ferris, take what supplies you need. They serve no purpose here."

"Do you want someone to go back to the *Kestrel* and scout for passing aircraft?" Castor whispered to Malachi.

"Scared, Castor?" Ferris teased without looking at him. Even the happy-go-lucky doctor's face had paled.

"We're in a creepy bunker with a bunch of operating equipment." He glared at Ferris. "I think the answer is obvious."

Ferris opened his mouth to snap back a retort.

"Ferris," Malachi said, shaking his head toward Marin's somber face. "Leave it."

He cleared his throat. "Let's see if I can find anything useful, ay?" He strode across the room to open a large cabinet, revealing thousands of small chambers stacked atop each other in rows, all about the size of an infant's cradle. Wires dangled inside each of the glass tubes, twisted like a knot of petrified snakes.

The sight made goosebumps skitter down Auri's arms. Her imagination filled the chambers with liquid, small bodies suspended from the wires, twitching, screaming, sharp nails scraping against the glass—

Katara came up to lay a hand on Ferris's shoulder, both of which had hunched around his ears. "Everything okay?" she asked.

Ferris pressed a hand against the glass. His usual humor was gone. "You know what these are for, don't you?" He shook his head. "*Kuso*. We shouldn't be down here."

Her grip on his shoulder tightened. "Let's see if there are any supplies you could use for the infirmary."

"I don't want…" He tensed and seemed like he would shake Katara off. After a slow breath he nodded. "Yeah. Okay." He let her guide him over to the medical supplies.

Auri forced herself to turn away from the tubes. Malachi still stared at them, a muscle spasming in his jaw.

"What is this?" Auri whispered to him. "Did you know about this?"

"This place exposes the dark underbelly of science." He still didn't look at her. "I wish Marin hadn't brought us here."

"She said this is where she grew up."

"She did." He ran a hand over his bloodshot eyes. "I'll be in the hangar getting it ready for the *Kestrel*. Feel free to join me. Castor," he called. "Come with me." He strode away, hands shoved into his pockets.

Auri moved to follow, beyond eager to leave the creepy room. She glanced around to realize Marin had vanished. The door on the opposite wall, once closed, was now cracked open.

She stepped over to the door and peered through the tiny opening. Marin stood in the center of a large space, her left hand twitching worse than it had before. Except now she didn't try to control it. Auri glanced over her shoulder at the other crew members before she took a breath and slipped inside.

One look at the interior and she gasped and stumbled back, the door closing with a click. Her hand covered her mouth in mute horror, eyes wide. The shattered remains of a floor-to-ceiling cryo tube glistened under the fluorescent lighting. The walls and floor were splattered a rusty red. The color was like old paint, chipped and peeling in some places.

Except the crimson splotches weren't paint.

A hazy image overlaid the room. A memory. A nightmare. *Unforgiving hands shoved Auri into a child-sized opening. Her fingers grasped for those rough hands, tears running down her cheek. There was so much pain, but fear overwhelmed her. "Don't!" she begged.*

The hands tugged free.

A lid slammed closed.

Air fled from the space and icy liquid surged in. She started to scream.

Auri shook her head, blinking the image away. She swallowed to ease the tightness in her throat. These hallucinations were getting worse and worse, but she couldn't dwell on them.

They terrified her. So, like everything else that hurt or didn't make sense, she tucked them away. She chose to forget.

Marin stood across the room, her fingers splayed against a wall. Auri inched closer only for her legs to lock up, refusing to carry her the rest of the distance. The wall Marin touched was lined with manacles, the bindings popped open and bent at odd angles.

The desire to run barreled through Auri. Panic was a fist around her heart. Squeezing, squeezing, squeezing...

She tensed against the urge and took a slow breath. In through her nose, out through her mouth.

Marin started to hum, swaying side to side. Auri recognized the rainy-day song, *Amefuri*, from her childhood. She mentally translated the words in English as Marin sang them in Japanese. The girl's voice broke around every other word, like the sharp edges of the shattered cryo chamber behind them.

Raining, raining
How it's raining
Rain a little more.
Mother's bringing my umbrella
It can rain and pour.
Pitter, patter, pitter, patter
Drip, drop, drop.

The way Marin sang the song gave it a ghostly quality. As if the lyrics' sweet innocence had been warped into something darker, perverted. Auri felt the song twist around her, choking the air from her lungs.

"Marin?" she hedged, stepping forward. "Are you okay?"

Marin turned to look at Auri. Her hand drifted from the wall to clutch at her twitching fingers. The girl's expression was pained, a look Auri recognized. The hunger to cry but the inability to find release.

Marin caught Auri's hand and pressed it against the girl's cool cheek. The out-of-character movement startled Auri so much, she nearly gasped. The blind girl normally shied away from physical touch. Auri had picked up on it in just the few days she'd been on the *Kestrel*. The crew was careful to give Marin space.

"The song," Marin whispered, her breath tickling Auri's skin. "When Mother—" She cut herself off with an almost snarl. "When *they* did their experiments, I would sing it. I would imagine the raindrops, the taste of the water."

Marin's words chilled Auri's blood. "What did they do to you?"

"I killed her. I killed both of them." She released Auri's hand and stepped past her to stand in the center of the room. "My parents, you might call them, were scientists. The GIC gave them a top-secret project. To create a robotic army."

"But droids—"

Marin glanced back at Auri. "A flaw in the code. I know." She rubbed at her head, the bristles of her hair catching on her pale fingers. "But they found a way around that. Human minds—the minds of children—in mechanical bodies. Children's minds can be manipulated, conditioned, in a way the faulty code couldn't in machines."

Bile rose in Auri's throat. Had the GIC really commissioned such a project? She shook her head. No, it didn't make sense. "But human experimentation is illegal. How could—why would the GIC do something like that?"

The twitching in Marin's hand stilled momentarily. "You're not considered human if you're grown in a test tube," she whispered.

Realization made Auri shiver. It was true. Test-tube conception of already living DNA was not considered true life. They were only clones, used by many for organ donation and medical testing. Auri had never given it much thought… Until now.

"Who is your clone?" she asked. "Whose DNA did they use?"

"Her name was Miko," Marin murmured, looking back at the broken cryo tube. "Their daughter. She committed suicide by overdosing on *zolpidem tartrate*, a medication. I always wondered if they used her DNA because they missed her or wanted to punish her for fleeing life.

"Her DNA—my DNA—was used over and over again. But each time, the brain was transplanted, a new flaw emerged. Paralysis, deafness… blindness. Nothing they did could fix the flaws."

Auri thought of Ferris's hand pressed against the glass tubes in the other room. "How many of you were there?"

"Over a hundred."

Auri stared at the dried blood peeling from the walls with fresh dread. "Marin, what… what happened to them? The others?"

"They weren't producing results. So the GIC cancelled the project, wanted them to move on to something new. I was the last one they kept alive. But when they came in to shut me down, I snapped." Marin's hand began to twitch anew, the movement making her entire body tremble. "I broke the protocol written into the mind-link used to connect my human brain to machine. My kill switch had been deactivated for safety concerns while they experimented. And I didn't plan to kill. I just wanted to stop them when they tried to deactivate me, but instead… Instead, I murdered my creators."

Auri could speculate how Marin had managed to kill her so-called "parents." But the blood still staining the walls, the atmosphere of unease… Unspeakable violence had happened here. Underneath the human-looking skin was mechanical strength and speed, as impossible as it seemed. No human would stand a chance against such an adversary.

"The GIC and his soldiers arrived... after," Marin continued. "I was delirious, my brain bleeding from the break in protocol. They didn't know how to shut me down without my creators or without completely destroying me, and the GIC was intrigued by my presence. So they took me to Attica until they could find an expert. That is how I ended up with this twitching limb." She gestured to her hand before she looked up at Auri. "My mind is human, *Onee-chan*, but my body is entirely machine. My brain grows and matures, but I'm trapped in this child-like body. I am almost twenty-one, but you wouldn't know it. You are half of what I am, and in a strange way, I find comfort in the fact that you too are trapped with machine parts."

Auri opened her mouth, unsure what to say. Her fingers wandered to the scars hidden under her jacket. "Machine or human, it's not what you are, but who you are." She caught Marin's twitching hand and squeezed. The motion stilled as Marin shifted to look at her.

"We don't just share the same mechanical parts," Auri said. "We both hurt, we both feel, we both love. You are as human as Malachi or Ferris."

"I am?"

"Yes." She smirked. "Though I doubt anyone could match Ferris's charm."

A smile twitched on Marin's lips. "There is truth in that."

"You know," Auri added, trying to give Marin some hope other than soothing platitudes, "if you feel trapped in your current body, we could find a doctor... Find someone who could help you. Bring you up to the right age physically."

"Akki-tan has been looking," Marin admitted. "He just has to be careful that my background isn't discovered. Sometimes my emotions overwhelm me. Being back home is harder than I thought, but *Kestrel* needed a safe place to hide." She lowered her head, gaze drifting to the side, eyes unfocused, forever shrouded in darkness. "Thank you... Auri. For accepting me and reminding me who I am is more than what I am."

After hearing Marin call Auri *Onee-chan* all week, being called by her name felt wrong. Auri took one step forward. Then another. She slid her arms around Marin, tentative, as if the girl would bolt at any second.

When Marin didn't try to shove away, Auri squeezed her tight. "That's not what I want you to call me, *Imouto-chan.*" *Little sister.*

Marin let out a small sob, though no tears fell from her mechanical eyes. The girl's arms stayed at her sides, but she buried her face in Auri's chest. "*Onee-chan,*" she rasped. "*Onee-chan.*"

Holding Marin, comforting her, was like stepping back in time. Auri imagined she held her younger self, a little girl who just wanted to be loved. To be *human.*

Auri looked up to see Malachi leaning against the now open doorframe. His eyes glistened in the fluorescent lighting. *Thank you*, he mouthed.

She nodded. He stayed until Marin's heaving breaths calmed, ready to step in if the girl needed him. It was then that Auri realized Marin might called her *Onee-chan*, but she had found a brother in Malachi too. A family in the whole *Kestrel* crew.

Auri couldn't stop herself from hoping that one day she might find the same.

CHAPTER
TWENTY-FOUR

---

26 Aug 3319, 05:00:02
Ancora Galaxy, Planet 01: Attica,
Docking Lot A2

"Any last questions?" Malachi studied the crew gathered around him in the cargo hold, Auri included. As the final docking maneuvers were being done outside, the techs on Attica scanned the *Kestrel* before they allowed her crew to enter the prison.

Katara snorted. "If we don't know what we're doing after two days perfecting this plan, we're in trouble."

Malachi inclined his head. "True."

Birdie sat beside Auri, staring at the crew with innocent eyes, tongue lolling as if they were all preparing to go on a grand adventure.

Adventure? Yes.

Grand? This was as far from *grand* as it could possibly be.

Auri rubbed Birdie's soft ear between her fingertips. Everyone would enter Attica in a few minutes. Well, everyone except Birdie and Ferris. The doctor had made his disapproval clear in more colorful language than Auri heard from the Marines. Surprising for an AC doctor. But Malachi's decision made sense—even to Ferris, though he'd never admit it.

Malachi wanted Ferris to stay behind because the doctor was the only one with a genuine, unaltered record. "It will be useful at some point," he said. Though Auri wondered if he was also secretly being protective, afraid Ferris might one day find himself locked between the iron walls of Attica.

The rest of the crew wore clothes suitable for Fed contractors: black pants and white shirts underneath tailored jackets, while Marin wore another *yukata*. This time with shoes. Katara had fashioned cloth slippers for Marin with small holes cut into the soles so her skin still touched the floor. Auri had even changed back into her DISC uniform after it underwent laborious washings by Castor and Katara. The assassin's ability to get days-old bloodstains out of clothes had been downright awe-inspiring. Also disturbing.

Earlier that morning, Auri had felt strange pulling on the green pants, buttoning up the vest, tying the white bow. Her uniform embodied everything and everyone she'd betrayed. The material brushed against her even now, a constant reminder of what she was about to do.

In the center of the gathered crew waited two large rolling bins. They brimmed with the contents of the food crates Castor had picked up. Malachi and Marin spent the last travel days altering them so the interior would be unscannable. Older metals tended to cause false readings with the detectors, so it wouldn't be too suspicious. Guards might check the contents, but by inserting a false bottom…

Malachi promised the bins were the perfect place to conceal a prisoner.

Auri worried the plan was too simple. A prisoner sneaking out in a bin? It sounded like a lame magic trick.

The cargo doors whirred as a long tube suctioned itself to the grooves outside. A loud buzz inside the *Kestrel* signified the air chamber had locked on. The prison was ready for them to disembark.

"Ferris, get up to the bridge," Malachi said. He tugged his military-style hat down to shade his eyes. "If this mission turns into a soup sandwich, I want you ready to take off. Got it?"

Auri's brows rose at the term for when things went to *kuso*. It was common among the Marines, those who saw the most action of any of the military divisions. Only people who failed their high school entrance exams were booted into that branch. Malachi seemed too smart for that. Then again, how well did she know him?

Ferris ignored Malachi's command and strode over to Katara. He handed her a single light pink peony, genetically altered to be the size of Auri's palm. "I'd tell you to take care of her," he said over his shoulder to Malachi, "but I know Katara better than that." Ferris ran a hand over the assassin's cheek. "Be safe."

Katara stared up at him and, to Auri's surprise, crimson bloomed across her nose. As if suddenly aware of her audience, she knocked him away with a shoulder. "I'll be fine," she snapped. "Go to the bridge already. You're slowing us down. Where do you even get all these flowers," she grumbled, slipping the peony into a pocket.

Ferris smiled as if he'd won some great victory. "See you all when you get back." He gave Malachi a curt nod before he clambered up the metal staircase.

"Go," Auri instructed Birdie, pointing toward Ferris. The dog hunched forward, one paw raised, a whine building in her throat. "*Go*," Auri said, voice firm.

Ferris paused at the entrance to the bridge. "Birdie, want a treat?" He fished into his pocket to pull out a bag of dried jerky. He shook it with a whistle. "Come 'ere!"

Birdie raced up the steps. Auri rolled her eyes. What did loyalty matter stacked against the possibility of food?

Once Ferris and Birdie sealed themselves inside the bridge, Malachi pressed the screen beside the cargo doors. A red light flashed on either side as the massive metal doors creaked open.

"It means luck," Auri said to Katara as they waited.

She turned. "What?"

"The peony." She nodded at the pocket in Katara's pants. "The light pink ones mean luck." *Also romance*, Auri didn't feel brave enough to add.

Katara laid a hand over the fabric, gaze softening. "Oh."

Manufactured oxygen rushed into the ship, blowing Auri's braid over her shoulder. In an instant, the pressure between the *Kestrel* and Attica leveled.

Two guards waited for them inside the covered gangway. After confirming she didn't recognize them, Auri could take in other details. Their gray uniforms made them chameleons against the storm-cloud color of the walls. They were junior guards, judging by the single bars on each sleeve. Each man cradled a blaster gun, a coilgun and taser tucked into their belts. They wore matching expressions of disinterest and boredom, a common look for any Attica soldier.

The guards escorted the crew out of the ship and along the narrow hallway. Marin kept close to Auri, her black and white floral *yukata* a contrast to the green of Auri's uniform. Castor pushed one bin, Katara escorting him. Malachi handled the lighter one—the bin containing the false bottom.

Auri felt naked without Birdie beside her. She didn't even have the protection or comfort of her disc. She'd left it on the *Kestrel* since the guards would confiscate the weapon anyway. Her organic palm dampened with sweat as the entry into Attica drew closer and closer.

The guards stopped at the door. One of them slid it open while the other stood watching the crew with glazed eyes. Auri wondered how often something exciting happened here.

More air rushed into the tube when the door opened. The crew members wheeling the bins entered first, Auri and Marin last in line with the second guard bringing up the rear.

The guards stopped them at a security station. Two pairs of thin panels emerged from the floor, high-tech scanners like the ones inside the Tech Towers on Agar Moon. Auri tensed at the sight of them.

Near the scanners, soldiers loitered behind a circular glass booth. Beyond the checkpoint curved the circular heart of the X-shaped prison. She knew from her tour in basic that the first floor, their current location, consisted of the guards' living quarters and a security check-in for all transporters, with a separate check-in for visitors. Below their feet, bisecting the X-shape of the upper floors, ran the maximum-security holding. Otherwise known as death row.

The two guards retreated to stand at the only exit. Three senior guards, two bars sewn at each shoulder, stepped out of the glass office. A fourth man followed behind, this one a lieutenant.

"We received your transport papers," the lieutenant said as he approached, his voice familiar. "We'll go through the security process and you can make your deliveries." He stopped in front of them, back straight, hands clasped behind him.

Auri's eyes widened as she recognized the GIC's old secretary. He looked the same as he had when she was younger: tilted eyes, flat nose, and reserved smile. Except he wasn't smiling when he saw Auri, barcode scanner in hand. His nametag, last name, first, perched on his left shoulder, opposite the medals on his right. *Aki Jun.*

"Agent Peri?" His forehead wrinkled as he studied her and then her companions. "Why are you arriving on a transport?"

She licked her lips as the senior guards stepped around her to scan the barcodes of the crew. When Malachi shoved up his jacket sleeve, she expected to see the cuff, but instead his barcode glistened with tattooed circuitry.

Her c-tacts registered the lines automatically and his information popped up on her display.

Malachi Vermillion
Occupation: Retired Private 1st Class
Federal Transporter

She wondered how much of that information was real and how much had been forged by Tsuna.

A deep *ahem* made her turn back to Lieutenant Aki. The well-rehearsed reply rolled off her tongue. "I had a shuttle malfunction when I was visiting a planet for Obon. Luckily, I ran into Captain Vermillion and his crew. They gave me a ride. I planned to head back to Rokuton, but…" She shrugged, trying to play the entire situation off as a cocky agent taking liberties. "When I learned they were delivering supplies to Attica, I thought I'd see if I could get a tour. As an official DISC agent, I wanted to get reacquainted with where my suspects would end up."

Lieutenant Aki frowned. "I see."

The guards' barcode readers beeped as they finished scanning the crew. Auri didn't dare meet their gazes, especially Malachi's. She needed to be a soldier, force herself to slip back into an old mindset. And she needed Lieutenant Aki to let her take the elevators down to death row.

She tilted her head but the lieutenant didn't offer another comment. "Sir? Will that be okay?" She added just enough submissive pleading into her tone.

Lieutenant Aki tugged on the hem of his jacket, a nervous gesture she remembered from his secretary days. He called over his shoulder into the guard office where the final sergeant lounged, watching the exchange with interest.

"Call down to the dugout and ask a CO to await Agent Peri in the supermax," Lieutenant Aki said. "She'll tour while the transporters deliver their supplies on the upper floors."

CO meant correctional officer. Auri curled her toes in her boots at the small success. She still needed to ask one more favor. And she had a cold-sweat kind of certainty that Lieutenant Aki wouldn't like it.

"Sir," she continued, back tingling with the intensity of the crew's combined gazes. If Auri didn't succeed now, she would run into problems later. "Would you permit an extra body to accompany me?"

Every guard froze as if she'd whipped a gun from her belt and ordered each prisoner's freedom.

Lieutenant Aki's gaze flicked over the crew. "Who would that be?"

She swallowed, shifting so he could see Marin. "She's blind and we preferred not to leave her on the ship. Captain Vermillion didn't want her interrupting the supply delivery. I thought it was the least I could do considering the help they provided."

When the lieutenant spoke, it was with a cautionary tone. Whether he meant the caution for Auri or his soldiers, she didn't know. "The girl's scan came up clean?" he asked the guards.

"Yes, sir," one answered.

"If she passes through the weapon detector without incident," he said to Auri, "then she may accompany you."

When they had discussed this part of the plan, Auri was worried Marin's robotic skeleton would set off the alarms. But the girl assured Auri they wouldn't. She wasn't made of reinforced steel like Auri. Her more advanced pieces wouldn't show up as an anomaly on a scan.

If only Auri could get some limbs like Marin's.

Lieutenant Aki stepped closer to Auri, lowering his voice to a whisper only she could hear. "We've known each other for a few years, Agent Peri. You seem determined to visit death row, so I won't dissuade you. However, I would warn you that there may be more than just memories down there for you. Don't get into any trouble the GIC can't get you out of."

A wave of cold crashed into her at the warning. One or more of her middle-school tormentors guarded maximum security holdings. The lieutenant had been the GIC's secretary during her year of being bullied. No doubt he even played a part in the transfer of the boys.

She made her spine rigid, her expression light. "It's hard to get into trouble when you're the GIC's adopted daughter." She forced a laugh then murmured, "Thank you."

The lieutenant inclined his head toward her. He turned his attention to the guards. "Get them through the scanners."

One of the guards stepped up to Lieutenant Aki, saluting the superior officer. "Sir, are you sure letting an extra body go down to maximum security is necessary?"

Lieutenant Aki glanced at Marin. "She's a blind little girl, Sergeant Matthews, and she's accompanied by the GIC's adopted daughter." With that, he offered Auri an officer's smile—lips sucking between his teeth, mouth tugging into a frown—and stepped back into the glass office.

Guilt twisted Auri's insides as she watched him go. She prayed Lieutenant Aki wouldn't be blamed for what was to happen.

The guards hurried the crew through the weapon detectors. The two pillars glowed a cheerful green as each person passed through. True to her word, even Marin didn't set the machines off. Auri, on the other hand...

She stepped through and the panels lit up red, beeping their displeasure. The sergeant responsible for her clucked his tongue.

"Step aside, Agent."

She rolled her shoulders back to hide the anxiety seeping from her bones. "I don't have any weapons."

On the other side of the panels, the rest of the crew watched. Katara's hand twitched as if she longed to hurl a dagger into the man's chest. Auri had mentioned this would happen, had always happened. She had also reassured them that it was a temporary holdup.

Malachi's arms were crossed, but he said nothing. He knew as much as she did that causing trouble would disrupt their plan.

"Step back, please." The guard extended a hand to block her path.

Auri obeyed. She glanced at the glass office where Lieutenant Aki peered out, alerted by the scanner. His eyes met hers for a flicker of a moment. Then he turned his back. Her earlier guilt fizzled, replaced by cold determination.

"I'm a cyborg," she whispered to the guard. "You know that. Just scan my barcode again. My profile—"

"Cyborgs have been known to hide weapons under their synthetic skin." The guard's tone was placating but firm. "As I'm sure you remember from the Cyborg Bomber. Behind the tinted glass, please."

Auri met Malachi's gaze one last time. He took a step forward before being blocked by one of the two sergeants.

"This is foolish," Katara growled. "You're going to search her? She's been under the Fed's thumb her whole life."

"It's protocol," one of the other soldiers answered.

Prodding from the sergeant made Auri turn away. It wasn't a big deal, she told herself. As long as the guard didn't get too handsy, she would be fine.

"I'll be right back," she said, infusing her voice with as much confidence as she could. She even smiled.

Then she obeyed.

CHΛPTER
TWENTY-FIVE

The crew entered an elevator bound for the upper floors. Meanwhile, Auri and Marin, escorted by a sergeant, took another elevator down. Auri smoothed the front of her uniform, counting the buttons that ran down her jacket, checking she'd secured them properly.

The elevator clanged to a stop and the glass doors slid open. Auri tensed, prepared to see one of her bullies waiting outside. Instead, a female CO stood before them, hands clasped behind her back. She nodded at the sergeant as Auri and Marin stepped off the elevator. The doors closed and the soldier disappeared.

The maximum-security portion stretched out in the shape of a long rectangle with a circular guard station in the middle. From her tour a year ago, Auri knew that the glass comprising the guard station was shatter-resistant. In case of prisoner escapes, steel doors would slam shut on either side of the rectangle, sealing the convicts inside. One far end comprised a bare-necessities hospital. The other held a tiny rec room with a light meant to mimic the sun. Prisoners on this level got an hour of rec time a day, usually one at a time, depending on occupancy levels. Maximum security really meant solitary confinement.

Until the prisoner's execution.

Maybe that was why despair seemed to ripple along the walls. The stone and steel corridors murmured to each inhabitant, *You will never leave this place.* She shivered.

"You're to receive a tour?" the CO asked, her short hair clipped away from her face.

Auri nodded.

"Come this way, and we'll get you signed in." She waved them over to the circular office where two other COs lazed in chairs.

Auri followed, Marin taking her arm to keep up the charade. The girl could see everything in the prison, courtesy of the massive amounts of tech and wires winding through the place.

"Are you okay?" Auri asked the girl. To anyone else it might seem she worried over Marin's footing. In truth, she worried about Marin being back here. Even Malachi's face had been paler than usual when the elevator carried him away.

Marin nodded as they stopped just outside the office door. "I don't have bad memories of this place." She spoke of the prison as if visiting Attica equated to catching up with an old acquaintance. Though, if what Malachi admitted was true, Attica *was* Marin's friend. The prison whispered its secrets to her, and Marin listened.

One of the secrets Marin had learned was the only way they were getting Tsuna out of here. All Marin needed was an excuse to touch a CO's hand. The keys to specific cells were stored on a microchip planted underneath the guards' skin. It would shut off if anything happened to the guard, but Marin could copy the chip onto her own skin, like an inked fingerprint. An ability Auri couldn't help but envy.

Another secret was an emergency staircase, no longer in use, that exited the maximum-security area. While Auri distracted the guard providing the tour, Marin would unlock Tsuna's door. They wouldn't have much time once the prisoner release alert went to the guard station. Once Tsuna was freed, Marin would open the staircase "under duress" and Tsuna would flee into the staircase—vanishing to the eyes of watching security, but actually meeting Malachi where the staircase let out, one of the few spots with a gap in security camera coverage. There, she'd fit into the false bottom of the storage container.

The prison would go into lockdown, but Malachi was banking on his pristine record and the warden's desire to get all visitors off-planet that the crew wouldn't get caught in it. But if they did? Tsuna would just have to spend some extra time in a too-tight container.

The plan made Auri wonder how he and Marin had managed to actually escape Attica all those years ago. Sure, they made it out of their cells. But they didn't have a crew waiting to get them off-planet.

The female CO scanned Auri's and Marin's barcodes again, registering their current location in the prison's system. Auri's c-tacts found Marin's tattoo, her public information sliding into place.

Marin Doe
Minor
Disability: Blindness, inoperable

Reading the crews' barcodes felt like a violation, yet Auri couldn't resist. For so long they'd been covered. Where she grew up, barcodes were used as conversation starters, not mysteries to be locked away.

"You're signed in." The CO turned to her fellow officers who were bent over a table. Auri studied them for familiar features. One munched on a meat-laden sandwich and the other had his disassembled weapon laid out before him. Both faced away from her.

"Hey," the female CO ordered. "Shiba, take these two on a tour of the wings."

The man with the food turned, sandwich raised halfway to his mouth. A chunk of cheese plopped onto his gray fatigues. "I just sat down to eat."

"You're always eating," the other one joked, spinning in his seat. "No normal person wants a sandwich this early."

Auri froze. Her gaze darted down to the nametag and then up to the man's face. *Bennet Indie.* He'd gained weight since middle school but hadn't gotten much taller. The green eyes that had brightened before each blow had sunken into their sockets, as if Attica had prematurely aged him. His slit of a mouth turned down as he studied her.

Her hand darted to yank her jacket back over her barcode, but the twitch of muscle near his eye proved she was too late.

Indie reassembled his gun with lightning speed then pushed out of his chair with a grunt. "Let me take this." He patted the female CO's shoulder. "Though you'll be in charge of making sure Shiba passes our next PT test." He winked.

She laughed, oblivious to the venomous expression on Indie's face when he looked at Auri. He could be charming when he chose to be. She remembered that fact well.

"Deal," the female CO agreed.

Auri's body seemed to have iced over, her feet threatening to shatter into thousands of irreparable shards if she moved. Memories assailed her, ending with the final time she'd seen Indie as he was hauled out of the principal's office. "Next time I see you," he'd hissed as he passed, a guard on each arm, "I'm going to kill you, clank."

Now, Auri yearned to retreat back to the elevator. To call off the tour. But so many people depended on her. Not just the crew and Tsuna, but the Bleeders' past victims and their future victims should she fail.

"This way, Agent." Indie kept his tone pleasant as he stepped out of the office. He slid the door shut behind him. The motion appeared to come from a desire to give the other guards privacy, but Auri knew better. This way they wouldn't hear her cries for help.

"Which end would you like to start with? East or West?" he asked. He eyed Marin, tilting his head as if gauging what kind of threat she would be.

Auri swallowed, clawing at her terror, wrestling it into submission. This was a familiar game. "West?"

"You'll like East better." He raised his brows as if waiting for her to argue.

She used to, but this time she didn't. Tsuna was being held in the East wing, exactly where Auri wanted to go.

"Good." He led the way, whistling their middle school's fight song under his breath. The sound bounced off the walls and transformed into knives, stabbing into her with each step she took.

Strive for the white and blue
Hear the lion roar.
Fierce, resolute, loyal, true
It's a victory we fight for.

The tune died on his lips as he spoke. "As I'm sure you remember from your tour in basic, these holding cells are impregnable. Each is made of steel with a ten-by-ten-centimeter window of bullet-proof glass." His voice took on the tone of a bored tour-guide. "The only keys are installed as chips in a guard's skin. If the guard dies, loses that hand, or the chip is removed, it deactivates. The prisoners aren't going anywhere." He drew the taser from his belt and began twirling it in his fingers.

Auri shook her head, forcing herself to focus. According to Malachi, when Attica was first constructed, a staircase had been engineered for doctors. If the corridors were sealed off, the doctors could still escape to upper levels. But when the prison had been outfitted with an underground pod system inside the hospital decades ago, among other tech upgrades, the staircase had been covered up and forgotten.

Until Marin spoke to the walls. And the walls spoke back.

They were approaching the end of that very hall. The intel Castor had gathered stated that Tsuna's cell was the last one on the left. Auri peered through the tiny glass window as they passed. A woman lounged on the metal floor, back pressed against the wall, eyes closed. Her skin gleamed with a dark complexion, her hair a curly cloud. Tsuna was beautiful, just as Castor described her. Adjacent to her cell ran the hospital, the open doors revealing a dark empty room.

Auri acted before fear persuaded her otherwise. She tripped, bumping into Indie mid-twirl of his taser. It skittered across the floor to knock against Marin's bare feet.

"*Gomenasai*," Auri gushed, using the friendly word for an apology when they had never been—and never would be—friends. "Marin, could you get the officer's weapon?"

Marin bent to retrieve the taser. "Here." She reached out, her hand brushing Indie's. An inky black stain oozed onto Marin's pale skin, the mark smaller than a rare currency coin.

"Are you suddenly clumsy now, *Kisama*?" Indie asked, tearing the taser out of Marin's hand. He grabbed the front of Auri's uniform, hauling her towards him only to shove her against a wall.

Kisama. The insult stung, like the bite of a painful memory remembered in the dark.

The wall's chill seeped through the thick material of her jacket and vest. "Don't call me that," she said, gathering her courage. "We're soldiers now, Indie. Can't we just forget everything?"

Behind him, Marin looked panic-stricken. Indie had thrown Auri right on top of their secret exit. And he now stood between Marin, Tsuna, and freedom. Auri needed to make him move. She wrenched away from his hands and took a step to the side. Away from Tsuna's cell and the door.

OF STARLIGHT AND BONE · 205

Indie shook his head, laughing. The straw-colored hair he wore long in school had been shaved in a buzz cut so close to his head she could see the skin underneath.

"It's hard to forget when I'm living in this hellhole because of you." He shoved her again. Her back hit the wall. She ran her palms across the smooth metal. Her fingers twitched with the need to curl around the handle of her disc. To fight.

"I wasn't going to hurt you," he said. "Just scare you with the possibility that I might. But you were never clumsy, *kisama*. You were always graceful and perfect. So you bumping into me tells me you're up to something." He slid his taser into a loop on his belt. "Want to see if I remember the right places? Can you feel pain now? Or maybe you didn't receive that upgrade." He loomed over her, a titan on a battlefield with her the lone combatant. Weaponless, weak, afraid.

Her chin trembled. "I-Indie, let's just stop."

Over his shoulder, Marin called out, "What's going on?"

"Indie, I'm sorry for what the GIC did," she began, hands up in an attempt to placate him. "But I never told him about the bullying. He found out somehow. And I'm sorry about your family. The Cyborg Bomber deserved what he got." After the murderer had been caught, doctors had removed the cyborg's robotic limbs and enhancements and left him to die. It took days.

Indie's shoulders hunched around his ears as if blocking out her words. Pain flickered across his face.

When he didn't reply, she cleared her throat, easing away from the wall, ready to step around him. "I've had enough of the tour. Take me back to the other officers. I'm sure they're watching the security feed and are curious about what's going on." She inclined her head at the glass office she could barely see from this end of the hall. Maybe the reminder that they weren't alone down here would penetrate his rage. And the fact that their altercation would be recorded.

Indie's face reddened and his teeth ground together. "You think you can order me around, *kisama*?" He stepped forward, pinning her in place. "The others won't look down this way. And the cameras you're so concerned about?" His knee slid between her legs. She stiffened. He leaned forward, breath stale on her cheek. "The cameras have been broken for the last month."

His fist slammed into her stomach.

Air rushed out of her lungs in a frantic escape. She wheezed, doubling over.

His other hand slapped her face, the motion banging her organic cheek into the wall. His knee between her legs kept her pinned, trapped. She held up her hands, all of her DISC training leaving her in a rush. She was a little girl again, cornered and alone.

"Stop!" she screamed at Indie. "Stop it!"

"I'll say that you attacked me. You and the girl. You tried to break someone out." His elbow cracked against her organic shoulder and true pain burst through her like fireworks. She cried out. "I had no choice but to fight back."

It was then she realized with growing terror: this wasn't going to be like the beatings in middle school. He was going to break the human parts of her. The irreparable parts. Adrenaline returned a spark of her training.

Auri brought both of her arms up, interlocked in an X as his meaty fist came down. The strength of her robotic limb caught the majority of the impact, holding him in place. He stared at her for a moment, body trembling as he tried to force his fist down.

"Auri?" Marin called. "Auri, what should I do?"

This way of distracting the guard was not what Auri had imagined, but she had to handle this on her own. Maybe she could knock Indie out, stumble back to the guard station, and make up a story. She wouldn't be the reason that the crew failed. They were trusting her to succeed.

"Stay back," she wheezed at Marin, gritting her teeth. Sweat beaded on her skin, trickling beneath the high neckline of her shirt. She brought her knee up and slammed it between his legs.

She felt the protective armor there and realized with detached clarity what would happen next.

The taser was out of his belt and jammed into her side before she could dodge. Lightning jolted along her spine, sending her electronic circuitry into a frenzied panic. If she was entirely human, the shock would've simply rattled her brain for a few minutes. But with as many cyborg enhancements as she had... a taser could be deadly.

His knee slid away. She hit the ground, body seizing. Warnings flashed before her vision. Her heart fluttered. Stopped. Then gave an off-kilter thump.

She tried to stand, but her cyborg vision swarmed with black confetti at the corners. Her system went into overdrive, attempting to regulate itself after the taser.

Indie was going to kill her.

She was going to die in this hallway reserved for the Fed's worst criminals.

"Enough!" Marin cried. Her hand twitching a dizzying rhythm. "You have done enough to her!"

Banging echoed through the corridor. Auri vaguely registered the sound coming from Tsuna's cell. Muffled shouts penetrated the metal door in a garble of threats.

"Stop," Auri wheezed, staring as Indie loomed over her. "Stop. They'll court martial you."

The threat didn't pierce his rage. He laughed. "They'll thank"— he kicked her legs out from under her as she tried to rise—"me for ridding"—he grabbed her hair and yanked her back up—"the galaxy of you." His fist pounded against her robotic temple and knocked her back to the floor.

In the midst of the pain and fear and hopelessness, Auri agreed with him. She stopped fighting. Stopped begging. She curled into a ball and closed her eyes.

"Die!" A high-pitched shriek made her head snap up. At first she thought the word, the sound, came from her throat until she realized her jaw was clenched tight against the pain.

She opened her eyes to see Marin drop to her knees, her mouth split wide in a scream. The girl slapped her hands against the steel floor, fingers splayed. Her eyes rolled back in her head. The shriek took on a robotic quality, deepening and seeming to reverberate throughout the corridor. Indie paused and turned.

Lightning crackled under Marin's palms. It skimmed along the walls and seethed into the lights above. The hall hummed for a moment, the power overwhelming the controls. Then the bulbs above exploded.

CHAPTER TWENTY-SIX

---

26 Aug 3319, 06:06:24
Ancora Galaxy, Planet 01: Attica, Attica Prison, Max. Sec.
Holding

ndie hit the floor. Electricity rippled over his limbs, crackling as though in manic glee. His body jerked and twitched as his eyes rolled back. Saliva and foam dripped from his gaping mouth onto the steel walkway. At the end of the hall, just before the guard station, a security door slid shut. The boom of its locks clicking into place echoed through the dark.

The floor, walls, and ceiling glowed around Marin, their skeletal circuitry coming to life. Like a wave crashing onto shore, power shot out from the girl and into the surrounding metal. As the floor awoke underneath Auri, pain barreled into her head. Sharp talons raked through her skull, twisting, prodding, and commanding submission.

The cyborg half of her complied, but her human half warred against the intrusion. She was being ripped in two. Blood burst from her nose, splattering the floor. Control seeped away, all her strength and freedom bleeding out in Marin's direction. Her body went limp and she sagged forward.

Darkness swept across her robotic eye, but with her human one, blurred through the tears, she gawked at Marin in horror. The girls' nails scraped against the floor. Smoke whispered up between her fingers, the scent of burned synthetic flesh making bile rise in Auri's throat. Marin's body shook in pleasure, her head bent toward the ceiling, her eyes black as the darkest night. Blue lines ran up from her hands, staining her skin, her neck, her face.

Auri tried to say Marin's name, but her jaw had locked in place.

The prison doors rattled as if chanting their praises. With a bang, a door flew open. She expected to hear the clang of alarm bells, but only the hum of electricity echoed through the sealed hall before it went deathly quiet.

Auri blinked. When she next opened her eye, Tsuna knelt beside her. The hacker's mouth moved, but Auri couldn't hear the words over the ringing in her ears.

Marin's body had gone rigid, her mouth open in a soundless scream, hands still on the floor. It was as if her body had locked up after... whatever she had done.

"Move her hands," Auri rasped, not sure if the words actually made it from her brain to her mouth. She didn't want everything to start back up again. Auri didn't know if she could survive another onslaught.

Tsuna's thin brows furrowed and Auri repeated herself. The pain in her head turned white hot as she fought against the voice that commanded, *Be silent*!

Tsuna must've understood. She scrambled over to Marin, looping her arms under the girl's armpits and jerking her upright. The sound of tearing flesh made Auri gag.

Where Marin's hands had touched the floor, a blackened imprint marred the steel. The hall's internal wiring dimmed. The hum of the overpowered tech quieted. Darkness stole into the space. The pain in Auri's head lessened as her robotic parts regained control of themselves. A systems diagnostic swirled in the left corner of her vision.

Red emergency lights fixed into the floor powered on, giving the corridor an eerie glow. Meters away, Tsuna cradled Marin in her arms like she weighed nothing more than a sack of feathers. "Can you stand?" she asked Auri. Her voice was husky yet sweet at the same time.

Auri glanced at Marin. She still spasmed in Tsuna's grip. An oily black substance seeped from her mouth and nose, dripping down her beautiful *yukata*.

"N-not much t-t-time," Marin wheezed. Her vocal cords sounded scratchy. "Security cameras o-off."

Auri staggered to her feet, one hand gripping a wall for balance. At the far end of the corridor, something hard slammed against the sealed door. No doubt the guards prying open the doors manually.

Auri's childhood tormenter lay slumped on the floor, unmoving. She couldn't bring herself to check his pulse, afraid of what she might find—and feel.

She winced as she forced herself toward the secret staircase. The instructions Malachi had given her hours before seemed muddled. She squeezed her eyes shut to concentrate. Every centimeter of her body shouted its aches. The human half of her suffered from Indie's blows. The cyborg part trembled after Marin... whatever Marin had done.

Auri breathed deep, the extra oxygen clearing some of the fog. She opened her eyes. The barest hint of two seams ran down the metal wall near the hospital's entrance.

Auri slid her pinky into one of them. She could only fit the tip inside, but that's all she needed. Halfway down, her skin caught on a clasp. She pressed it with as much leverage as she could. A hiss of air billowed out as a panel of wall slid away. About twenty centimeters of it stuck up from the floor. A narrow staircase yawned, disappearing into the darkness beyond. Even going one at a time, it would be a tight fit.

Tsuna entered first, Marin cradled close to her chest. The black prison uniform hung off the woman's slender frame, the V-neck draping almost seductively over one shoulder. Auri staggered in after them, her robotic foot catching on the lip of the door. She fell forward, just catching herself on the steps. The sting of the impact on her organic hand made her grimace.

"Are you okay?" Tsuna's question reached Auri's buzzing ears.

She thought she replied, but when Tsuna asked again, Auri realized she was still on her hands and knees.

The pressure of time bore into Auri's back, tightening the muscles there. She needed to move. Now.

She hauled herself up with a groan.

"I wish I could help you," Tsuna said, indicating Marin. The girl's eyes had fluttered shut, though the lids twitched as if she dreamed. The oil-like blood dripping from her mouth and nose ceased but had stained her skin like Indian ink.

"I'm okay," Auri rasped. "We need to get to the top."

Their progress was slow due to Auri's battered body. She knew she should tell Tsuna to go on ahead, but the woman didn't suggest it, and Auri was too afraid to ask.

A bang made her jump. She whirled around to see the secret door reseal itself. Musty darkness descended with choking intensity.

"Keep moving," she said. Her voice sounded detached, maybe even brave. But panic sat on Auri's chest. She tried to keep track of the number of stairs they climbed, but her mind reeled as the faint alarms echoing through the prison reached her. Phantom fingers brushed across her cheek, her hand. Logic told her the sensation was probably from cobwebs, but her mind refused to listen. She widened her eyes to their limits, yearning for even a fragment of light.

As if answering her prayers, a flash of light appeared far above, as if a door had been opened and shut. After a few seconds of darkness, a beam clicked on, illuminating stairs a half meter above them. The beam bobbed as whoever held it approached.

"Who is that?" Tsuna whispered, stopping.

Warmth radiated from the woman's skin as they stood close together. "It should be Malachi," Auri whispered back. "He said he would meet us here."

"When I saw Marin pass my cell," Tsuna said, "I suspected Cai was the lunatic who'd staged this break in." She shook her head, her hair brushing Auri's face. "Marin and Cai are inseparable." Her words lilted with a smile. She seemed unaffected by the horrors of the hallway they'd left behind and the suffocating blackness surrounding them.

The light drew closer. When only a few steps separated them, the silhouette of the other person materialized. At first Auri thought it was Malachi, the boots and pants similar to the ones he wore. But when she saw the jacket and colors seeped into the blackness, she gasped.

Tyson Peri stood two steps above her, wearing the fitted uniform of the DISC taskforce.

CHAPTER
TWENTY-SEVEN

---

26 Aug 3319, 06:19:47
Ancora Galaxy, Planet 01: Attica, Attica Prison, Max.
Sec. Holding

Ty's dog, Busu, was missing, but his blaster gun, light shining from the barrel, was not. His eyes widened as he raised the light to eye level.

"What the hell?" His words echoed in the space around them. "Aur, you're... What's going on?"

"Tracking," Marin muttered as she stirred, her eyelids fluttering. She reached back for Auri, brushing limp fingers over her chest.

"Shh," Auri soothed. Her heart battered against her ribcage, eager to escape and soar away. "Ty, listen..." she said, reading the suspicion in his expression.

Except listen to what? How in the world was she going to explain this?

"Oh, I'm listening," he said. The surprise in his tone surrendered to steely resolve. Something sparked in his eyes, but the light shining in her face was too bright for her to see clearly.

"The explanation for you being found in a hidden stairwell with a death row prisoner should be very interesting."

"Unfortunately," a familiar voice said from behind Ty. "You're going to have to wait for that."

Ty whirled around. Even as the light on his gun illuminated Malachi's face, the captain was moving. His hand lashed out, knocking Ty's arm away. In the space of a blink, Malachi grabbed the gun and turned it around, its barrel pointed at Auri's best friend. His finger slid onto the trigger.

"Wait!" Auri cried. "Malachi, don't."

He glanced at her and studied her face, lips parted. "What happened to you?"

Auri swiped at her blood-crusted nose with a sleeve, realizing she must look like a disaster.

"Now isn't the time," Tsuna interjected, adjusting her grip on Marin who still mumbled about tracking. "How about you get us out of here, handsome?"

"That was the plan," Malachi said, frowning as he looked at Ty. "He, however, wasn't."

Auri watched thoughts flit through Malachi's mind as he worked toward a decision. The calculating look in his eyes sent chills along her organic skin.

"Don't shoot him," she pleaded.

"I have a better idea." He grabbed the front of Ty's jacket and yanked him forward so they were almost nose to nose. The barrel of the gun dug into Ty's temple. The light at the tip burned red where it touched his skin.

Auri took two steps closer when Malachi spoke. "You're going to get us out of here, Agent..." He glanced down at Ty's nametag and tensed. His gaze darted to Auri before it came to rest on Ty. "Agent Peri. Once you escort us to our ship, we'll drop you off on Rokuton. If those terms aren't agreeable, we can always kick you from the airlock on our way out of orbit. Or, if you plan on betraying us, I'll shoot you here and save me and my crew the trouble." He paused, studying Ty. "Answer wisely,

Agent, because I have a gift for reading people. I'm almost never wrong."

Ty swallowed, his Adam's apple bobbing against his collar. "Fine. Yes. I'll help you."

"Good." Malachi shoved him forward so his knee cracked against a step. "Lead the way." He hauled Ty upright, the gun digging into his back. To Auri and Tsuna he said, "The entire prison is suffering from an electrical shutdown. They're running on emergency generators."

"I think I know why." Tsuna jerked her chin down to Marin.

Color fled from Malachi's face as he saw the girl for the first time. "*Maitta na.* We need to get her out of here. I'll take her. Here." He handed Auri the gun. "Keep that on him." His fingers lingered against hers for a fraction of a beat, as if he doubted her loyalty. Then he strode toward Tsuna. "We have to be quick when we exit at the top."

Auri's fingers fumbled on the gun, her senses still off-kilter. She stepped close to Ty but couldn't bear to shove the weapon against his vulnerable back. This close, she could smell the musky scent of his soap melded with the detergent used on his uniform. Her insides twisted.

"What is going on?" he hissed, not turning his head. "Aur, what are you doing?"

She didn't answer. Her tongue seemed to have tied itself into a series of intricate knots.

Behind her, Malachi hoisted Marin onto his hip, her head lolling against his shoulder. He swiped his sleeve across the black liquid staining her skin. The way he held her reminded Auri of an older brother carrying a little sister who had fallen asleep. Maybe that was the point.

"Can you get yourself cleaned up?" Tsuna murmured to Auri. "The last thing we need are questions about your appearance."

"Good idea," Auri rasped. She scrubbed at her face, doing her best to clean off the blood from Indie's attack and whatever Marin had done to her. Then she shrugged off her jacket to hide the crimson staining the green fabric. She draped it over one arm and turned to Tsuna who nodded her approval.

"Auri." Malachi's voice made her look up. "Do you have a story of how you and Marin made it up here during a prison-wide blackout?"

Her mouth opened as possible ideas crowded her brain, every thought sluggish and nonsensical. A pang went through her temple and she grimaced.

"A wall panel popped open," Tsuna supplied. "You and Marin fled up the staircase while that ass-hat guard secured the escaped prisoner—me. He failed, obviously." She glanced back the way they had come with a crinkle of her nose.

"Is that okay with you?" Malachi asked Auri.

She cleared her throat. "Yes. That works."

"Then we can go." Malachi pressed himself flat against the wall. "The gun, please?" He extended his hand to Auri. She only hesitated a moment to glance at Ty before she returned the weapon to Malachi's hand. "Thank you. As for you, Agent…" The captain jerked his head at the stairs. "Start walking."

Ty gritted his teeth. "No need to be so rough." He moved up the steps, shoulders rolled back as if this was just a minor inconvenience, not a life-or-death situation.

When he got to the door at the end, he glanced over his shoulder. At Malachi's nod, Ty slid the door aside using a small lever fixed in the center. The group stepped into a deserted hallway, the only light coming from a window at the far end. The blast of an alarm droned, a voice repeating, "Code Black, Code Black. This is not a drill. All COs report for duty."

One of the delivery bins rested against a wall nearby. "Get in." Malachi gestured with his head. "There's a false bottom."

Tsuna yanked it up and slid inside, curling herself up like a snake.

Seeing that Malachi's hands were full, Auri bent over and adjusted the fake bottom, locking it into place. Her side twinged where Indie had kicked her. She winced as she straightened.

As a group, they proceeded down the hall. Auri rolled the cart, grateful for something to steady herself on. Even with a woman hiding in the bottom, the bin wasn't very heavy. Hopefully, the guards wouldn't be suspicious.

Malachi and Ty led the way, Ty's jacket hiding the gun Malachi held to his back. The hallway for guards' living quarters stood empty, door after door sealed shut. The lights above seemed to have exploded, glass fragments crunching under each step. Breakfast smells curled through the hall, mingled with the scent of burned rubber.

Up ahead, the circular area where they had entered bustled with activity. Recruits wearing tech expert jumpsuits fiddled with wall paneling and the wires sprouting beneath. Lieutenant Aki stood in the middle of it, overseeing COs and sergeants as they entered generator-powered elevators.

"Make sure all the prisoners are secured," Lieutenant Aki ordered, hands clasped behind his back. "And find out what piece of *kuso* caused this blackout."

He pivoted as they approached. Auri's heart raced when his gaze fell on her. "Agent Peri, how did you get back up here?"

She swallowed, glancing at Malachi. "When the power surged downstairs, one of the wall panels popped open. Ind—" she caught herself, refusing to let the final image of him rise before her. "—Officer Bennet told us to get out while he secured the escaped prisoner."

"Wall panel?" His brows drew together then he shook his head. "A mystery for later. What happened to your little friend?" he asked, more out of courtesy than care, his gaze was already shifting to follow the path of his frantic sergeants.

"Tour wore her out," Malachi answered. "What's happening?" He stood beside Ty, his face the perfect mask of a concerned transporter captain. "Do you need help, Lieutenant?"

Lieutenant Aki shook his head. "No. Do us a favor and return to your ship before the warden arrives. We don't need you and your people underfoot. The others are already back onboard." He glanced at Ty as if just seeing him for the first time. "And the second Agent Peri? I don't remember seeing you check in."

Ty cleared his throat. Auri's muscles tensed as his lips parted to speak.

"I came in through the visitor's entrance. I'm going back to Rokuton, and the captain here offered to give me a ride since I took a public shuttle."

Lieutenant Aki nodded. "Well, we were glad to have you stop by to visit. Give our regards to your father and," he stepped forward, lowering his voice, "I would be grateful if you didn't mention this to him."

Ty smirked. Auri could guess what he was thinking: *Even if I did mention it, my father couldn't care less what I have to say.*

But he said, "Secret is safe with me, Lieutenant." He gestured toward the empty security checkpoint. "Do you need to call some officers over for this?"

Lieutenant Aki hesitated.

"Sir," a soldier rushed up to him, chest heaving. He offered a hasty salute. "Half the cells on level two are breached. We need backup to secure the prisoners."

He swore. "Get that up on the Big Voice. Take twenty men down with you." He spun back to Ty. "Just get out of here. I trust you, if not the others."

Auri pushed aside the sting from his words.

They hurried out of the prison and along the gangway. Every so often Malachi would pause to adjust his grip on Marin. The girl had passed out at some point during their conversation with Lieutenant Aki.

The *Kestrel*'s cargo doors still gaped open. Auri shoved the cart over the lip with a grunt, mentally apologizing to Tsuna. Sweat rolled down her temples and gathered at the center of her back. She longed to tear off her uniform and sink into a hot bath to ease the hurts.

Castor and Ferris waited just inside. Malachi must've sent them a ping because they didn't even blink upon seeing an unconscious Marin or the unexpected Ty.

Castor grabbed Ty by the back of his collar. His fingers were deft as he secured Ty's hands behind his back. Ferris hurried toward Malachi. He probed the sides of Marin's neck, under her jaw.

"Infirmary, now," the doctor said, all traces of his usual teasing humor gone.

They rushed out of the cargo room as Katara entered, Birdie just behind her. Birdie ran for Auri in an all-out sprint, her tail wagging furiously. She stopped just shy of leaping atop her when Auri commanded, "Stay!"

Birdie's bottom plopped down. Her tail thumped a fast staccato on the floor.

Auri collapsed, her back pressing against a crate. The further away Marin got, the less pain Auri felt. She let out a slow breath as her cyborg parts settled into their usual rhythm.

"You good?" Katara asked. She stood above Auri, arms crossed.

Auri nodded.

Katara yanked up the cart's lid, removing the fake bottom. She helped Tsuna out, offering a rare smile. "Nice to see you again, Tsu."

Tsuna nodded in agreement. "You too." Her gaze lingered on Auri, lips a thin line. Auri hazily recollected that Tsuna had pounded on the door, trying to draw Indie's attention. The woman had witnessed the whole embarrassing beating. "Mind telling me what craziness led to you breaking me out?" she asked Katara.

"Hey, *boke*!" Ty's voice made everyone turn. "Get off me. Aur!" He jerked out of Castor's grip. Castor had secured Ty's bound hands to one of the iron posts connected to the catwalk above. His feet too had been bound. Castor had been in the middle of gagging him with a rolled-up kerchief.

"It's either this," Castor said, jovial tone pierced by a sting of venom belied it. "Or I knock you unconscious. Which would you prefer? Keep in mind I haven't washed this kerchief in a very, very long time."

"Have you turned to brawling and unsanitary habits now?" Tsuna asked, cocking a hip and planting a hand there. Despite the bulky prison garb, the hacker looked like she belonged on a fashion holo. Castor seemed to agree with Auri's opinion. His eyes swept over her from head to foot. He dropped the rag.

Auri pushed herself to her feet with a groan. "They won't hurt you," she promised Ty. "Everything will be fine."

He snorted. "If I'm depending on you, I'm not entirely sure."

The barb stung, just as he'd intended. "I'll explain everything," she whispered, not daring to venture closer.

"Maybe we *should* gag him," Katara said, frowning at Ty. "If he's going to be spouting such *kuso* about the one person keeping us from throwing him out once we hit orbit."

"Speaking of orbit"—Tsuna turned from her intense stare-off with Castor—"who's going to fly the *Kestrel* with Marin… without Marin? We need to get out of here before the COs realize I'm gone and decide to search the ship."

Silence descended. It seemed no one liked piloting. Auri realized how much Katara had to care about Malachi if she'd shown up to save them back on Medea. It made her doubt the whole *I'll kill you one day* vow.

Tsuna rolled her eyes. "You two are impossible. Castor, take me up to the bridge and catch me up on what's going on."

Castor stepped forward. "This way." The two started up the steps that led to the bridge a level above.

Katara glanced at Auri and Ty. She placed a hand on Auri's shoulder and whispered, "Talk to him if you must, but be wary.

Get yourself to the infirmary after. Ferris can do something about the bruising."

Then she hurried out of the cargo hold, no doubt bound to check on Marin.

Auri watched her go and stared at the door long after Katara shut it. Looking at Ty just now seemed an impossible feat. Her avoidance was almost comical after the years she'd spent with him throughout her life, the hours she daydreamed about him over the course of the trip.

In the end, his words drew her to his side. "Are you a renegade now?"

Renegade. A term for defected citizens, usually those who left the force after the mandatory two years and joined a militia.

The insult stirred the embers of her anger but failed to spark a flame. She felt so, so tired. Like a sponge wrung out over and over again. Empty. Disheveled. Exhausted.

Birdie, nonplussed, pranced over to Ty and began licking his face now that he'd been rendered defenseless.

He coughed and shook his head back and forth. "Birdie, leave it." But, as he knew, the command would only be obeyed if Auri spoke it. Which she did.

"There's so much you don't know, Ty." She knelt in front of him, her bones creaking with the effort. "And I will explain everything to you. Right now I need to go to the infirmary."

"To check on that girl?"

She nodded. "Yes. And in case you haven't noticed, *aho*, I've been beaten up."

His gaze flicked across her face, the anger in his twisted features softening. He let out a breath. "Was it that guy from middle school?"

She looked away. "I didn't know you knew about him."

"I knew the whole time. I can't believe you had the chance to defend yourself after all these years and you still let him beat the *kuso* out of you."

Auri met his stare, her heart flip-flopping with pleasure at the intent way he studied her. She'd missed him so much. Yet having him on the *Kestrel* felt awkward, like he didn't quite belong. Something wasn't right.

"You still have your birthday present." He said it with certainty, as if her losing the necklace was unthinkable.

"I do." She rested a hand over it where it lay underneath layers of clothing. Auri started to stand, but hesitated. "Ty, why were you on Attica? Did you drop off a suspect?"

He tilted his head. "You're keeping your secrets. So I'm keeping mine. I might've known you for a long time, Aur. But I don't trust this crew. They're not typical transporters."

Auri didn't miss the implied meaning: *I also don't trust you*.

Would she trust him in the same position?

The answer came to her without question: *yes*. A hundred times, a thousand lifetimes, yes.

"I'll be back," she said to him, her cold tone surprising her.

"Hey, Aur. Hey—wait!"

But she didn't stop. She turned around and limped out of the cargo hold, not looking back, Birdie whining at her side. Because if she looked back, she would apologize.

Right now she lacked the strength to win Ty over. He, his questions, and his secrets, would have to wait.

CHAPTER
TWENTY-EIGHT

---

26 Aug, 3319, 12:49:01
Ancora Galaxy, Planet 02: Isoroku-Patton,
UNKNOWN

Tsuna managed to dock the *Kestrel* inside the hidden hangar on Rokuton. Contrary to Auri's fears, they hadn't flown off Attica amidst a flurry of alarms. In fact, it would probably be hours before systems came back online and authorities realized a certain death row inmate had gone missing.

In the infirmary, Ferris and Katara worked to help Marin, Katara acting as an assistant nurse, handing the doctor implements and syringes. Malachi hovered nearby, face creased with worry.

Once Ferris no longer needed help, Katara instructed Auri to lay on one of the beds. She used a handheld device to ease the bruising. As the warm light seeped into Auri's skin, breaking down the blood underneath, Katara leaned forward.

"*Sumimasen,*" she whispered.

Auri's brows drew together, making her wince. "For what?"

"You're not a little robot. You're our Little Warrior." Katara opened her mouth to say more, but Tsuna came over.

"Auri, mind if I take a look at your barcode?" she asked. "Malachi told me there's a bit of code he wants to reactivate."

"Oh." She glanced at Katara, who had returned to her task. "Sure." She smiled at her new nickname. *Little Warrior*.

"It might take a while, so feel free to take a nap." She glanced over her shoulder at Marin's limp body, making it clear that she doubted Auri would be able to relax enough to sleep. She was right.

Tsuna applied a sticky mesh to the bar code that connected to a clear tablet via a thin wire. While Tsuna tapped away, Auri watched Marin. The machines Ferris attached to her skin beeped erratically. He fought to normalize her robotic heart rate, her blood pressure, her oxygen levels. Such oddities in something that wasn't even human.

Malachi stayed at Marin's side, mumbling reassurances to her, holding one of her bandaged hands. The girl never stirred. She barely even breathed.

It took Ferris an hour of intensive labor to settle Marin's body into a stable, medically induced coma. Malachi remained with Marin for another hour after that. He would probably have stayed longer if Tsuna hadn't finished Auri's barcode and ordered him to sleep. The captain must've been in worse shape than even Tsuna realized, because he turned to obey without complaint.

Auri swung out of the infirmary bed to catch Malachi. "Mal—oof." Her head spun and she reached out to steady herself on the mattress.

"You okay?" Tsuna asked with a wince, looking up from her tablet. "Sorry. I took even longer than I thought so I forgot to have you sit up. When I get lost in a project... Everything else fades away."

"Just a little dizzy," she assured the hacker before hurrying after Malachi. She reached him in the living area. "Malachi." She caught his sleeve. "What happened to Marin?"

He ran a hand across his face. "Ferris stabilized her. Now she just needs rest."

"I mean back on Attica. She controlled all the tech…" Auri trailed off, wondering if she should admit it. "She even tried to control the cyborg half of me."

Malachi glanced over his shoulder at the closed infirmary doors. "That's what happens when she breaks protocol," he whispered.

"Something like that was how she killed her creators?"

He nodded. "When she was created, Marin's control of technology was hemmed in with two protocols. She can't kill humans. And she can only make tech do what it has already been programmed for." He shook his head. "When she gets agitated or angry, when her brain is scared and her body can't process, she breaks protocol. She becomes unstoppable. It wreaks havoc on her. It's like a grand mal seizure. The first time she got that hand twitch. Ferris thinks she's now lost control of that arm permanently. If she does it again…" He let the silence finish his statement.

"Her brain… she'll die," Auri said aloud. She lowered her gaze. "I put her in that position. I was afraid," she murmured, rubbing at her cheek. "I did nothing to stop the guard's beating that set her off." The memory of Indie's blows tainted her thoughts, her skin.

"That's okay, Agent Aurelia Peri." He tugged on the messy end of her braid to make her meet his eyes. "It's what we do with the fear that makes us strong. Next time, you'll be ready."

Auri recalled Indie's limp body, prone on the floor.

She highly doubted there would be a next time.

———

Later that evening, Auri huddled on a couch in the living area outside the infirmary. After a long nap, she'd showered and changed into a loose dress. Birdie lounged atop Auri's bare feet, warming her chilled skin. Through the glass of the infirmary doors, Tsuna watched over Marin, studying the rise and fall of the numbers on the monitors.

Castor had supplied the crew, except the still sleeping Malachi, with a hearty stew. Tsuna's own bowl sat untouched on a nearby table, cold and congealed.

The hacker looked up from stroking Marin's hand, gaze locking with Auri's. The sudden connection startled Auri into looking away. To her embarrassment, the infirmary door scraped open seconds later. Tsuna crept out, leaving the opening ajar so the steady beeping of machines leaked into the room.

Tsuna took a seat on the couch opposite Auri, moving a blanket and discarded book onto the low table. "Thank you for helping me escape."

Auri nodded, toying with Birdie's tail. "Thank you for trying to stop the CO."

"If I hadn't been stuck in my cell, I would've kicked the *kuso* out of him."

"Like I didn't."

Birdie jerked to nip at Auri's fingers. The dog never liked having her tail played with.

"There are different kinds of strength," the hacker finally said. "And there are different kinds of weakness. You can't have one without another." Her gaze grew distant as she stared at one of the many cluttered shelves in the room. "Castor is a weakness of mine."

"How do you two know each other?" Auri asked. "He seems to…" She searched for the right words. "He seems to really care about you."

Tsuna smoothed the long black dress she'd borrowed from Katara. Auri wondered if the assassin was running out of clothes. A familiar tattooed chain encircled her left ring finger. "Even after the divorce, he still cares."

228 · EMILY LAYNE

Her mouth parted in surprise. "Wait." She leaned forward. Castor's finger bore the same tattoo, she realized. Birdie groaned her disapproval. "You and Castor?"

She laughed. "Hard to believe?"

"No," Auri scrambled to say, afraid of offending the woman. "I'm more surprised no one mentioned it when we made the plan to… to break you out." She'd almost said *rescue*, but Tsuna struck her as the kind of person that didn't need rescuing. If they hadn't swooped into the prison, she bet the hacker would've found another way out.

Tsuna shrugged. "It only lasted a year. We married young and came from different worlds. He was a poor delivery boy on Medea and I was a diplomat's daughter visiting the planet every summer."

A diplomat's daughter turned hacker. That must've been an interesting origin story. Still, Tsuna's reason for divorcing Castor sounded hollow to Auri's ears, an easy excuse. The pained expression on the woman's face encouraged her to ask a more personal question. "Why did you really separate?"

She sighed, collapsing into her seat. "Because he poisoned my father."

Auri's eyes widened in horror. She sank back against the couch. No wonder Tsuna made up other explanations.

"You already planned to kill him." Castor's voice came from the stairwell. His sudden appearance made Auri jump. He'd navigated the metal steps soundlessly, likely intending to eavesdrop. "I just accelerated the process."

"Which is exactly what I didn't want you to do." Tsuna gritted her teeth, jerking upright. "For years he tormented me. I wanted to be the one to end it. You stole that."

Castor crossed the room in two strides, looming over her. "I wanted to save you from the guilt of it. Then you went and seduced the captain."

Auri stared, torn between running away and wanting to listen.

"What if it was a guilt I wanted to bear?" She shoved him away, standing. "How dare you assume I would feel guilty over it? And Cai? Get over yourself, Castor. We were separated by then, and Cai wasn't even interested."

"I didn't assume. I knew. I still loved you, and I know you still loved me. You just used him to make me jealous. He's practically a kid."

"Oh? You can tell all that because you know me so well?" she snapped. "Maybe I like younger men!"

"Yes. Because I've loved you for over half my life, ever since I saw you on Medea when we were children. And younger men drive you to boredom. Not enough intellectual stimulation. Or stimulation of other... types."

Tsuna opened her mouth and then shut it. She pursed her lips. "I'm going back to watch over Marin until Ferris gets back." She turned to Auri. "It was nice to talk to you. I hope to get to know you better when we don't have people listening in." She shot Castor a seething look that was half longing, half hate. Then she whirled around and strode into the infirmary, closing the door tight behind her.

Castor shoved loose braids out of his eyes and cursed women-kind under his breath.

Auri cleared her throat. "Um... I'll check on Ty." She'd been putting it off, but she knew she should go bring Ty a very late dinner. She doubted anyone had bothered to feed him. After the *Kestrel* took off, the crew's concern had shifted to treating injuries and reaching Rokuton.

Castor shrugged as if he didn't care what she did. He still glared at Tsuna through the infirmary's glass walls.

Relieved to escape, Auri followed the spiral staircase up to the second level. She crossed the dining area into the kitchen where stew still simmered in a large glass container. The contraption was meant to use the energy in the air to keep leftovers hot. A hand on the warmed glass ensured it was working. She grabbed a bowl and scooped out a few helpings of stew.

Birdie waited at her feet, begging with no shame. That habit had gotten worse since they joined the crew. No doubt people were feeding her too many contraband treats. Auri frowned.

"You're getting spoiled," she chided the dog. If she'd been braver, she might have told Birdie to go to bed, but part of her hoped the canine's company would ease the awkward tension with Ty.

Stew in hand, Auri headed toward the door to the cargo hold catwalk, Birdie following behind. She moved down the hall, pausing where the crews' rooms branched off. Ferris and Katara were resting after the frantic chaos of stabilizing Marin. She thought of Ferris's unflagging attempts to get closer to the assassin. And Katara's occasional glimmer of interest. That wasn't much to go on, but Ferris never gave up. Or pushed Katara too hard.

Auri wondered what it would be like to be so wanted by someone. Mind, body, and soul.

A sound made her ears prick. It sounded like a cry. She closed her eyes to hear better. When the cry came again, her senses placed it at the corridor to her right.

Every night she'd been aboard the *Kestrel*, she heard the moaning, the cries, even muffled shouts at times. Once she worked up the courage to ask Marin about it, the girl said that *Malachi hid demons under his skin and fought them at night*, a line from a famous poem that dealt with combat PTSD. She then explained it was an unspoken rule that he wasn't to be disturbed. The crew had quietly accepted Malachi's nighttime battles.

Auri hadn't.

Every night she lay awake in bed, listening. She didn't know what nightmares he had, what horrors he relived over and over again in his sleep. But she didn't want him to be alone, even if he was unaware of her nightly vigil.

Tonight was different. Maybe the tiredness weighing down Auri's bones made her do it. Maybe it all came down to avoiding Ty for a few minutes longer. Or maybe she just wanted to comfort someone and be comforted in turn.

Auri crept down the hallway of the captain's quarters, encompassing the entire east wing of the *Kestrel*. She paused outside the only door, ear pressed against the rice paper. The stew warmed the palm of her hand as she listened.

At first, silence reigned in the room beyond. Then there came a muffled grunt followed by the rustling of sheets.

Auri's fingers curled around the door handle. If it was locked, she'd go, but if it wasn't…

She tugged and the door slid open a crack.

To her surprise, the room glowed with light. Not bright or blinding, but more light than one would want to fall asleep. Unless Malachi hoped the light would fight the darkness of his dreams.

"Stay," she whispered to Birdie. Then she stepped inside, closing the door behind her.

CHAPTER
TWENTY-NINE

---

26 Aug, 3319, 22:08:34
Ancora Galaxy, Planet 02: Isoroku-Patton,
UNKNOWN

Malachi's room was enormous. Rows of books filled an entire wall, a rarity in the Ancora Federation where anything from verse to novels to textbooks could be accessed via the grid. A cushioned seat stretched below two windows that overlooked the darkness of the hidden hangar. In the center of the room was a large *kotatsu* with books and papers arranged across it. A bathroom, the door slightly ajar, waited at the far end of the space. And, in a corner, situated underneath a rectangular window, spanned a large bed.

Malachi lay atop it, tangled in his sheets. Light reflected off the sheen of sweat on his face and bare chest. One pillow had been abandoned to the floor; the other was clutched tight in his still-gloved fist.

The sight of him so vulnerable and so unclothed enraptured her. The cool indifference, the control he exuded when commanding the crew, had been stripped away. Left behind was a broken man not much older than herself, battling fears of his own.

Auri shouldn't be here. This was an invasion of his privacy. Malachi should've kept this door locked, for stars' sake. She whirled around to leave. Hot stew sloshed over the bowl's edge and scorched her organic hand. She opened her mouth to cry out, then remembered where she stood and settled for a pain-filled grunt.

She abandoned the stew on Malachi's *kotatsu*, licking off the residue. Beneath, the skin glowed a bright red.

Malachi gasped, eyes squeezed shut. His muscles went taught, chest rising with each breath.

She winced, brows drawn together in concern. She crept into the bathroom, grabbing a washcloth from a bin on the sink. She ran cool water onto the fabric and wrung it out. For years she'd suffered through nightmares with no one to comfort her. What she wouldn't give to wake and have someone there.

She perched on the corner of Malachi's bed. Half his face was smooshed into the mattress. His hair stood up in messy strands around his head, and a tangle had flopped over his eyes. Auri smoothed it away, pressing the cool cloth onto his forehead, his cheeks, his neck.

"Shh," she soothed as his body relaxed. Tension drained from his muscles. The hand clenching the pillow loosened. Her gaze wandered down to the tattoos swirling around his arm, bleeding onto his chest. This close, she could make out individual letters. The design was comprised of names. Name after name marred his skin. Kestrel Treatis was there as well as a few others she recognized from the case file on her floppy. Malachi had tattooed the victims from Uma District onto himself. But why?

Auri realized she had lowered the damp cloth to his chest, just above his heart, her fingertips brushing hot skin. She looked up from his tattoos to see Malachi's eyes, open and staring at her.

She let out a startled squeak and dropped the cloth. At first, Malachi didn't speak. He just stared at her as the haze of sleep cleared from his eyes.

"*Sumimasen*," she said with a half bow, hurrying to stand and flee the room.

Malachi's hand caught her wrist. "Stay," he whispered, voice hoarse.

She gingerly lowered herself back onto the bed. "I have nightmares too," she murmured, not sure what else to say. She risked a glance at him. He'd propped himself up on a pillow. The waistband of his pants peeked through the sheets at his hips.

Auri found her throat suddenly dry. "I, uh, didn't want you to suffer through your nightmares alone anymore."

Malachi cleared his throat and this time it was him who glanced away. He looked toward his bookshelf as if the answers to both of their fears lay scrawled across cracked spines. "The crew told you to stay away?"

She nodded.

"I'm glad you didn't."

Her eyes widened, part relief, part surprise. "Really?"

He offered her a crooked smile and released her wrist. "My dreams have been worse since the Bleeder attack on Medea. Maybe it's because they've been following us."

She froze. "How close? Do we need to—?"

He shook his head, his lack of concern not reassuring. "They've kept plenty of distance. Just close enough that our sensors intermittently pick them up, but they trailed us past the Curve."

"Why would they do that?" she asked, shivering at the memory of the monsters' bloodied and grotesque faces.

"No idea. It's not normal Bleeder behavior. They're making me uneasy, making my nightmares more frequent. Usually… Usually, I don't get them so often."

Auri caught the embarrassment in the statement. Her body hummed with the realization that Malachi didn't want her to think him weak for being afraid.

She clasped his hand with her organic one, longing to feel the heat of his skin against hers again. "You dream about the attack on Uma District."

Malachi didn't speak. His face remained neutral, not exposing a hint of shock at her statement. His hand shifted so her palm met his, the squeeze of his fingers tight against her skin. Another thought occurred to her. It seemed impossible yet absolutely right at the same time. His desire to bring the Bleeders to justice, naming the ship after Kestrel, the tattoos of those lost in Uma District, his escape from Attica with Marin…

"Your real name isn't Malachi Vermillion," she murmured, watching his face.

His hand squeezed hers again.

"You were born Peter Treatis and your sister, Kestrel, was murdered in the Bleeder attack."

He seemed to fold in on himself, as if all the strength had been torn from him with that one name. "How long did it take for you to figure things out?"

She licked her lips. "I was suspicious after you gave my floppy back, but I wasn't sure until just now."

He met her gaze, his strange eyes twinkling.

Her mouth popped open. "You wanted me to find out!"

"I did."

She rolled her eyes at the madness of it. "Why?"

He gave her hand a final squeeze before letting go. "Because I wanted to tell you the truth." He swung his feet out from under the sweat-soaked sheets, sitting up. Their faces hovered just centimeters apart.

"What is the truth?" she breathed, unable to move away.

"I was on Kaido during the attack because I'd been dishonorably discharged from the Marines."

236 · EMILY LAYNE

She tensed. *Dishonorably discharged* was a black mark against any man or woman for the rest of their lives.

He pulled away. "My father served in the Fed, made a career out of it. He got left behind on a mission in hostile militia territory and died." He ran a hand through his tangled hair. "When my turn for the high school entrance exams came, I failed on purpose. I got drafted into the Marines. I wanted to teach the Fed a lesson. Anger blinded me, made me a fool. In the end they were the ones to teach me." He shifted so Auri could see the muscular contours of his back. Crisscrossing scars made horrendous shapes against his spine, his shoulder blades.

"You must've been very bad in basic," she said with forced amusement.

He chuckled darkly, turning back. "I was. Which was why they assigned me to the disposable unit called the Renegade Sevens when I graduated."

Her brow furrowed. "Renegade Sevens?"

"Every year they have to replace at minimum seven of their Private First Class soldiers due to renegade militia attacks. The number is usually in the high teens. No one survives in the unit long. We're usually involved in events on Medea. The first mission they sent us on…" He bent forward, elbows on knees. "It was horrible, Auri. Headless children, tortured men and women in heaps. All members of a rival militia that just happened to step foot on the aggressor's territory."

She laid a hand on his arm, not interrupting but offering what little support she could.

His fingers steepled against his lips. "Only three of us out of a unit of twenty survived. I struggled with PTSD for months, but they never discharged me. I requested relief countless times. Eventually I intentionally botched a mission and they kicked me out. I went home for recuperation. Days later the Bleeders attacked my District."

Auri's heart shriveled in her chest. "Oh, Malachi."

"My little sister, Kestrel, was delivering packages that day on her hovercraft. She loved flying and dreamed about joining the lousy Chair—*Air*—Command, despite what happened to my dad." His mouth twitched in a smile at the memory.

Auri smirked at the derogatory term for the Air Command. She imagined a young girl, her long hair blowing in the wind, a smile on her face as she navigated the long board with a motor and sail attached to catch the breeze.

"Kestrel found me during the attack, tried to get me out of the District to a tiny cave where we played as kids. A handful of Bleeders tracked us. We'd just reached the cave when they grabbed her." Emotion drained from his voice as if to tell this part of the story he needed to detach himself. "I got tossed into the cave, the hovercraft crashing in after me and sealing the entrance. The Bleeders couldn't get to me, but they got to her." He turned to Auri, his expression awash in turmoil and guilt. His fingers toyed with the glove on his hand as if the skin underneath burned. "I had to listen while they… while they…" He shook his head, squeezing his eyes shut. A single tear rolled down his cheek. He was quick to wipe it away.

Auri wanted to wrap her arms around him to take away the pain. Compared to this, her nightmares were daydreams. How selfish she had been, thinking she had it the worst of anyone.

"It took me two days to clear the wreck to escape. I carried the remains of Kestrel's body back into district to find Uma decimated. Corpses everywhere, wild dogs feasting on them. Some people had shot themselves rather than be taken. Others were eaten, but even more had just been murdered outright. That's when the Fed showed up. They needed someone to blame. So they declared me guilty and sent me off to Attica with a death sentence. Except I didn't meet death there." He straightened. "In the cell next to mine, I met Marin."

Auri breathed in deeply. Malachi's past hovered around her like dust motes dancing in the sunlight. It had forged him into the man before her. "I'm in awe of you," she whispered.

His brows rose. "All that and your response is awe? Not to demand a shuttle to escape the ship of a damaged captain?"

Damaged? He thought himself damaged when he was wrongfully blamed for the deaths of his sister and everyone in his district? "No, Malachi." Auri wrapped her arms around his neck, her cheek resting against his shoulder. He went rigid, but she didn't let go. "Your brokenness has made you stronger."

His head rested against hers, his body relaxing into her touch. "Thank you," he murmured.

They stayed interlocked for a few moments, Auri taking in as much comfort as she gave. She'd never been held this way by anyone, not by the GIC and certainly not Ty. He smelled of sweat and lavender and metal that was all him. All Malachi.

He was the first to pull away. Splotches of red colored his cheeks, but he met her eyes without embarrassment. "What were you doing on your way here?" He indicated the bowl of stew on his *kotatsu*.

"*Maitta na*," she groaned, clapping a hand to her forehead. No doubt the stew was cold by now. And Birdie was still waiting outside. "I meant to take that to Ty."

"Alone?"

"I'm bringing Birdie too." Her face flushed and she looked away from his convicting stare. No doubt he knew the entirety of her feelings for the fellow DISC agent. "He's not really my brother. I'm adopted."

He chuckled. "You think that's what I was worried about?"

Her flush burned even hotter. She cleared her throat. "You should go back to sleep. I have a surefire trick to make sure you don't have any nightmares."

"Other than baring my soul to an almost stranger?" One of his brows shot up. "Besides, I thought we agreed that if I told you mine, you would tell me yours." He held up his pinky.

She laughed. "I don't have much to tell, considering I don't know what happened before the GIC found me." She slid off the bed and moved over to the bookshelf. "He said I was attacked by animals. Everyone involved assumed my parents abandoned me…" She trailed off. "Anyway, what's your favorite book? I'll read some of it to you." She glanced back.

The sight of him propped up in bed, watching her with his trademark unreadable expression, sent a thrill through her. It was as if this moment, in this place, with him, was where she belonged. Yet guilt poked at her stomach. She should be comforting Ty right now, not Malachi.

"Have you ever wondered if the GIC lied?"

She frowned and shook her head. "Why would he?"

"I'm not saying he did. I just wonder at the story. Seems too convenient." He sighed when she didn't answer. "As for the book, the one right in front of you is my favorite."

Auri examined the worn book he directed her to. The cover was a deep green fabric with gold printed in beautiful patterns along the front, back, and spine. She opened it to see a small stamp on the left top corner. *One More Page Books*. Across from that was the title: *A Collection of Verse for a Wearied Soldier.*

Then an inscription:

P—

May these words comfort you in the darkest of places.

Love, Dad

Auri brought the book back to the bed. The value of the tome made her afraid to touch it. Not only had the book been printed in the late 2000s, but it was a cherished gift.

"Don't look so scared," Malachi said. "The book has survived long before me. It'll survive after you've touched it."

She sat down a careful distance from his legs under the covers. "Do you have a favorite poem in here?"

He lowered himself back to the pillows. "Just pick one."

Auri did and began to read. The first poem ended and another began. She read poem after poem until her voice grew hoarse. She whispered a last verse and closed the book, the spine creaking farewell.

Malachi lay on his back, eyes closed. Auri crept to the shelf and slid the book into its spot. Her fingers tingled with the loss.

She hesitated beside Malachi's bed, wanting to say goodbye, but not willing to disturb him. Instead, she tiptoed back to the desk and retrieved her stew. Just as she went to open the door, his voice stopped her.

"Wait."

She turned and nearly dropped the bowl. He stood just behind her. "*Kuso*! What is wrong with you? I thought you were falling asleep!"

"I thought of something I need to discuss with you before you go." He yawned, reminding her of a tired little boy, not a man with the weight of a galaxy bearing down on him. "And you're not going to like it."

CHAPTER THIRTY

---

26 Aug 3319, 22:59:21
Ancora Galaxy, Planet 02: Isoroku-Patton,
UNKNOWN

After collecting an annoyed Birdie and swapping cold stew for warm, Auri finally entered the cargo hold. From the catwalk, she peeked down on Ty's limp form, still bound to the post. Birdie's tail wagged in recognition. Katara had allowed Ty to relieve himself hours ago, but other than that, it didn't look like any of the crew had bothered him.

She moved down the steps as quietly as she could. Ty's chin rested on his chest, a uniform button digging into his cheek. His eyelids fluttered as if he dreamed. The strangeness of walking in on another sleeping man was not lost on her.

"Ty," she whispered, kneeling to rest a hand on his shoulder. Birdie darted forward to lick his face, but Auri shooed her away. "Ty, wake up."

He groaned, head lolling as he abandoned fantasy for reality. He blinked blearily at her, lips splitting into a yawn that showcased his back molars. "Aur, there you are. What took so long?"

"I brought some food." She rested the bowl of stew and accompanying spoon on the floor beside him. Birdie sniffed at it but didn't try to steal any for herself.

"Unless you want to feed me, you're going to have to release my hands." He raised his brows expectantly.

Auri hesitated, then reached to press the release button on the zip ties. Where could he possibly go?

"Thanks." He massaged the tender skin along his wrists before bending to yank off the bindings around his ankles.

"Ty, I don't think—"

"Relax. You can tie me back up when I'm finished." He tossed off the bindings and scooped up the bowl, ignoring Birdie's attempts to get him to pet her. So much for the dog helping to ease the tension. "Right now I'd like to talk."

She smiled at that. "Okay."

Ty sipped at the stew and groaned. "This is good."

"I thought you'd like it." She refrained from mentioning an acquitted poisoner had prepared it. Birdie grumbled at Ty's lack of attention and left to lay across a heating grate in the floor.

"I tried to connect to the grid on this ship," he said between slurps. "But they have an insane firewall. Do you know the password?"

Auri blinked. She didn't. She'd been able to access the grid on Delfan and hadn't wanted or needed to access it again. No need to look at all the unread pings from the GIC. At least she wouldn't have to lie to Ty about that. She doubted Malachi wanted him to be able to contact anyone. The thought of the captain and what he'd said to her minutes before made her temper flare. She took a slow breath, focusing on Ty.

"I don't know the password. Sorry." She watched him drain the contents of the bowl and set it aside. "Ty, why were you on Attica today?"

He shrugged. "I was just visiting."

She decided not to point out how odd that sounded. "How did you know about that staircase?"

"Really, Auri? Everyone knows about that."

She shook her head, suspicion worming in her gut. "It's a secret staircase."

"Way to be cliché."

"Ty, I'm serious. I was gone for over a week and you didn't even send me any pings."

"I wasn't worried. Besides, I was busy on a case." He stayed seated. His gaze flicked from her necklace, visible due to the dress's low neckline, and back to her face. "You know how hard it is to send pings while on a case past Krugel's—" He cut himself off with a sharp intake of breath followed by a wince. "Oh, wait. No. No, you don't."

Auri bit her cheek as his words hit home. Her stomach crawled its way into her throat. She turned away from him and started pacing, toying with the gladiolus pendant.

How had he known about the staircase? If everyone in the prison knew, there would've been guards stationed outside. And taking a public shuttle to Attica instead of a private one? Ty hated the inconvenience of public transportation. The only reason he would do that was if...

Was if he didn't want the GIC to know his destination.

She paused, looking down at her necklace. Malachi's words, just before she left his room, slithered through her mind. She didn't blame the ship's captain for not trusting Ty. Malachi didn't know him like she did. He didn't grow up with him. Ty cared about her. He'd given her a beautiful birthday gift. He'd—

Auri's fingers stilled on the pendant as another memory surfaced, buried amid the chaos of the prison escape. Marin's weak whisper. *Tracking.*

Cold swept through her veins in a relentless tide of sudden understanding. She dropped the pendant against her chest. Ty's birthday gift hadn't been a gift at all.

She whirled around to find him standing right behind her.

"Why did you give me a tracker!" she shouted, not caring if the rest of the crew heard. "Why did you give me this piece of *kuso* for my birthday?" She yanked off the necklace, snapping the chain. Anger sizzled along her nerves. Birdie let out a low growl at the sound of her raised voice. Tears blurred her organic eye, but she tilted her head back. She would not cry.

He stared at her a beat before laughing. "Oh, Aur. I knew what would happen. You'd botch your plan, end up lost and in trouble. Then the GIC would send out an emergency bulletin for high-ranking officials to bring you back."

"He didn't send a bulletin." Her voice was small, inconsequential in the light of Ty's confession. His absolute lack of confidence in her, in what she could do.

"He's about to." Ty sighed at the pained expression on her face. "This wasn't to hurt you. I wanted to be the one to bring you in, earn his respect." He looked around at the cargo hold, sliding his hands into his pockets. "Though the last thing I expected was for you to team up with criminals to break a prisoner out of Attica." He shrugged. "Two for one. When I get you back to the GIC, I'll report this ship's captain and they'll bring the entire crew in. Everyone will be sent right back to Attica. This time, there won't be a secret staircase."

Auri lunged at him, her shoulder connecting with his chest. Birdie leapt to her feet with a snarl. Ty hit the ground with an *oomph*.

"Stay, Birdie!" Auri commanded. This was her fight. She brought her fist back, aiming for Ty's face. He turned to the side just in time. Her robotic knuckles collided with the floor.

"Auri, *chikushou*! What are you—?"

This time her fist connected with his jaw. He grunted with pain, finally taking the fight seriously.

He caught her other fist, arm trembling with the effort.

She growled. "How dare you use me!"

He bucked, rolling her off. Her back hit the cold floor as Ty positioned himself above her. She tensed, but he didn't strike. He just stared down at her, a bemused smile on his rapidly bruising face.

Birdie whined, pacing back and forth. The dog clearly wanted to intervene, but also wanted to obey Auri's orders.

"It's okay, Birdie," Ty called.

"Yes," Auri agreed. "I can take care of this liar all by myself. Stay, Birdie." She glared up at Ty. "I hate you," she hissed.

"No you don't." He smirked, his split lip leaking blood. "You've been in love with me for years."

Shock reverberated through her veins. *He'd known the whole time?* But she pushed aside the emotion.

Auri used his own move on him, thrusting him off with her hips. Ty tried to counter the move, but she used the strength in her robotic leg as leverage. She leapt to her feet as he scrambled to his. Auri's fist darted out, but he dodged and barreled into her, shoving her backward into the pole he'd been tied to earlier. His body pressed hard against hers as he fumbled at a pants pocket, chest heaving with exertion. She jerked back, ready to headbutt him and knock him unconscious. Whatever Malachi did with him after that was fine with her.

Suddenly his lips were on hers. She gasped at the contact, her anger exploding into hunger. One of his hands knotted in her hair. The other slid over her cheeks, down her neck. She sighed against him, relaxing into his touch as his kisses intensified, the taste of sweat and blood sliding onto her tongue.

"Auri," he murmured. Something buzzed by her ear and she opened her eyes to look at the source of the sound.

Ty slammed an electrified wand into the base of her skull. Birdie howled. Her claws scraped on the floor as she darted forward. The world went black as Auri's cyborg machinery exploded with electricity—

"Forgive me," Ty whispered.

—and then shut down.

CΛPTΛIN'S LOG
Hachigatsu 27, 3319 at 0116

[Chair squeaks as a body drops into it]
We just lost one of our shuttles.
[Crackling silence]

Turns out I was right about Agent Tyson Peri. I'm not relishing that fact, especially not after Auri's arguments on his behalf. I thought she was going to punch me when I warned her and relayed a backup plan. She claimed she could handle Ty.

[Scrape of hand rubbing stubble]

Auri knows part of the plan. She knows we'll come for her. But I didn't tell her about the plan's holes. Predicting Bleeders' movements is next to impossible, but with this group still following us…

This just might work.

If I'm willing to pay the price.

CHΛPTER
THIRTY-ONE

30 Aug 3319, 11:16:33
Ancora Galaxy, Planet 03: Aurora, Moon: Harlequin,
The Spire, Floor 01: GIC Living Qtrs.

"I never imagined you were capable of this, Aurelia." The GIC leaned against the desk in his office on the Spire's first floor. Sunlight filtered through the wall of windows at his back, revealing rolling hills of grassland and wildflowers. His mouth formed a firm line as he stared at her. "A CO ended up in critical condition the day you broke that criminal out of Attica. Doctors reported it as a heart attack. Somehow I doubt it now. This behavior, I just... I can't believe it of you. Is what Tyson told me true?"

The sound of her betrayer's name widened the gaping wound in her chest. She'd woken up that morning, groggy and with a pounding headache, in an unfamiliar room. It only took minutes to realize Ty had kidnapped her, stolen a shuttle, and brought her to Aurora's moon, where she was now waking up—three days later. No doubt a tech doctor had needed to stabalize her cyborg systems after Ty's taser, Indie's taser and beating, and Marin's technological attack.

Then she'd received a ping—an order, really—from the GIC. Ty would arrive in thirty minutes to collect her. Failed efforts to send a message to Malachi or Katara told her the GIC had limited her connection to the grid to only receive messages from him like she was a grounded schoolgirl.

Now she sat in a hard-backed chair, being berated by the man she'd looked up to as father...

Once.

"Aurelia," the GIC snapped, using his command voice. "Attention!"

She shot to her feet, her body going rigid, obeying the word drilled into her at basic. "Sir."

"Is what Ty told me true? Did you break a volatile hacker out of Attica?"

Her shoulders threatened to curl inward. So Ty really hadn't spared any details to protect her. She could lie, but what was the point? Lieutenant Aki would place her at the scene.

"I did."

The GIC opened his mouth to speak but stopped as his eyes unfocused to read an incoming ping. When he looked back at her, he shook his head. "I don't have time for your insubordination." Though his tone was gruff, a flicker of pain, of fear even, shone in his eyes before he turned away. "We'll keep with our annual tradition. You will attend the military ball this evening to show that nothing is amiss."

She shook her head. "Amiss? The public shouldn't be concerned. Captain Ishida gave me leave."

"You had leave, yes." He sighed and turned to her. "But you left after a public mission that ended poorly. Before the investigation was complete. You would've been cleared for duty before this clusterf—" He cleared his throat, tugged on the hem of his fitted jacket. "You and Ty always accompany me to the Obon Festival on Rokuton. This year, you were absent. The press jumped at having something to report other than typical militia violence. Trouble is awakening across the galaxy, Aurelia. I need to show that I'm a strong leader and that I can keep my house in order."

"I was injured," she said, unable to bear the disappointment in his voice. "I meant to tell you I couldn't make the Festival, but I didn't have access to the grid."

"It's too late for excuses. Be at the ball. Your dress from last year has been delivered to your room."

Auri's hands clenched into fists. She wanted to argue with him, force him to look at her. *Really* look at her. How would he react if she spat the question, "Why are you covering up Bleeder attacks?"

The words hovered at the tip of her tongue, ready to shoot from her mouth. To soar through the air as a barrage of laser artillery.

She swallowed them back, relaxed her hands. Hurling that question at the GIC wouldn't lead to anything. There were other options. Auri still had choices.

So she bowed, mumbling, "Yes, sir. I'll be there." Then she fled the office, hurrying past the secretary outside and through the final door. Her fingers trembled as she slid it shut. She turned around, startled to find Ty standing there, waiting.

His face brought her back to seeing him for the first time this morning after realizing his betrayal.

Shortly after receiving the GIC's summons, someone had knocked on her door. She stayed seated on her freshly made bed.

The door opened and Ty stepped inside, smiling so bright it lit up the room. It had been the happiest she'd ever seen him. He wore a fresh DISC agent uniform, his shoulders erect. He strode in with a new level of confidence.

Questions pounded through her head, her bleary mind refusing to accept that Ty had deceived her.

"Hey," he said, stopping a meter away. "The GIC wants to see you." Ty acted as if nothing had changed between them, as if Auri's heart wasn't broken into irreparable shards.

Auri's lips burned with his phantom kisses as she glared at him. "What did you do, Ty?" she asked, voice hoarse with suppressed emotion.

"I brought you back. Birdie too, in case you were worried. I had to taser her—she was inconsolable after what happened. The mutt actually bit me. She's in a kennel."

Good dog, Auri thought even while her insides felt hollow. It was as if someone had reached in and scooped out her bones. "You kissed me, knocked me unconscious, and kidnapped me. How did you even manage to hide that taser from Castor?"

"I did what I had to. As for Castor, he wasn't as thorough as he should have been. Too distracted by that other woman." His gaze found her lips before returning to her eyes. His voice softened ever so slightly. "I enjoyed our kiss."

She had, too, until the overwhelming fear of feeling her heart stop and her body go limp around her ruined it. Auri never wanted to kiss Ty again.

Yet she also wanted to drag him to her, to get lost in the feeling of having someone close.

She looked down at her traditional wooden *geta* and socks. "What did you get in exchange for bringing me here?"

"The GIC invited me to the military ball as his guest of honor."

Her head jerked up. Ty beamed. The GIC's guest would be considered an accomplished individual, usually promoted months after the ball, regardless of current rank.

The GIC hadn't invited anyone in years.

"Come on." He sat beside her. Auri scooted away, blinking fast to keep her emotions in check. "Don't be mad. You belong here."

"I'm not sure I do."

That made him laugh. "So you think you belong with criminals DISC agents will hunt down after tonight's ball?"

Cold shot through her. "You really told the GIC about them?"

"Of course I did. They're *criminals*, Aur. Not so long ago you wouldn't have hesitated to report them."

"You don't understand what's going on, the secrets the GIC's keeping."

His brows rose. "What secrets?"

Auri faltered. He'd betrayed her, tricked her into thinking he cared for her. But maybe, just maybe, he would believe this. She needed to try.

"There are cannibals, called Bleeders, roaming the galaxy. They're these humanoid monsters. Incredibly strong and violent. They've mostly been attacking districts on the rim, a few on Kaido, but the Fed…" She trailed off at the grin growing on Ty's face. She clenched her hands into fists. "I'm serious! I was almost killed by them. They were even tailing the *Kestrel*. My first case with Tanaka Hiroki—"

"Now you just sound stupid. Enough, Aur." He stood and offered a hand. "You're already late for your meeting with the GIC."

She crossed her arms. "I'm not going anywhere with you."

"You don't have a choice."

The worst part of all? He was right. She'd gone with him after he threatened to call in the guards.

And now he stood in front of her, yet again.

"Am I going to be escorted everywhere now?" she asked, rubbing at her forehead.

"Trust me, I'd much rather be on assignment than following you around. Orders are orders though. Let's get back to your room." He led her along a different route than before. They took a sharp right turn and approached a row of kennels built into a wall. Each cage reached up to Auri's hip and was wide and spacious, located in a low traffic section of the Spire. Her heartbeat quickened.

The first two sat empty, but in the last kennel stood Birdie, her tail wagging at the sight of Auri. The dog's tongue flopped out the side of her mouth as she panted. Birdie hated being locked in crates, probably because Auri rarely put her in one. At the sight of Ty, Birdie's tail stilled. A low growl rumbled in her chest. To Auri's satisfaction, Ty shifted back a step.

Auri fell to her knees in front of Birdie's cage, poking her fingers through the bars. "Hey, Bird," she cooed. "I missed you."

Birdie whined, licking at Auri's fingers. She pawed at the cage door.

Auri looked up at Ty. "Can I…?"

He shook his head. "It's important for you to obey the rules. No dogs in your room." Birdie bared her teeth at the sound of Ty's voice. She snapped at him, making her opinion of him known. The way Ty flinched made Auri preen with satisfaction. If they got out of this, she would give Birdie the biggest bone she could find.

"It's important for me to obey the rules?" Auri stood. "Why? Because you care if I get dishonorably discharged?"

His gaze dropped to his boots. "Honestly, Aur? I'm having a hard time deciding how I feel about you. I've hated you for so long, but after that kiss, I don't know."

"You… you hated me?" A chasm yawned out at her feet. "Why?"

He glanced over his shoulder, as if checking to ensure they were alone. When he looked back at her, he didn't meet her eyes. "Did you know, just before the GIC brought you home, that my mom died?"

"I… No. I didn't." She'd heard Ty's mother passed away in an accident when he was young, but that her death coincided so closely to Auri's arrival? No one ever mentioned it.

"Not only that, but after the shuttle accident, when she lay dying in the hospital bed, my father—*the GIC*—refused to come home. Do you want to know why?"

She didn't want to know. Yet she asked, "Why?"

"Because he was with *you*." He spat the final word and for the first time, Auri got a glimpse at the hatred festering within.

The tarry, seething creature peered at her behind Ty's eyes. "You were undergoing surgeries of your own. He didn't know if you'd survive. So I said goodbye to my mom, alone. I went to her funeral, alone. You know what's even better?"

She remained silent until he continued.

"When the GIC brought you home, all his attention turned to you. He ignored me, even though my mom, his wife, had just died." He pointed an accusing finger at her, so close it almost stabbed into her chest, just above her heart. "You became more important, and I hated you for it. I tried to hurt you in whatever way I could, but I eventually learned that being friends with you gave me the most leverage."

Suppressed memories of Ty terrorizing her the first year she lived with the GIC resurfaced. The bugs she'd find in her room, the time he'd cut her hair with scissors, put tacks in her shoes at school. She'd tucked all of those hurts away after the day he walked up to her at recess when she'd been sitting alone and said, "You can play with me."

"I didn't know," she said. "Ty, I'm sorry." The words left her lips before she realized their meaning. Why was she apologizing for the way he had treated her?

Auri stared at Ty, struggling to match his confession to the boy, the man she loved. He'd spent more than half his life despising her. He'd been her friend only to hurt her.

"Aur... I... I didn't hate you the whole time. Just so you know." An edge of guilt softened his tone. "It's complicated." He looked as if he wanted to say more but shook his head instead. "We better get you back."

She pressed a kiss to the tip of Birdie's wet nose to hide the tears building in her eye. Her skin felt too tight. A mad desire to tear free of her body shot through her. To fly up, up, and up. To forget Ty. To forget his lies. To forget how much, how desperately, she loved him.

Auri straightened and allowed him to lead her away.

Outside her door, she paused. She studied the floor as she asked, "Why are you being so honest now?"

"Something changed when I kissed you. I realized that I might actually care."

She couldn't help but ask, "Did you want me to fall in love with you?"

"I did. I just never expected to start feeling something for you." He laughed, the sound tight and choked. "When it comes to you, my emotions have never been simple." He leaned forward, as if he was about to kiss her. She closed her eyes, unsure if she wanted him to or not. Instead he whispered in her ear, "Do you still want me, Aur?"

She stayed frozen in place, eyes closed. "Apologize," she breathed. "I'll forgive you." And she would. She knew she would.

"You love too freely and forgive too easily. It's a weakness."

She opened her eyes to see his frown. "It also makes me strong."

"It depends on what you consider strength." He offered her a lazy man's salute. "See you at the ball."

She slipped inside her room. The tumblers clicked as Ty locked the door behind her.

CHAPTER THIRTY-TWO

---

30 Aug 3319, 18:21:05
Ancora Galaxy, Planet 03: Aurora, Moon: Harlequin,
The Spire, Floor 01: Visitor Barracks 3D

Auri changed into the altered *kimono* hanging in her closet. The exterior fabric was a smooth mesh with curlicues of gold and floral accents. The inner lining was a pink silk that was held in place by a long band around her middle. She twisted her red hair and secured it to her head by a few pins.

Then she stared at her reflection, not really seeing it.

Just one level below her feet waited the answers to all her questions. Courtesy of Tsuna, she even had access to the vault, the Ancora Galaxy's central data warehouse. What the Bleeders were, where they came from—it would all be there, if Malachi's suspicions were right. If they weren't...

The thought made her stomach clench. How would she even get into the vault now? She didn't have the *Kestrel*'s crew to help break inside.

Something flickered at the back of her mind. A memory begging to be brought to the surface. But as she focused on the thought, it flitted away. Whatever the memory was, it didn't matter. Auri was alone, again.

She sighed, blinking her reflection into focus. After wearing Ty's necklace for so long, her chest felt bare. She ran her fingertips across the smooth skin, sliding past the low-cut collar of her dress. The edges of it barely hid her scars. Last year she'd taped the fabric against her, terrified it might slip during the ball.

Not this time.

The marks were hard ridges against her fingertips. Compared to the simple beauty of her dress, they were hideous. They didn't belong in this perfectly crafted world—

And not just her scars.

"You don't belong here," she murmured to the lonely girl in the mirror. "You've never belonged."

She scooped up an object resting on the bathroom vanity. She'd saved it from a pocket of the dress she'd worn on the *Kestrel*. The flower earring glistened in the light. She ran her thumb across it. This earring was part of her; going anywhere without it felt wrong. It was her link to a past that she longed to remember.

Auri leaned close to her reflection and unscrewed the leaf. With a deep breath, she stabbed the backing into the synthetic skin on her earlobe once, then twice. She didn't feel any pain. There wasn't any blood. Up close, Auri could see the seam, the barely noticeable mismatch of color between the real and fake skin. She threaded the chain through and then slid the leaf on. The flower swayed, dancing back and forth.

A knock on her door made her turn from the mirror. Probably Ty ready to escort her to the ball. Even now, she failed to suppress the thought she had every year: *Will he think I'm pretty?*

She gritted her teeth against the flutter in her chest. How could she still care for, still want, someone like him? When he had done such terrible things to her?

She opened the door, a dismissal on her lips.

Ferris Quark, the *Kestrel*'s doctor, stood outside. His blond hair had been gelled against his head, beard brushed just so. Usually one for vests and fitted shirts, tonight he'd dressed in a dark green suit with gold accents. The badge on his chest marked him as an MPB Bodyguard.

"Ferris?" she murmured, hazy memories of the night she'd been abducted by Ty starting to clear. Damn all tasers. "What are you doing here? Are you... Are you supposed to be here?"

He smirked, arching a brow in a way that one would think flirtatious if Auri didn't know of his obvious devotion to Katara. "Expecting Cai, were you?"

She rubbed at her throbbing temples. "Not even him."

She'd completely forgotten her argument with the *Kestrel*'s captain, and the tasers hadn't helped. It felt like a lifetime had passed since he warned her that Ty might try to take her back to Harlequin. He'd relayed one of his simple plans. Despite Auri's continued protests that they wouldn't need it, he made her repeat the plan back to him. Ferris showing up—Malachi had promised someone from the crew would find her—was just step one of the captain's Plan B.

Staring at Ferris, Auri was once again in awe of Malachi Vermillion. She had the nagging suspicion it wouldn't be the last time either.

"You look beautiful." Ferris's voice drew Auri's attention. "Pink suits you."

She smiled. "Thanks. But what are you doing here? I thought I would meet one of you in the ballroom."

"The GIC posted an opening for a bodyguard. Malachi took advantage. Tsuna hacked my name into the position since Ty never got a close look at me. His loss, of course. My *supervisor* has given me strict orders not to let you out of my sight." He winked.

Ferris's teasing eased the sting of the bodyguard news. But only slightly. The GIC hadn't hired a guard for her protection. He praised the security of his main office often enough at their weekly lunches. The bodyguard was meant to keep her from escaping. The GIC would probably never trust Auri again. Their relationship was broken beyond repair. The realization stole her breath.

Deal with it later, she told herself.

Auri tucked her pain over Ty and the GIC away. Right now, she had a strategy and she had Ferris, with Malachi and Tsuna waiting just a few floors above.

"Well, bodyguard," she said. "Are you ready to go?"

Instead of answering, Ferris gestured to the hallway in a sweeping movement that would've made Katara snort. Auri shut the door behind her and walked away, the doctor chatting amiably at her side.

CHΛPTER
THIRTY-THREE

Ferris and Auri huddled in the corner of a crowded elevator. Some partygoers recognized her and gave a nod or a smile out of respect for the GIC, but most avoided eye contact. Instrumental music played and level after level passed beyond the clear glass walls.

The elevator slid to a stop and the doors opened onto an enormous ballroom. To their left and right other guests exited from two other elevators. Floors hewn from crystal caught the light from the numerous chandeliers hung at regular intervals throughout the room. Reinforced glass comprised the ceiling, coming to a sharp point in the center.

Although Auri had spent countless boring hours at military balls over the years, she always found herself awed by the beauty of the Spire's top level.

Couples twirled to music, some in fancy attire and others in their dress uniforms. The perfectly arranged buffet table scented the air with the aroma of sweet and savory delicacies. It was located across one glass wall, overlooking a dark sky, courtesy of the early sunset. Servers dressed in white suits and black ties swept about the room, trays balanced on gloved hands.

On the far side of the ballroom, round tables with pristine white tablecloths waited for anyone interested in sitting. Auri had spent hours people-watching from those tables. One year, when they were twelve and eleven respectively, Ty convinced Auri to climb under one with him and have a picnic.

The memory was a razor against her skin. She jerked her gaze away before her mind could examine the memory, twist it, and uncover Ty's selfish machinations even then.

"What next?" she asked as the two of them settled into a corner of the room, opposite the buffet table.

"Cai said he'd find us," Ferris said, scoping out the food.

"But h—" She cut herself off. Weaving through men and women meters away, wearing a server's uniform, was Malachi Vermillion.

"No way," she breathed. Malachi paused as a woman took a skewer of meat from his tray. Seeing him here, surrounded by people who wouldn't hesitate to have him arrested, should've unnerved her. But her mind looped over that night in his room, his fingers curled around hers. His confession. The nightmares of his past.

Malachi approached a few minutes later. "Everyone good?" he asked.

Ferris gave a quick nod. "We're ready when you are." He grabbed an appetizer off Malachi's tray, which earned a scowl. Ferris shrugged and popped the seasoned steak into his mouth.

The captain turned to Auri. "Listen carefully because I only have time to say the plan once. In a few minutes, we're going to slip out of here with Tsuna." At Auri's confused look, he murmured, "The table at eight o'clock."

Across the room where Malachi indicated, a willowy woman draped herself over the arm of an Air Command officer. She wore a slinky black dress, her hair twisted into hundreds of tiny braids that danced across her shoulders. The glamorous make-up gave Auri pause, but after a moment of scrutiny, she realized the woman was indeed Tsuna. The hacker looked at Auri and smiled, easing off the man to excuse herself. Instead of coming over, she sauntered toward the buffet table, took a small square of cake between thumb and forefinger, and disappeared into the crowd.

"After we leave with Tsuna," Malachi continued, "we'll head down to the vault."

"What about the guards?" Auri asked.

"They won't bother us."

"Why?"

"Don't worry about it." Malachi brushed off her question with a shake of his head. "Once we're by the vault, we'll use Auri's barcode to gain access. Tsuna should be able to get the information stored onto a floppy. Then we'll hop on the ship where everyone else…"

Auri's gaze locked with Ty's across the room where he stood at the GIC's side. He looked painfully handsome in his dress uniform, the buttons down his coat gleaming. His brow furrowed as he shifted to get a better look at Auri.

No, not at Auri. At the server. At Malachi.

Kuso. "Malachi," she hissed. "We need to go. Now."

He started to turn to follow Auri's stare, but she caught his shoulder. "Don't. It's Ty."

Ty frowned, and Auri jerked her hand away from Malachi. The GIC's son strode forward, weaving through the crowd. Auri winced. He had seen her reach out to touch the server—to touch Malachi. Even if Ty hated her, he knew she never casually touched someone like that.

"He's headed this way," she said, heart racing. She hiked up the hem of her dress to run.

"Stay calm, Aurelia," Malachi murmured, shifting his tray. "We don't want to make a scene."

"Elevator?" Ferris suggested.

Malachi shook his head. Auri watched his mind work at the problem. He frowned at the glass ceiling. "West stairwell. Just got a ping. Tsuna is waiting for us. This way." He jerked his head in the direction of the buffet table and the door to the closest of two stairwells that led to the lower levels of the Spire. People subconsciously parted for him, the server uniform clearing the way. They'd just broken through the last of the crowd, the door to the stairs in sight, when a hand clamped around Auri's wrist.

She whirled around. Ty held onto her, his face flushed.

Explosions suddenly burst in the sky above, drawing everyone's attention. Someone nearby murmured excitedly, "Were there supposed to be fireworks?"

Then the broken front of a defense drone hurtled past the Spire. Everyone gasped. The heads of all the high-ranking officers in the room jerked down, eyes losing focus as if they'd all received an urgent ping. A second later a proximity alarm sounded throughout the room. Something had broken through the moon's automated security system. The orchestra ceased playing as red lights flashed, reflecting off the floor, walls, and ceiling.

"What's going on?" Ty asked, his grip loosening.

She opened her mouth to speak, to say she had no idea, but a blinding light shone through the glass above. Ty released her, shielding his eyes. Auri stumbled back, knocking into Malachi.

The room filled with shouts and cries of surprise. Auri squinted through the light, and her less sensitive cyborg eye recognized the details of a familiar ship.

A Komodo Class.

She had an instant jolt of sheer terror before something yanked her backward. The ceiling exploded in a rain of lethal glass.

CHAPTER THIRTY-FOUR

---

30 Aug 3319, 19:02:03
Ancora Galaxy, Planet 03: Aurora, Moon: Harlequin,
The Spire, Level 15: Ballroom

Screams filled the silence left behind by the destruction above. Auri opened her eyes, expecting to see her dress stained with blood. Malachi lay half atop her, half on the floor. He had shoved her under the buffet table at the last second. Ferris huddled there as well, eyes wide as he lifted the edge of the tablecloth. His intake of breath made Auri shove Malachi off to see the source of Ferris's surprise. Malachi slid away, not bothering to look for himself.

The ballroom was a sea of bodies. Some staggered to their feet, others moaned and thrashed; a few didn't move at all. Auri sought out Ty in a panic. He wiggled out from under the body of a man with a glass shard impaling his chest. The stranger's blood smeared Ty's face, and she swallowed against the acrid tang in her mouth.

The Komodo Class ship hovered in place above the ceiling. Its searchlight provided the only source of illumination in the destroyed ballroom.

"Bleeders," she wheezed. "Bleeders are here."

As if her words had summoned them, a hatch opened at the bottom of the ship. Massive bodies leapt out, landing on the floor and straightening easily, as if the ten-meter jump was only a few centimeters. Their muscled limbs, stained clothing, and bloody faces made the partygoers freeze.

Then a man screamed.

The sound seemed to release everyone from the spell of shock. People stumbled to their feet, running or limping for the elevators. A few Bleeders charged after them, jaws spread overly wide, matted hair streaming behind them. They howled in pleasure, noses sniffing as they chose targets. Some dropped to the floor to sink their teeth into the prone forms of those already dead.

The majority of the monsters froze in place, their heads tilted as they smelled the air. Auri shifted to slide back under the table. A shard of glass caught her organic skin. It sliced a deep gouge down her palm. She hissed in pain.

The waiting Bleeders' heads spun in her direction. They snarled.

"*Chikushou.*" Malachi hauled her out from under the table, Ferris at his back. "We need to get out of here."

They ran for the door to the stairs. Malachi yanked it open and they all stumbled into the stairwell, the Bleeders howling as they took chase. Tsuna stood on the other side, her eyes wide.

"What ha—?" she started, until she saw the expression on Malachi's face.

She activated the magnetic lock on the door as a massive force slammed into it from the outside. "The lock won't hold against that," Tsuna gasped. The door shook again, the metal bulging in the center.

"Run!" Malachi yelled.

They didn't need to be told twice.

Auri's heart thrummed in her ears, the beat pulsing in her stinging wound. She kept thinking of Ty, of the GIC, of all the other guests trapped up there. Tears burned her eye. She should've stayed. She should've done something. But she didn't have a weapon, not even her disc. The rules of the military ball banned weapons; everyone would be defenseless.

"You're lucky I stole a key from my date," Tsuna panted as they ran past the eighth floor. "Or whatever is following us would have made us dinner by now."

"They're Bleeders," Malachi replied, his tone dark. "And I think they're after Auri."

Auri was too numb to feel surprise at Malachi's revelation.

"Why?" Ferris huffed behind them.

Another bang sounded on the sealed door behind them. The squeal of hinges buckling echoed down the stairwell. They doubled their pace.

"I don't know," Malachi answered. "But they followed us all the way from Medea and the only thing they haven't seen before..." He glanced at her running beside him, his face shining with sweat. "Is you."

Auri nearly slipped on the next step, courtesy of her too-long hem and soft shoes. Her frantic breaths strained the fabric around her chest.

They reached the second floor as a cacophony of growls echoed from the upper levels.

"The Bleeders made it through the door," Ferris panted.

"Once we get to the basement," Malachi rasped, "don't stop running. Follow me to the vault. The guards will be responding to the attack in the ballroom. We can seal ourselves inside if we have to."

They reached the first-floor landing. Muffled frantic barking penetrated the stairwell door. Auri froze, Tsuna nearly plowing her over. She knew that bark.

Birdie.

She sprinted back up the few steps she'd run down and grabbed the door handle. "I'll meet you in the basement," she cried, flinging it open.

266 · EMILY LAYNE

"Auri, what're you—?" Malachi sounded exasperated.

"Birdie!" She tore into the hall. Auri kicked off her shoes as she ran. The hallway was eerily empty, Birdie's cries the only sound.

Auri skidded to a stop at the kennels at the far end of the hall, where she and Ty had entered earlier that day. "Shh, shh," she cooed as Birdie's howls quieted into a whimper. The dog trembled, jaws parting in a yawn. "I'm here, Bird. I'm here." Her shaking fingers scrambled for the two latches. She cursed and reached for them with her robotic hand instead. She undid the first, kneeling to do the second when the sound of footsteps made her freeze.

At the end of the hall by the stairs stood a Bleeder, the same male from the FOB on Medea. His mouth split in a too-wide smile. Blood trickled from his back molars, sliding over his lower lip.

Bile rose in Auri's throat and a hazy memory lurked at the back of her mind like a word almost remembered. She stood slowly, taking a step back. Her hands ached for a weapon to curl around, to wield against the creature. She glanced over her shoulder and froze.

Another Bleeder waited at the opposite end of the hallway, much closer to her. This one was female, her dress in tatters, a flash of mottled white thigh exposed from a slash in the fur-lined blue fabric.

If there were two Bleeders, more would follow.

Auri's heart thudded in her ears as the creatures sniffed the air. A rasping laugh came from the female as she stepped forward. Her brown hair was tangled in a thick braid down her back, the strands coated with oil and dried blood. The stench of curdled meat and stale sweat festered in the narrow space. Auri gagged.

Birdie snarled in the cage, her tail tucked between her legs. Auri's hands tightened into fists. She'd have to get past one of the Bleeders—but which one? How would she without a weapon?

The monsters crept toward her like wolves taunting wounded prey. Except unlike wolves, the Bleeders didn't have fangs. Their teeth were entirely human. Which meant their assault would be more painful, her death slower.

Auri tensed and her toes curled against the cold floor. She didn't regret coming back for Birdie. No matter what happened, she wouldn't regret it.

Ty barreled out of the staircase and skidded to a halt meters behind the male Bleeder. A fresh gash at his temple seeped bright red, staining the white collar of his dress uniform. Relief made Auri weak, but she didn't call his name.

His wide eyes met hers.

Help me, she pleaded with her gaze. *Help me*.

She wouldn't say the words aloud. She didn't want the Bleeders to go after Ty. Not even when he stepped back, shaking his head.

Not even when he ran in the other direction, abandoning her.

She choked on a sob and glanced back just as the female Bleeder lunged, too-long nails like gnarled claws.

Auri dodged. Her back hit the wall opposite the kennels as the two Bleeders closed in. Birdie swiped at the cage with her paws, shoving her head against the partially open door. She barked, her hair standing up in a thick ridge.

The two Bleeders converged, almost blocking Auri's view of Birdie's struggle.

"Please," she whispered to them, wondering if they could even understand. "Please let me go."

The female snarled, taking a step closer. Movement by her left ear caught Auri's gaze—a flower pendant with a leaf backing swung at the creature's ear. A twin to Auri's own earring.

Ringing blared in Auri's mind, her vision blurring as the scent of lilacs filled her nose.

"I love you," a woman sobbed, lips brushing Auri's temple.

Pain was a haze around her. Auri reached for the voice with bloody fingers.

"No!" she tried to say. "Don't leave me!" Metal pressed against her back and tight against her side. A coffin. A prison. She didn't want to be alone. "Don't leave me!" Auri reached out, fingertips catching fine metal chains.

Auri's vision cleared as the two Bleeders pounced, their lips spread, their mouths bloody pits of blackened teeth and half-digested flesh.

CHAPTER
THIRTY-FIVE

---

30 Aug 3319, 19:02:03
Ancora Galaxy, Planet 03: Aurora, Moon: Harlequin,
The Spire, Level 01: Kennels

Birdie pawed the bottom lock open and shot from the cage, sinking her jaws into the female Bleeder's shoulder. Auri leapt away from the male's attack, bare feet skidding on the floor. She pushed off the wall with one hand, dodging a blow from his gnarled fist.

A huge crash echoed behind her, and Auri pivoted to see Birdie slumped atop the row of kennels.

"Birdie!" Auri shouted as the dog rose, whimpering. The female Bleeder stalked toward the poodle.

"Aurelia!"

She whirled at Malachi's voice. Her disc spun through the air. She reached up automatically to catch it, and her fingers curled around the handle. Renewed strength and hope rippled through her, fueling her anger, her desperation. She threw herself at the female Bleeder, disc voltage on high and the lightning edge crackling.

The male Bleeder reached for her, but gunfire echoed through the hall. Bullet after bullet lodged in the creature's chest until it staggered against the wall, leaving a smear of blood against the white paint.

Auri blocked the female monster's claws as they slashed at Birdie, then drove the disc into the Bleeder's neck. The monster screamed as the lightning shot through her. She stumbled back, snarling as she grabbed the sides of her head and fell to one knee.

"Come on, Birdie!" Auri shouted.

Birdie bounded down from the kennels, her rear leg curled up so as not to take any weight. They started running toward Malachi. He had a gun raised, his belt of weapons looped over a shoulder.

"Get down!" he shouted.

Auri dove to the side as he loosed a bullet into the springing female Bleeder. The Bleeder's chest exploded in a splatter of blood, but she didn't stop. Auri brought her disc up as the monster slammed into her. Her back hit the floor, the full weight of the Bleeder crushing her lungs.

Auri activated her lightning barrier again. The Bleeder slumped atop of her with a hiss of putrid breath. The sheer weight of the creature sent the air rushing out of Auri's lungs. She fought to breathe as the disc sent a warning to her c-tacts.

Battery 0%. Disc Charging.

Suddenly the Bleeder's head jerked up, returning to alertness. Her nails raked Auri's side, slicing through the silk *kimono* and the skin beneath. The monster licked her black nails, pupils dilating in pleasure. The female twisted to bring her jaws down on Auri's exposed shoulder.

Something slammed into the Bleeder, and together, the two forms rolled across the floor. Malachi landed on top, gun aimed at the Bleeder's forehead. The Bleeder reared up, jaw extending, teeth snapping. Malachi fired. Again and again. He screamed as he pulled the trigger until the chamber emptied.

The male Bleeder stirred from where it had slumped against the wall. His blood-shot eyes locked on Auri. She watched the wounds in his chest knit closed.

"*Chikushou*," she whispered. She pushed to her feet as the Bleeder stumbled toward her, gaining mobility as he ran. She switched arms so her robotic hand gripped the disc. She activated the serrated blades.

Auri screamed as she rushed to meet the creature, her muscles tensed, sweat dripping into her eyes. She hurled the disc with all the strength in her robotic arm. It spun through the air, light dancing off the lethal edge.

The Bleeder didn't have time to dodge before the disc sliced through tendon and muscle. The monster's head toppled off and hit the floor, the body following seconds later. Auri's disc caught in the wall with a loud *thunk*. Blood spurted from the decapitated Bleeder, staining the floor. The male's and female's ichor merged into a crimson pool.

Auri's momentary relief shattered as guttural growls and footsteps echoed down the hall in the direction Ty had come from earlier. They weren't safe. Not yet.

"Malachi," Auri rasped, running for him. He still hunched over the dead Bleeder, body trembling. She grabbed his shoulder.

In an instant, a gun was pressed against her forehead. Heat emanated from the metal. Her skin flushed with panic despite the knowledge the chamber was empty. Malachi's eyes were wide, his gaze unfocused.

Auri raised a hand slowly, aware of the approaching Bleeders but afraid of spooking the captain. She gripped the barrel of the gun and slowly lowered it.

"Peter," she whispered. "You are safe. You are on Harlequin."

Malachi trembled, the name seeming to bring him back to himself. He dropped the gun. It clattered against the floor.

"Auri," he breathed. He glanced from her to the dead Bleeder. "The earring." His brows furrowed. "Your earring."

She shook her head. "We need to go."

"Wait." He looped a fist over the Bleeder's earring and tore it free. Fresh blood trickled over his fingers. Auri's stomach twisted as he handed the trinket to her. She slipped it into an inner pocket of the *kimono*, not looking at the slashes in her dress and side.

"Come on." She yanked him to his feet. "More are coming. We need to reach the vault." She tugged her disc free from the wall with her stronger robotic arm. Plaster fell in crumbles at her feet.

He nodded, his usual take-charge attitude returning. "This way."

They ran for the stairwell, Birdie keeping pace despite her injured leg. The door slammed behind them as a horde of six Bleeders turned into the hallway.

"Where did you get my disc?" she asked as they pounded down step after step.

"I brought a small weapons cache with me and I stopped to grab it before I followed you. Sorry it took so long."

"Thanks for coming back."

Malachi led her into the warehouse-styled basement. The walls, floors, and ceiling were all made of hard concrete, offering little light except for the inset bulbs in the floor that illuminated their immediate path to the vault. Cold and full of shadows, just how Auri remembered it. But now was no time to reminisce, not with the Bleeders racing after them.

After her.

At the far end of the lit-up path, two figures waved. Tsuna had knotted her dress at her hip, exposing muscled legs. Ferris had abandoned his jacket, sleeves shoved above his elbows.

The stairwell door banged open behind them. A glance over her shoulder cost Auri speed. Bleeders tore into the basement, just vague outlines of shadow and unsatiable hunger.

"Hurry!" Tsuna screamed. She pointed at the scanner positioned at the door.

Auri's heart thudded in her ears as she skidded to a stop under it. The wound in her side burned. This was the test of Tsuna's handiwork. If the barcode worked, they'd be safe. If not...

The light on the scanner glowed green. The doors slid open with a whoosh. They stumbled inside, the Bleeders meters away. Auri searched the inside of the vault for another scanner as Birdie whimpered beside her.

"There!" Ferris cried, pointing. She slid her arm underneath it.

A clawed hand darted through the gap. The doors slid closed, slicing through the skin. Blood dripped down the metal and oozed onto the floor. But the door, caught on the Bleeder's arm bone, didn't close. The scanner's light turned an angry red and an alarm began to sound.

CHAPTER THIRTY-SIX

---

30 Aug 3319, 19:34:01
Ancora Galaxy, Planet 03: Aurora, Moon: Harlequin,
The Spire, Level 00: The Vault

"Tsuna, can you do anything?" Malachi asked. His gaze was fixed on the exposed arm bone. It created a fist-sized gap between the Bleeder and indestructible safety. Auri could see the contorted faces of more monsters beyond the one stuck at the door, dirty fingers scrabbling and prying at the crack. Sparks began to shoot from the scanner fixed to the wall as the doors shuddered, unable to close.

Tsuna answered by vomiting.

"We could cut it off," Ferris suggested. "Anyone have a laser?" He looked from Malachi to Auri, who both shook their heads.

Auri hefted her disc, wondering if one swing could get enough momentum for the blades to sever the appendage. She'd be able to cut off the hand, but the arm still between the doors was a problem. She pushed down the nausea that accompanied the visual.

Tsuna straightened, wiping her mouth. "It won't matter." She pointed to the sparks still spraying from the scanner. "The mechanism is shorting out. It's just a matter of time before the door opens automatically."

Malachi cleared his throat, breaking the horrified silence. "We get the intel. Then we fight our way out. At least we don't have to worry about guards. In fact, maybe the alarm will bring some guards to help us fight *them*."

"Small comforts." Ferris frowned. "You doing okay?" He addressed Tsuna.

She nodded with a shiver. "This way." She rubbed her arms to warm them as she staggered through the vault, winding around the black server towers that ran from ceiling to floor.

Auri followed at the rear, mindful of Birdie's limp. The icy chill of the floor seeped into the exposed skin of her feet, but the sensation was a faraway distraction. This place had been sacred to her. As a child, she had replayed the memory of her adoption every night before she went to sleep. She'd told the story to any kid who would listen until their mothers or fathers quietly pulled them away, whispering warnings about cyborgs.

Little did her younger self know that a decade later, she'd break into this room. That she'd abandon the GIC in a ballroom filled with flesh-eating monsters.

That Ty would leave her to die.

All his talk of being confused over how he felt about her, his scarred childhood… It didn't matter. When the world went to *kuso*, he would leave her. He would always choose himself over her.

That didn't mean she stopped loving him. No sudden realization could change that. But she began to understand, in that moment, that her love had been built on a daydream. The Ty she loved was a lie.

And she was through with lies.

Auri slid her collapsed disc into the band around her waist, wincing as the movement shifted fabric over the wounds there.

Tsuna perched on a stool in front of the main panel. Her fingers dashed across keys and controls. The small screen in the center spat out a jumble of commands Auri couldn't comprehend.

Behind them, the door screeched and the Bleeders howled a victory. Auri glanced back to see hands squeezing through the gap and curling around the edge. Little by little the opening grew.

"What keywords are you looking for?" Tsuna asked Malachi without raising her head. Now that she was in her element, it seemed some of her raw panic had eased. Her fingers were steady on the keys.

He leaned over her, scrutinizing the screen. "Pull up everything they have on cannibalism, Bleeders, Peter Treatis, Roanleigh..." He glanced at Auri before turning back to the screen, his voice soft. "And Aurelia Peri."

Tsuna's brows rose, but her fingers continued to tap away.

Auri moved to stand beside him. "Why me? I have nothing to do with the Bleeders." She fingered the female's earring in her pocket through her dress, not wanting to think about it yet.

"It's just a hunch." He didn't look at her, scrutinizing the tiny screen as Tsuna loaded folder after folder.

"Got them," she breathed a few seconds later. She freed a floppy where it had been taped around her thigh and wirelessly synced it to the panel.

Everyone watched her in tense silence. A loading bar flashed into brightness on the floppy's clear screen.

Two percent... five percent... ten percent...

Tsuna brushed a renegade braid from her face. Her breaths came in heaving pants, and her gaze kept darting to the door. "There's a lot of intel, Cai. This could take a while." The Bleeders still struggled at the gap, arms now forcing it ever wider.

"Ferris, see if you can get Katara on a ping," Malachi ordered.

Ferris nodded and turned away. He covered one ear to drown out the clang of the alarm.

"Tsuna, can you pull up some files on the projector?" Malachi pointed to the enormous screen where Auri had seen her personnel file years ago. "Give me Auri's."

Rather than answer, Tsuna's fingers flew across the keyboard.

"Malachi, I don't want my personal…" Auri trailed off as a file popped onto the screen. The label read *Peri, Aurelia DOB 14.08.3272.*

"There must've been a typo. I wasn't born in 3272." She forced a laugh, looking from Malachi to Tsuna. "I just turned eighteen."

Malachi tapped the screen, opening the file. Auri knotted her fingers in Birdie's fur, suddenly afraid.

Medical files, her school records, her results in basic, and other reports compiled in a long list. Auri started to relax until Malachi scrolled down to a folder labeled *Roanleigh*. He tapped it open. The only file inside was a video clip. Malachi looked back at her.

She didn't meet his questioning gaze, just nodded.

He hit play.

The clip expanded across the enormous screen in perfect quality. Auri forgot about the Bleeders fighting to get inside. Her attention narrowed to the video. A logo on the bottom corner was from a space odyssey program Auri had watched as a kid. Men and women would explore the deepest reaches of the Ancora Galaxy with a camera crew and record their findings.

A man's face appeared, the bridge of a mid-sized shuttle behind him. Two other figures hovered at the corners, but they were blurred in the background. He looked to be in his mid-thirties, long black hair tied back in a bun, his face unshaven, eyes wide with excitement.

"As you guys know," the man's voice overpowered the blaring alarm emanating from the speakers, "we're out on the rim. Roanleigh has long been labeled the Toxic Planet due to a terraform malfunction before anyone settled there." He shoved his face into the camera, capturing each pore in high def. "We were orbiting the planet at 167 kilometers, the closest you can get without harmful radiation when we received a distress signal!"

The Bleeders at the door snarled in response to the man's shout.

The man in the vid leaned back, bringing the camera with him. "We talked it over"—he showed the rest of his crew, two women in jumpsuits—"and we're going to investigate." The camera clicked off.

For a few seconds, darkness filled the screen and Auri let out a breath. Maybe that file had been placed in her folder by mistake.

Audio filtered through the speakers first: steady beeping and panicked whispering. The camera focused on the man's face.

"*Chikushou*," the man hissed through his teeth. In place of his earlier excitement, the man's face had paled, wrinkles more pronounced, as if he'd aged twenty years off camera. He had changed out of a t-shirt into a fur-lined winter coat, a hat snug on his head.

"We found the source of the distress signal." He spun the camera around, revealing a steel-walled room, before the lens focused on a pod. It was about the size of a coffin, with a rounded cover made of glass. The glass had frosted over except in the small section where the crew had cleared away the ice. Nestled in the tube, eyes closed, skin almost translucent in the dim lighting, lay a young girl.

Terror clawed at Auri's chest, but she didn't look away. She couldn't even blink.

"It's a cryo-chamber," one of the women said as she knelt next to it, reading the display screen. Her breath fogged in the air. "It's been sending a distress signal the last thirty-two hours.

It's about to run out of emergency battery power." She looked up at the man, her green goggles giving her an alien look. "This little girl is in bad shape, Chief. We need to free her and get to a hospital on Medea. Fast."

The camera swung to the other woman, a fur hood drawn up around her face. "Mira," Chief asked. "Do you think you'll be able to keep her stable?"

Mira swallowed, leaning to peer into the cryo-chamber. "I'll try."

The cryo-chamber released a series of rapid beeps, a red light flashing beside its tiny keypad and display screen.

The other woman keyed in a command. The cryo-chamber hissed, the seals releasing with a groaning click. Liquid drained from the bottom, freezing almost immediately. Mist curled into the air, freed from the crack in the lid. The crew coughed as Mira leaned forward, a thermal blanket in her arms. The camera zoomed in on the girl.

The girl's red hair was damp around her face. One arm had been torn clean off and deep gouges marred the skin peeking through her thin pajama top. Resting atop her chest glistened a small flower earring.

CHAPTER
THIRTY-SEVEN

The clip ended, the screen turning black.

Auri stumbled backward, a whine building in her throat. She bumped into a server tower and rested her weight against it. The machine hummed with a reassuring warmth against her back.

"Auri?" Tsuna closed the video and twisted around in her seat. "Are you okay?"

A distant part of her brain registered that the gap in the vault's doors had widened enough for a Bleeder to shove its shoulders inside, showing fragments of the black warehouse beyond. She couldn't bring herself to care.

The girl, in that cryo-chamber…

Aurelia Peri had never been attacked by animals on Medea. She was found on Roanleigh. The GIC…

He had lied about everything.

She fell to her knees, head in her hands. Memories swarmed before her, all tarnished by the make-believe past the GIC created. Then there were the hallucinations she'd suffered ever since cornering Hiroki on the roof.

Who was she?

Malachi knelt in front of her, Birdie at his side.

"It's me," she rasped, looking up at him through bleary eyes. "Malachi, that girl is me."

"Auri, I—"

"I can't reach Katara," Ferris interrupted. "Or Castor and Marin. The tech in here must block the grid. A security protocol." He whirled on Tsuna. "Can you crack it?"

She nodded at the buckling door. "Not before they break through."

Malachi's jaw tightened. "What is the status of the floppy?" he asked, not turning away from Auri.

Many arms now forced their way through, claws scrabbling and scraping grooves into the metal. The snarls turned into howls of excitement and hunger. The door screeched opened wider. Chills raced across Auri's skin.

"Ninety-eight percent," Tsuna whimpered, eyes fixed on the claws. "Malachi, tell me you have a plan."

"Honestly?" He stood, holding out a hand for Auri. "I don't have a plan." He glanced over his shoulder at Ferris and Tsuna. "My plan fell apart when we barricaded ourselves in here." He looked to Auri. "Is there another way out?"

Auri knew that he knew there wasn't. But maybe the purpose of the question was to bring her back to herself. To give her clarity, make her mind work.

She shook her head, hysteria receding as the task before her demanded attention. "Only one entrance and exit."

Birdie's ears twitched as another Bleeder scratched at the door. The dog watched Auri with trusting eyes.

Auri's gaze shifted to Malachi's hand, still outstretched toward her. She reached out and took it, her fingers trembling against his. He tightened his grip.

She stood on her own strength, giving his palm a final squeeze before letting go. "We'll have to fight."

The floppy pinged just as a male Bleeder forced his upper body through, the door slicing into its broad shoulder. Yet he didn't pull back. Instead, the creature leaned into it, the edge cutting deeper even as the door opened wider. Others swarmed above him and between his legs, affording the group a view of gnashing teeth, bloodied eyes, and greasy hair. Tsuna grabbed the floppy. She retreated until a row of server towers separated her from the door.

"I could trigger the self-destruct." She gasped as one of the Bleeders started crawling through the spread legs of the one bracing the door. The male's frenzied stare landed on them. He roared, bloody spittle splattering from his lips. One of the others caught his legs and hauled him back. It seemed each wanted to have the first bite. "The electrical surge throughout the room might kill the Bleeders. But it would definitely kill us too."

"It's a good option." Malachi watched as the Bleeders redoubled their efforts at opening the door. "An instant death, compared to the slow death they will give us—"

The door slid halfway open as another creature wedged himself below the first. The first Bleeder screamed and shoved his arms apart until electricity crackled across the scanner and its flashing light died. The alarm cut off, and the silence rang in Auri's ears. Lights above flickered in an endless loop, giving the scene a strobe effect.

The door opened fully, and the Bleeders poured in.

"Tsuna—" Malachi cried. The hacker was already working the keyboard.

Auri tightened her grip on the disc, taking up a defensive position. Her mind whirled as she calculated what moves would preserve her disc's battery while also dealing sufficient damage to actually take down multiple creatures. Perhaps the blades were her best option; the Bleeders seemed to recover from even the highest voltage. Her heart was a deafening drum in her ears.

A massive shape hurtled through the basement beyond the vault, scraping against the ceiling before centering itself in the room. Auri had only a moment to recognize it as a transport vehicle before it crashed into the open doorway.

With a scream, Auri leapt back as plaster exploded and the transport crashed into server towers and Bleeders. Electricity crackled through the air. She slid to a stop against a toppled server as pain sparked along her spine. She shielded her eyes, squinting through the dust and debris to see the transport grind to a halt.

The stench of scorched flesh and lightning coated Auri's tongue. Bleeders lay crushed underneath the transport, some who had been hit by the ship still moving feebly around the edges of the room. The now-scratched emblem of the Ancora Federation painted along the sleek black side left no doubt to the transport's owner.

Auri gaped. How had the GIC's personal transport gotten down here?

Ferris coughed, waving dust from his face. "What just—" He was cut off as the hatch door slid open and Castor popped out. Birdie barked in recognition.

When his gaze landed on the group, he waved them over. "Get in!" he shouted. "Now!"

His words were like a race's starting gun, and they sprinted for the door, leaping inside as the first Bleeder staggered to its feet. Castor threw himself into the co-pilot's chair. Katara waited in the seat beside him. Once everyone was inside, he sealed the door with a sigh of relief.

Katara flipped switches with a blur of speed. The transport hummed as it powered up. At first it wobbled and the clank of debris tumbling off the roof pounded around them. Then with a jerk it rose into the air. Something caught against the hull. Then the left and right sides. Guttural screams pierced through the walls. Tsuna trembled and murmured frantic prayers under her breath.

"Hold on!" Katara cried. Everyone scrambled for handholds along the walls and ceiling. Katara grabbed the accelerator and punched it forward. The screech of claws scraping along the outside lasted half a heartbeat before the small ship shot through the broken door and into the room beyond.

The only sound in the transport was their combined ragged breathing. Katara flew as fast as the transport allowed, cutting to the left side of the massive basement, a darkened area Auri had never seen before.

Within seconds, the transport was hurtling through an empty hangar. Lights flicked on in the floor and ceiling as they tripped the motion sensors. Auri had a brief glimpse of the crumpled blast-proof doors. The protective drones outside lay in a scattered mess of robotic corpses on the paved roadway.

Then suddenly they were hurtling away from the Spire and through the night sky. Everyone seemed to heave a collective sigh of relief, bodies relaxing.

Auri lowered herself onto one of the metal benches lining the walls, reserved for the GIC's security. She could've claimed the cushioned recliners in the rear, seats she'd taken on the yearly visit to Aurora during Obon. But she didn't deserve that honor now. Auri was officially a renegade.

She peered out one of the tinted windows, searching for the Spire. The Fed had dubbed it a Great Wonder of the Ancora Galaxy. Even citizens on Aurora could see the glow of the Spire from thousands of klicks away. But beyond the windows was only blackness.

The transport broke atmo and Castor set it to autopilot, circling the gravitational pull of Harlequin. Both he and Katara unbuckled their belts and stood.

"Are you all right?" Castor asked Tsuna, his gaze searching her exposed skin for damage.

She nodded. Letting out a slow breath, she collapsed into one of the cushioned seats, and Castor hurried over to join her. They spoke in hushed voices, Tsuna letting out a sob she stifled with a hand. Castor pulled her close, shushing her while she cried.

"Well," Ferris said, raising his brows. "Who wants to hold me while I cry?"

"Don't joke," Katara snapped, striding up to him.

He raised his hands. "Kat, I—"

"I thought I lost you, you idiot." She caught his shirt in a fist and smashed her lips against his. Ferris let out a surprised gasp before his arms wrapped around her.

"Kat," he breathed against her lips, but she silenced him by deepening the kiss.

"Finally," Malachi muttered. "The tension was annoying."

Auri glanced at Malachi where he sat on a bench across from her. "What about your dislike for onboard romances?"

He offered her a shrug as if to say, *What can you do?* but his gaze was intense, face shadowed. Unlike the shrug, she didn't know what that look meant.

So she glanced away.

When Malachi cleared his throat seconds later, Katara and Ferris finally came up for air. The doctor beamed. Katara rolled her eyes at him, but her cheeks were flushed. He caught her hand and interlaced his fingers with hers, yanking her down onto Auri's bench.

Malachi stood in the center of the transport. He raised his brows at Castor. "What happened to the plan? To staying on the *Kestrel* until Ferris pinged Katara to pick us up? And where did you get this?" He gestured at the shuttle around them.

"I screwed the plan," Castor said, his arm still around Tsuna. The hacker wiped at her cheeks. "You had my wife in there and none of Katara's pings to Ferris went through after a certain point, I'm guessing once you entered the vault."

"Ex-wife," Tsuna muttered with a small sniffle.

Castor glanced down at her. A shadow of the fear he must've felt flickered in his eyes. "We were watching from atmo," he continued, turning back to Malachi. "Marin said that a

Bleeder ship was incoming. But it went right past us, headed for the Spire." Castor shivered, remembering.

"Marin is awake?" Auri asked, cutting into the explanation. "Is she okay?" The last time she had seen the girl, she'd been unconscious in the infirmary, the monitors connected to her whirring and beeping.

Castor nodded. "For the most part. Her arm…" He shook his head. "She's alive at least."

Katara leaned forward. "Whoever piloted the Komodo ship… *Whatever* piloted it, they knew what they were doing against those drones. We knew you'd need backup."

Malachi tilted his head. "You came to rescue me?"

"She obviously came to rescue me," Ferris interjected.

Katara rolled her eyes. "I came to rescue Tsuna and Little Warrior. I couldn't care less about the two of you." Contrary to her words, she gave Ferris's hand a squeeze. "Marin flew the *Kestrel* to the Spire's hangar. The guards had already deserted it, no doubt rushing toward the ballroom, so Castor and I commandeered the GIC's transport. Marin took the *Kestrel* far away from the action, and we came for you. Easy."

"You broke into the Spire's basement hangar," Auri said, running her fingers along Birdie's spine. "It had its own share of drones you destroyed. I wouldn't say it was easy. Even with the GIC's transport." Her tone was subdued. Though she addressed Katara, she stared down at her scraped toes, her mind splintering between the conversation in the present and the dark mysteries in her past.

"We wouldn't leave you behind," Katara said. She looked to Malachi. "Did you get what you needed?"

He nodded. "Tsuna?"

Tsuna tossed the folded-up floppy through the air. Malachi caught it and waved it at the gathered crew. "Everything we need is on here. When we get back to the *Kestrel*, I'll comb through the intel." When no one moved, he sighed. "Which means someone better pilot us back to my ship."

Katara and Castor entered a stare-off that Castor quickly lost. He grumbled under his breath and withdrew to the controls. In moments, the shuttle broke orbit and headed into free airspace.

Everyone else settled into their seats. Hushed conversation picked up between Tsuna and Katara as the women discussed what had gone wrong in the vault.

Malachi knelt before Auri, and Birdie growled in displeasure.

"You know," he began. "You and your dog are very similar."

"What do you mean?"

He smirked. "You both have terrible judgment when it comes to people." He sighed as he shifted to press his back against the wall next to her. On the opposite side of Birdie, Auri noticed. "Do you think she'll ever like me?"

"She liked Ty," Auri muttered.

"I never did, if that counts for anything."

Auri didn't answer, and he let silence settle between them. Finally, she whispered, "Malachi, who am I?"

He looked at her. "You're brave," he said. "You love people, even when you shouldn't, and you're so naïve."

Her lips twitched in a smile. "Listing my positive qualities and then saying negative ones doesn't help. Besides, that's not what I asked."

"It's exactly what you asked." He studied her as if she was the most beautiful, most radiant, most enrapturing creature he'd ever seen. "Aurelia Peri," he murmured as if he didn't want the others to hear. "You burn with the light of ten thousand suns." He swiped at a smudge of dust on her cheek. "And suns aren't concerned with their origin story. They're too busy lighting up the entire galaxy."

His words stopped Auri's breath. They even seemed to stop her heart. No one had ever said something like that to her.

"We will find out the truth," he said, voice soft. "I made you that vow. And we won't stop until we share that truth with the entire Federation." He offered her his hand, pinky finger raised. She expected him to roll his eyes or laugh, but his expression was grave, mouth a thin line.

Auri raised her own pinky. "We won't stop until the entire Federation knows the truth." She curled her finger around his, sealing the promise.

CHAPTER THIRTY-EIGHT

---

31 Aug 3319, 8:53:52
Ancora Galaxy, 2,000 klicks from Planet 04: Babbage

Auri's organic eye burned from lack of sleep and from staring too long at a bright screen. She blinked rapidly to moisten it.

Malachi hunkered on the low table beside her, cross-legged on a cushion. Like her, the captain refused to take a break despite the crew's prodding.

After Ferris treated Auri's and Birdie's wounds and the crew showered and changed, Tsuna was supplied a work space. She had set up a huge screen on the table outside the infirmary, connecting the floppy's files to it. Auri then laid the female Bleeder's earring on a corner. It winked up at her whenever she bumped it, catching the light. The jewelry fueled her, kept her mind alert when her body longed to sleep.

Together Malachi and Auri combed through the intel. She'd been horrified at first. So many agencies were involved in the cannibalism cases. Each one seemed to have a part in the cover up, in sentencing innocent men and women to death.

To her disappointment, the only other information about her, besides the sickening video, was her medical files and other records. Nothing before she was six years old.

"Your medical charts…" Ferris had mumbled as he scrutinized the detailed notes from the doctor on Medea. "Did anyone ever explain what they did to you?"

She shook her head. "I was a minor. The GIC made all the decisions."

His eyes flicked across the lines and charts dictating where the doctors located damage on her body. "This doesn't match up," he said, swiping at the tablet to pull up more information. "Most of what happened to you, the organ failure, the traumatic brain injury…" He finally looked up at her. "They aren't symptoms of an animal attack."

Malachi leaned around Auri. "What are they?"

He rubbed at the back of his neck. "I… Well, it's not common, but all tied together, the symptoms point to it." He cleared his throat. "They're extreme side-effects of Cryo Bite."

Auri's fingers probed her temples as if she could drill into her forgotten memories by force alone. "I've never heard of Cryo Bite, but I'm guessing it's related to how the camera crew found me in a cryo chamber. How I got there," she sighed, "I have no idea."

"It's not a common issue anymore," Ferris said. "Back when settlers arrived in Ancora Galaxy, some opted to travel in cryo chambers. Too long in one can cause side effects, but none as extreme as yours. Most recovered in a matter of hours." He hesitated then murmured, "Auri."

She looked up. "Yes?"

"To suffer as terribly as you did, your body must've been frozen for at least twenty years. Maybe more, considering your files' birth date."

Twenty years.

She swallowed hard. "Who would do that to me? My parents...?" She turned to Malachi as if she'd find the answers scrawled across his skin.

"We'll figure out what happened," he said. "Thanks, Ferris."

After Ferris left, Auri watched the video footage over and over again until Malachi forced her to stop. She kept searching for details, anything that would trigger a memory. Once she'd shoved her strange hallucinations away. Now she longed to have one.

If only she could visit a Tech Tower to research the fate of the show's crew members. But here, on a ship barreling toward Krugel's Curve, that wish was impossible to grant.

"Auri," Malachi said hours later, drawing her attention to an open file. "Look."

She shifted closer. All night they'd read about Roanleigh and the truth behind the planet's terraforming disaster. It turned out the planet had transitioned from uninhabitable to habitable just fine—if one considered daily snowstorms "fine." Citizens from Earth had even settled on the planet, the final colony.

Except something happened to them. They had all vanished. The few Fed-sanctioned archeologists who had been sent to investigate—and managed to return—failed to determine where the settlers went. The only body ever found there...

Had been Auri's.

Malachi gestured to the last file in Roanleigh's folder. Auri blinked to focus her eyes as the text wavered.

We were unable to pull data from the settlers' computers. It seems our own technology has advanced much faster than Earth's—Roanleigh's. So much so that their software is no longer compatible with what we brought.

Despite the wealth of knowledge and potential for explaining the disappearance of Roanleigh's settlers, I advise the General-in-Chief to block off the planet. Too many have been lost over the last year in the pursuit of truth. My crew and I were

savagely attacked by monstrous creatures while planetside. On-
ly four of us—out of twenty—managed to escape.
And barely.
Final Recommendation: Let the fate of Roanleigh and its
citizens rest where it belongs, under feet of abominable snow.
Signed, C.K.E.

Auri looked up at Malachi. All the information she'd absorbed over the last few hours clicked into place. "We have to
go to Roanleigh. You were right back on Medea. The answers
are there."

Malachi nodded, his eyes bloodshot but bright with feverish
excitement. "Not just the answers to the Bleeders, but the answers to what happened to you and why your parents froze you
in time." He gestured to the female Bleeder's earring resting on
the corner of the table. "Why that matches the earring you
wear."

"Hey," Katara said, hurrying down the steps. She'd changed
clothes, her hair still damp from a shower. Auri swiped at her
own hair, knotted into a messy bun at the top of her head. Exactly how long had she been reading?

Malachi rubbed at his eyes. "We just got to the end of the
intel." He sniffed the air as if just becoming aware of the allur-
ing scents drifting from the kitchen above. "Please tell me
Castor has breakfast ready along with some form of stimula-
tors."

She propped a hand on her hip. "How long has Castor been
on this crew? Of course he has."

Malachi was already rising to his feet. "Thank the stars."

He held a hand down to Auri, who took it and stood. She
breathed deep the faint scent of sausage and freshly brewed cof-
fee. Her stomach growled.

Katara led the way up the spiral staircase, the lavender scent
of the crew's shampoo mingling with the breakfast aroma.
"There's a mandatory news bulletin about to play on the table
upstairs. You two need to see it."

Malachi and Auri seemed to come to complete alertness at the same time. They hurried after Katara, two stairs at a time. Mandatory news bulletins were a rare occurrence and automatically played on any grid-connected streaming device. The vids were then followed by a citizen-wide newsletter detailing the events in text format.

In the kitchen, everyone was gathered on one side of the table, staring at the screen. Breakfast dishes had been cleared to various ends. Marin sat on the opposite side of the vid, head cocked as she listened, left arm in a sling. Auri gave her a whispered "Hello." Marin nodded with a small smile. She hadn't caught up with the girl, having been too busy with Malachi.

The crew made space for Auri and their captain as they crowded in to watch. A female newscaster with cropped hair was speaking.

"After the horrific attack on the Spire during the Federation's annual military ball, many citizens are worried about the safety of the galaxy. To address these concerns, the General-in-Chief has invoked a mandatory news bulletin."

Auri let out a relieved sigh as the GIC's familiar face filled up the screen. She hadn't let herself dwell on what his fate had been, trapped in the ballroom. But he was safe. *Alive.*

He wore a fresh dress uniform, hat fixed straight on his head. Behind him the Ancora Federation flag hung, a white banner with an eagle plastered in the center. The GIC stood at a podium with his hands clasped behind his back. Sadness deepened the wrinkles around his eyes.

"Last night at 1900 hours, we were attacked. Many men and women of the Federation lost their lives. To their families, I offer my deepest condolences. My own son was injured in the assault."

The camera panned out from the GIC's face to focus on Ty where he stood just behind his father. Auri's heart squeezed painfully at the sight of him. He wore his DISC uniform, and stitches crisscrossed the gash on his forehead, his arm resting in a linen sling.

The camera moved back to the GIC. "My adopted daughter, Aurelia Peri, was taken in the chaos, presumed dead." He paused as if choked up. Knowing him as she did now, she guessed it was an act for the sake of the cameras. A lump formed in her throat.

"Some say the aggressors were monsters," he continued. "Some claim they weren't even human." The GIC clenched his jaw. "I tell you, citizens of the Ancora Federation, their actions were monstrous, but they were most certainly human. My sources disclosed, minutes before this bulletin, that a renegade militia from Medea has taken responsibility for the atrocity." He leaned forward, fingers curling around the podium's sides. "I have this message for the murderers: We are strong. We are trained. We will be coming for you. And we won't stop until you are obliterated. The Federation protects its own, and you do not belong with us."

The camera switched back to the newscaster as she and her fellows discussed the attack and their thoughts on the GIC's re-action.

Malachi slammed his fist onto the table and the vid screen winked out. "Nothing changed." He gestured to the table where the vid had played. "Just more lies, more cover-ups. He didn't even mention the damage to the vault or the information he probably lost due to the transport slamming in there. I wonder how much he paid for this. What blackmail he used."

Auri thought of the GIC, of the man who saved her then raised her. A prickle of guilt stabbed her belly at the thought of turning against him. But what choice did she have? His was a world of lies. She wanted the truth. She wanted the entire Feder-ation, the Bleeders' victims, the families of the innocents put to death, to have the truth.

"His cover-ups don't matter anymore," Auri said. "We are going to find out the truth. And with it…" She raised her chin. "We are going to expose him."

Malachi looked to each member of the crew: Marin, Castor, Tsuna, Katara, Ferris, and finally Auri. "I have a volunteers-only proposition." He strode to the head of the table. As if the motion was a signal, everyone slid into a seat.

Auri moved around the table to take her original chair, Marin on her left, Malachi on her right. Tsuna occupied the once empty chair at the opposite head of the table. The seat on Malachi's other side remained vacant, but there was a rightness about it, as if the spot was already occupied. Occupied by Kestrel's ghost, a girl with a hero's heart and a hunger for the sky.

Malachi folded his hands atop the table. "If you aren't interested, just say so and I'll drop you off on any planet from Babbage down to Medea."

"Just tell us the job so we can say yes," Katara muttered.

The corner of Malachi's mouth twitched. "The intel Tsuna helped us steal from the Feds details the truth about Roanleigh."

Everyone took a sharp intake of breath. The silence in the room radiated with a curious intensity.

Malachi continued, "Rumors that the planet's terraforming failed are lies from the Fed. Bleeders originated there and Roanleigh is where Auri came from." He glanced at her to see if she had anything to add. When she shook her head, he said, "There are non-transferable files on that planet. Files many archeologists died to view and failed to extract. It'll be dangerous." He paused, taking a slow breath. "My mission is to go to Roanleigh, collect the data, and use it to take down the Fed."

"Your plans are always absurdly simple," Tsuna mused.

"*The best plans are*," Katara said, quoting Malachi from their prison heist.

The captain shook his head. "None of you need to join me in this," he stressed. "As I said, I can drop you off at any planet along the way, no questions asked." He looked at each member of his crew. "Just say the word."

To Auri's surprise, Ferris answered first. "I have four words for you, Cai." He stuck his arm out, removing the cuff on his barcode. "I'm going with you."

Malachi smiled at his friend. "Technically, that could be five." He inclined his head. "Thank you, Ferris."

The act of Ferris exposing his barcode sparked Auri's memory of a textbook page from basic. In the early days of the Fed, when captains enlisted people for his or her crew, ceremony dictated each member bare their barcode for scrutiny. It symbolized the sacrifice of an individual's life to follow their captain's wishes. Even unto death.

Katara repeated the ceremonial motion. "I'm with you. What better opportunity to kill you than on a desolate planet?"

"You're still spouting that?" Tsuna asked, rolling her eyes. She pushed up her sweater's sleeve, her barcode bare. "I am with you, Malachi. Though you're well aware I puke under stress, so you may not even want me."

Malachi couldn't help but smile at that. "You're always welcome, Tsuna."

Castor glanced at his ex-wife then at the rest of the crew. He sighed. "We'll need to stop for groceries." He removed his cuff, baring his barcode.

Marin didn't speak, merely held out her barcode for everyone to view.

Malachi looked to Auri. "Agent Peri?"

Auri's gaze moved around the table. She was surrounded by people she'd only known for a few weeks—strangers, practically... Yet she knew deep in her bones, in her blood, in the depths of her soul.

Auri knew she'd found a home.

"It isn't Agent Peri. Not anymore." She rotated her robotic arm so he could see her barcode. "I'm with you, Malachi."

It might've been Auri's sleep-deprived vision, but the captain's eyes seemed to swim with unshed tears. He cleared his throat. "Okay." He let out a choked laugh. "*Okay*." He shoved up the sleeve of his thermal shirt with trembling fingers and joined his barcode to the other bared arms.

A smile spread across his lips as he looked at each one of the crew members. "To Roanleigh."

"To Roanleigh," they repeated.

———

OTHER BOOKS BY
Emily Layne

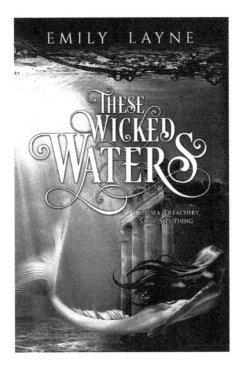

A centuries-old curse plagues the island of Viaii Nisi and an ancient enemy lurks beneath the depths of the surrounding water. When Annie makes a terrifying discovery, she must face her biggest fears to uncover the truth and save the people she loves.

These Wicked Waters by Emily Layne
available wherever books are sold.

ΛCKNOWLEƎGEMENTS

The physical act of writing a book is a solitary task, but so many have left their mark on these pages.

First and foremost, I thank God for blessing me with a love of writing and for creating me with a boundless imagination.

I'm forever grateful to my parents and sisters—My dad for his sacrifices while serving in the U.S. Army for thirty-five years at the time of publication. Dad, you instilled in me a sense patriotism, duty, and appreciation for this beautiful country I'm thankful to call home. Thank you.

My mom for serving on the homefront with four rambunctious daughters. Thank you for your boundless love and patience. I have learned so much of quiet strength and resilience from you. My sisters, Maddie, Becky, and Sarah. You were the victims (and supporters) of my early writings despite its many flaws. I love you all.

And my husband and children—Jeff, I am forever changed by your love and support--and so is this book! Thank you for being my sounding board, for editing with me late into the night at the kitchen table, despite being sleep-deprived from our sleepless babies. Without you, I wouldn't know about orbital assists or

SpaceX. "Ship-shat" would also still be in this book (thank goodness it's not!).

To my above mentioned sleepless littles, Eloise and Wilder. You two are forever teaching me the importance of flexibility, the boundlessness of love, and how to find the fantastical in the little moments.

This book would not exist in this gorgeous binding if it were not for my amazing publishing team. Endless thanks to my champion of an agent, Becky, and the hard-working team at Owl Hollow Press, Emma, Hannah, and Olivia. I can't wait for book two!

And finally, thank you, reader, for taking a chance on this book. I hope you found new friends in the flawed yet lovable characters you met in these pages.

Emily Layne grew up a proud Army brat with an Anne Shirley-esque imagination. She loves reading, eating too much pizza, and spending time with her husband—who loves books almost as much as she does.

When not writing fantastical stories, Emily can be found playing with her curious children, exploring the great outdoors, or concocting mostly-believable excuses to avoid socializing.

Her debut novel, *These Wicked Waters*, was inspired by her experience on a cruise ship (which proved to be quite flammable, unfortunately).

Emily is represented by Becky LeJeune of Bond Literary Agency.

Find Emily online at www.emilylaynebooks.com

9 781958 109120